Suellen

Dee DeTarsio

Suellen

HISTRIA
ROMANCE

Histria Romance

Las Vegas ◊ Chicago ◊ Palm Beach

Published in the United States of America by
Histria Books
7181 N. Hualapai Way, Ste. 130-86
Las Vegas, NV 89166 USA
HistriaBooks.com

Histria Romance is an imprint of Histria Books. Titles published under the imprints of Histria Books are distributed worldwide.

All rights reserved. No part of this book may be reprinted or reproduced or utilized in any form or by any electronic, mechanical or other means, now known or hereafter invented, including photocopying and recording, or in any information storage or retrieval system, without the permission in writing from the Publisher.

Certain characters in this work are historical figures, and certain events portrayed did take place. However, this is a work of fiction. Names, characters, places, and incidents are either the product of the author's imagination or are used fictitiously. Any resemblance to actual persons, living or dead, is entirely coincidental.

Library of Congress Control Number: 2024948100

ISBN 978-1-59211-542-6 (softbound)
ISBN 978-1-59211-554-9 (eBook)

Copyright © 2024 by Dee DeTarsio

"I never wait until tomorrow."

The Civil War may be over, but for thirty-year-old Suellen, the battle has just begun. After burying her husband and children, Suellen and her lifelong friend, Lucy, pack up secrets and set about rebuilding their lives up north. But as Suellen finally finds the love and security she never thought she deserved, Lucy disapproves of the match and threatens to ruin Suellen's chance at happiness.

Closer than sisters, neither can bear to part from the other until a train robbery changes everything. Lucy slips into Suellen's life, while Suellen is embroiled in her kidnapper's quest.

From bidding adieu to southern traditions to embracing love, compassion combats betrayal as Suellen and Lucy bravely face the future.

Chapter One

April 1877
Fremont, Tennessee, a small town outside of Nashville
Notes from my 30th year...

I haven't talked to my sister for nearly three years, though I hear about her from time to time, of course. Folks can't seem to resist wanting to stir up that honeypot, trying to catch me out sharpening my tongue on vengeful stories of her excesses; hoping her waist is the size of a pickle barrel, or that all her hair fell out. They'll learn none of that from me. "She's doing well, I expect," I always say.

My parents, especially Mother, would be most ashamed of me, the middle daughter, since I turned out to be what the God-fearing members of my family would charitably call a bluestocking. The less kind, perhaps not having a big enough vocabulary and an even more limited imagination, have tried to infer malicious perversions about me. So-called friends wearing lemon-pursed lips often try to comfort me, repeating the aspersions of sins long past in hopes of a ring-side seat to a drama of I don't know what. Sometimes it takes all my willpower not to start clucking like a chicken pecking at their skirts, or maybe even kissing them right on their dumb-bunny mouths to give credence to their shabby hopes of a mind gone 'round the bend. I try not to preen as I know others would, but there is solace to be had upon growing up with little expectation; surely my life could only turn out to be a pleasant surprise. The scales of justice, however, are weighted with the heaviness of lead, and the loathsome burden of my own misdeeds are no match for any mercurial chance at happiness, a quicksilver emotion in which I no longer believe.

I stilled my pen. The word happiness wobbled in a messy scrawl on the page before me.

Happiness? I would settle for amnesia.

Oh, Lord. Southern women may be short of sugar, flour and butter, though the accursed war ended years ago, but deprivations have not affected their memories in the slightest. What matters forgiveness when the delicious "never forget" is etched upon bitter hearts? Etched? It is my belief a lady of my acquaintance, Miss Sew A Fine Seam, embroiders the phrase on her petticoat. I want to forget everything. If I am successful at my endeavor, why then, what would there be to forgive? Pride may goeth before a fall, something these southern women should have learned from the ink not yet dry in history books, but like a hound dog on a pork chop they gnaw on their memories. Pardon me for stating the obvious, but memories do have a way of becoming polished into a diamond-bright fantasy, for who is there to call it a lie? What could-have-been becomes should-have-been through the would-have-been wounds of a scarred soul. When the worst has happened and you've lost everything that matters, what matters is something you never knew you needed.

After my husband died… My hand rested, as I waited for the passing of the hot shame that stole my breath and caused my heart to stumble out of its rhythm like a lame horse. I couldn't bear to think of him often, or the end, his end, and my role. God rest his soul. I ran away from home; from all that I hurt and all that I hated. I loathed the very ground that swallowed my babies, my sole chance for redemption, and cared not which gates of Hell I entered. I picked up my pen again. This saga wasn't going to write itself. I wasn't one who put off unpleasant tasks until tomorrow. I scratched out the line about my husband and began again.

I start this tale at the sunset of my years, as if reading a book backwards…

"Dear God, Suellen, you're five days older than me. I am not ready to jump into the pine box with you just yet."

I pressed my hands into the paper, taking care not to smear the black ink. "Lucy. This is a private matter. Please." I turned my head back to the desk.

"Your story is mine and mine is yours," she declared.

"Your solidarity is touching," I replied. "But we both know your desire for telling tales has yet to meet its match." I couldn't help smiling at her over my shoulder. My father used to tell her the sun would one day burn her tongue. "You know everything there is to know about me." I shooed her off with my left hand.

She clasped that hand, deliberately misunderstanding my gesture, and bent to wrap her arm around me. "As you know about me."

Our eyes met in my mother's mirror that hung above the escritoire, as if we recognized our declarations as false. Isn't it strange how no one can know the soul of another? Isn't it a relief?

Chapter Two

"I have resolved it is far better to be bored to death than scared witless. We have born far too much of the latter, and I, for one, look forward to settling into the former."

"As do I, dear friend." Lucy agreed with me. "Though it does sound a trifle as if you are trying to convince yourself."

"I welcome the peace. We've had enough tragedy for several lifetimes."

"Hush. Don't say such a thing." She looked around as if ghosts were eavesdropping, waiting to punish us for daring to say "enough." Perhaps I should have listened to her.

Lucy and I had taken residence in an old carriage house, situated well outside of the capital, Nashville. Refurbished of course, poorly, and fitted with as primitive mismatched furniture as one could imagine. To think I wasted precious moments yearning for a set of dining chairs that looked as though they came from the same tree. Though no amount of fresh wood and gently used carpet could convince my olfactory system to inhale deeply lest it smother in the smells of offal that seemed to lurk in the corners. Our "home" as Lucy proudly called it, wasn't much, but dear Lord, she had a hankering to actually name it, and was only silenced when I laughed at her pretensions. Lucy had been by my side from my first memory and it's no exaggeration to say we were closer than sisters.

"We should call it 'Hydrangea Haven,'" she had said, cheerfully scrubbing the floor boards as we settled in.

"Pigsty Station" would have been more fitting. I pinched my nose. The small two-story glorified barn was all that remained of an establishment that had once belonged to a distant relative, a misfit cousin. Escape though one may try, family has ever-so-long memories, honed into their version of truth, merely via repetition. No one had particularly cared for the man, though what his sin was I could not accurately attest. My cousin's misfortune, in that he died alone, became mine and Lucy's saving grace.

My cousin had favored me for unknown reasons. It is disturbing to think he perhaps found me a kindred soul, as I had merely served him a plate of food at a barbecue once, and that only under command of my mother. Most I remember of him was that he smelled as old as he looked. How my sisters had laughed at my discomfort, and, most likely, sullen presentation of that plate of chicken, potato salad and corn on the cob, and they had scampered out from my mother's sight.

Cousin Methuselah, as my sister referred to him, had pinched my cheek—rather hard—told me I was a good girl, and shooed me off so I could go enjoy the party. I succumbed to my guilty conscience, back when I still had one, and sought him out later that afternoon to proffer a slice of pecan pie along with a glass of ice-cold buttermilk, which I knew he liked. Lord, I hope I never live long enough to become an odiferous affront to small children.

After my husband passed, I would not, nor could not, survive on the farm, and it was with no small relief that we moved away. Lucy, (who had grown up alongside me and my sisters), and I had gratefully settled into our new life. We were on Hensel-Poorman Street, in Fremont, Tennessee, a small town a day-and-a-half's journey or so southwest of the great city of Nashville. Lest you are as ignorant as my neighbors, I am being sarcastic.

Nashville after the war, or as those very same neighbors exclaim, The War, was a deflowered southern belle, pillaged and plundered of all her good manners and upbringing, eager to embrace the first rapscallion with jingling pockets to save her.

I had sold nearly every last blessed possession as Lucy and I set forth to live out the rest of our lives, waiting for the death that was never there when you needed it. The upside to the ill-manners of Miss Nashville and her surroundings was that respectability was whatever one chose to make of it, not a protocol prescribed from days gone by. A welcome freedom from a past I will never miss. Armed with only a disused shotgun, standing sentry in the kitchen, and our old hound dog, Jasper the Third with nary a tooth left in his head, the two of us began the next chapter of our lives. Uninspired perhaps, but mostly unafraid.

I rarely thought of my husband, buried now so many years. The nightmare of his passing yet serviced my dreams with terror, but he and I had done all right together, I suppose. Work, hard work and harder work, beginning from the first morning's light, had been the sum total of our days. We had made my family's farm respectable again, though I care as little for farming as I do for poison oak rash. Nevertheless, I found myself possessed of a comfortable enough amount of

Suellen 11

money that, if handled with parsimonious care, as my sister had once taunted was my middle name, it should do to last Lucy and myself for a good long while.

With Lucy by my side, as she has been for all my life, we shall do quite nicely, I thought. My mother never cared for Lucy but had the good manners, of course, to hide her true feelings—just enough to make one wonder if perhaps we had misread her subtle clues of disdain. But my sisters and I, who had grown up with our mother's nuances engraved upon our souls, learned etiquette at her breast. When something occurs that's not supposed to occur, southern women pretend it never did occur at all. At Mother's knee, we composed our faces into masks, and practiced disguising those ill-bred looks denoting ill-mannered signs of how we were really feeling. "A lady never allows distress to manifest upon her features." I swear sometimes I can still feel her cool fingers slide down my forehead, trying to smooth out the fierce ridges that would form right there, just between my eyebrows.

Mother's etiquette was simply to pretend Lucy wasn't there. Since Lucy and I grew up almost inseparable, her glazed look often spilled over to me. At some point, I was as close to Lucy as if she were my own sister, closer, since I liked her far better than either of the ones I had been burdened with. I would speak that very same sentiment to Lucy upon occasion, at which point she would tilt her head and squint her eyes at me. I do believe I embarrassed her with my praise, so I endeavored to use it sparingly.

Lucy has mahogany hair, which is just as lovely as the word itself, conjuring up a decadent rich brown with hints of auburn that glistened in the sunlight. My poetic devotion is not hyperbole. Her hair was full and lively, and complain though she might when the hot and heavy humidity that is part and parcel of the geography of the South played upon its strands, it became a temptation to touch, puffed up like that. It was her pride and joy. When we were young and fashioned our corn husk dolls, instead of using the dried silk off the cob for our creation's hair, Lucy shared with me the loose strands of her own—a deep brown of soft angelic down that resulted in the most beautiful dolls in the County. In a sign of loyalty that alone would have determined my undying friendship, she would only split her bounty with me. My mind flitted back to that time when we played together with our halo-haired dolls; seeing a far-off romantic future, that couldn't have been more diabolically different had Satan himself intervened.

An unwanted memory of that doll surfaced. My sister had asked to see it. Pride does goeth before a fall was my lesson that day. Surprised by my sister's interest, and warmed by her praise, my shy, eleven-year-old self had handed it over. "Why, this is the beatingest corn husk doll ever," she said. She showed it to a few neighbor boys who had come to play. I didn't know why they laughed; I was just happy to be part of my sister's circle. Why, she does care for me, I remember thinking.

What I hadn't realized was that she had secreted a blackberry in the palm of her hand and had driven her thumb clean through to the center. She then pushed her purple stained thumb into the head of my corn husk doll, the small crescent of her nail spoiling its face with a frowning grimace. "It looks just like you, Suellen," she said and waved it in the air. When she began chanting "Grumpy Skirts" the boys had chimed in. Lucy had leaned over my sister's shoulder as if for a better view, but before I could lay claim to that grievous betrayal, Lucy had surreptitiously smeared mud on the back of my sister's yellow cotton skirt, right below her backside. The howling laughter of the boys transferred then to her, and did considerable for my injured feelings. You did not want to tangle with Lucy.

Lucy's river green eyes always seemed to sparkle. I had once heard my mother say her eyes were as demur as a sinner's ears hearing church bells. I had noted that gentlemen responded warmly to her, though it goes without saying she didn't have the social opportunities that I did. Women tended to ignore her, much as they did me, I suppose. Most of the time, I didn't mind it. Lucy and I were the only friends each other needed.

"I am the *lagniappe* to your claptrap," Lucy often interrupted some of my more outlandish notions. When I needed such soothing in my younger days, before I learned unfairness is simply the way of the world, she would remind me that most folks aren't that smart. "Who appreciates the beauty of Queen Anne's lace in a bouquet of roses?" Though I harangued her for implying I was a weed, truth be told, I rather liked Queen Anne's lace.

We had been settled into our new place in that smallish sized town—but large enough to have everything we needed—for only a few days before we earnestly set out to engage employment. "I do not have the slightest idea of where to begin," I said fretfully. "You have skills," I told her. "I was raised to be lady. The very idea of engaging in commerce seems degrading."

Suellen 13

She had stopped in her tracks. "And did you perhaps sleep late on the very day comportment was being taught?" She snorted most unbecomingly at my expense. I could practically hear my sister attach yet another label, Sanctimonious Suellen.

"That's not what I meant, and you know it, Lucy. I'm uncomfortable with this pursuit, that's all. And I can hardly think who would give a nickel for some as yet undiscovered talent of mine."

For those with short-term memory, dearth of ego, and ample supply of elbow grease, there was money to be made in reconstruction. I don't use the capital letter R for that word; I'll let the politicians, old timers, and newspapers argue that point, as if the rebuilding of an entire generation, sans some of the best and brightest, deserved an especially shiny term all its own. I have a better R word for it—Ruin.

"Chin up, Suellen. You'll figure it out." Arms linked, we were headed into town. We were barely out of sight of our front step when we were distracted by the raised voices of several women gathered on a porch several doors down.

"Shameless," we heard one of the women say. "After all we've done for her and her family?"

"And this is the thanks we get?" Another voice had chimed in. "She can whistle 'Dixie' until the cows come home before I offer her food from my table again."

"Do-gooders sure do have a mighty fine opinion of themselves," I said to Lucy. "And want everyone to know about it," she agreed.

"If I am to understand their rather loud complaints, to whomever they are doling out their wondrous charity, isn't behaving in a properly humbled manner. Somehow, I don't feel that's what the good Lord had in mind." My steps became brisker.

Lucy kept pace. "Judge not lest ye be judged." We shared a raised eyebrow at our own hypocrisy.

"Why, I have half a mind to educate those ninnies."

"Oh, my stars, Suellen, if only you could get a job telling people what to do."

We stepped up onto the wooden platform lining the establishments of Main Street. The heels of our boots pounded comfortably in time as we passed the barbershop, then, goodness, the saloon. We hurried by, of course, our gazes held forward, and were nearly at the mercantile.

Lucy's words had given me an idea. I halted and shook off her hand. "Stay here." I marched into the town newspaper building of *The County Consort* and exited with a weekly advice column to call my own. Of course, the editor, Mr. Calvin Coates, practically wanted to pay me in peanuts, but I had persevered.

Lucy, in her own right, had become a seamstress of renown, and she actually enjoys the task, if one can believe that. She had several orders lined up our very first week; two dresses, and a pair of front parlor curtains, and was as excited as I'd ever seen her. And now after only a few weeks, my journalistic enterprise also seemed right on course.

"Auntie Ques." Lucy paused as she held the newspaper that contained my debut efforts. "It looks as if some poor fool doesn't know how to spell," she observed. "Antiques." Lucy pointed at the headline.

I grabbed the paper and rattled it, pleased beyond belief at my very first foray into journalism. "It is clearly 'Auntie Questions,' which is abbreviated, to make it folksy and familiar."

Lucy snatched the paper back and settled into her seat as I poured us each a cup of coffee. I take great solace in the very word coffee, and like a hound called to supper, its mention serves to set my heart beating once again. I wonder if it is thus for those fond of strong drink? No perhaps about it, coffee is my very favorite necessity, returned to its place of honor and homage after the war, and more fittingly, was my first purchase from the earnings of my own hand. I loved our afternoon ritual. My mother had preferred tea, but my father embraced coffee. After the war, my biggest pleasure was grinding the coffee beans which finally made it back into southern ports.

The bitter brew, topped with the richness of thick, sweet yellow cream became a reminder to savor the day. If you must know, Lucy thought of that syrupy devotional, "to savor the day," and being under the warming effects of the potage, I let it pass.

Jasper came and lay at our feet between us. I leaned over to scratch the soft spots behind his droopy ears, then settled back in my chair. "Now, let's hear my column."

"Dear Auntie," Lucy read. "My friend," she looked at me, "it's always a friend." She continued. "My friend has fallen upon hard times. I do what I can to help out, offering up chicken from my own pantry, bread, and some of the leftover vegetables from my garden, after my family has been cared for, of course."

"Of course," I smiled.

"But I do not believe my gifts are truly appreciated." Lucy cleared her throat. "Oh, they never are, dear sanctimonious one."

"Hush." I nodded at her to continue.

"In fact, I saw her feed her dog bits of my chicken, but the worst insult is that my other neighbor saw her purchase candy for her children and an expensive pair of shoes for herself, at the mercantile. If she is so blatantly wasting the good money she has, why should I, as a good Christian, continue to encourage this shameful behavior?"

Lucy glanced up at me. "I cannot wait to hear your good and kind judgment, Suellen." I lifted my eyebrows in encouragement.

"Dear Shocked, The War has warped all sensibilities, hasn't it? As Socrates said, 'The unexamined life is not worth living,' but for goodness sake, please keep your eyes on your own page. It is not for you to know your neighbor's business, and perhaps you need to prescribe to the motto, charity begins in the home, and by charity, I mean kindness of thought. Your fellow acquaintances would much prefer an honest smile over begrudging handout. Good day.

"Sincerely, "Auntie"

Lucy laughed and read the final line.

"Auntie Ques. is available to answer all your questions and solicitations for hearth and home advice. Please send your letter to the editor of *The County Consort.*"

She folded the paper carefully and set it on the table. "Very well done, Suellen!" We raised our china cups to each other. They were the only two matching cups we owned, taken from home. They were part of our ritual and I dearly loved them. They had a white background with delicate blue flowers patterned beneath the rim. The fragile handles fit our forefingers perfectly, and they were sweet to gaze upon. They didn't match our dinner plates. I minded, Lucy didn't.

"I thank you for your help," I told Lucy. "You have a good eye for editing my goings on."

"You do go on," she said. "I still can't believe you get to do two of your favorite things: write and tell people what to do. And you get paid for it."

"Twenty-five cents for each posting they publish," I told her. "It will keep us in coffee."

"Maybe we should donate that sludge we used to have to drink. We still have some hoarded in the back cupboard. Maybe you can offer it up to Sanctimonious," Lucy suggested.

My practical nature, and memory of my stomach chewing upon itself, insisted on safeguarding provisions, such as they were. The sludge to which Lucy referred was a nauseating coffee substitute, of which certain odors could still conjure up the very taste. I refused to call it coffee and, to Lucy's amusement, I simply used to refer to it as "cough." My mother's people had taught her how to roast the nasty chicory root, along with acorns to create the foul brew which did not provide the happy heart I had grown to crave.

"There are two types of people in the world, Suellen. The coffee drinkers and the meek," Lucy said, helping herself to a spot more, and adding the rest to my cup. On special days, we would treat ourselves and split a piece of pie or cobbler, but most days we simply nibbled leftover cornbread.

Our addiction was the one constant in the day that made our spirits sprightly and allowed us to feel an incredulous hope about the world. Though coffee cannot protect against the insidious tortures that flair in the middle of the night, and in fact may even add to the apprehensions we could not quit, it was still a respite, allowing myself, for however short a time, a surcease of worry.

Lucy returned to the paper and skimmed the front page. "There are 35,000 miles of new railroad track, coast-to-coast, across our country," she told me. "Oh Suellen, don't you just want to jump on a train and go somewhere?"

"No, thank you," I shuddered. "I don't think they'd let Jasper on a train, anyway." Lucy laughed and tossed him some crumbs of leftover cornbread.

Lucy read on, "After the Panic four years ago, the railroad is the largest employer, right behind the farmers." She looked up at me. "Those railroad workers are a rough crowd. I know they work hard, but they sure seem miserable. They work the longest hours ever, and have been forced to take pay cuts. How can you raise a family on a dollar a day? Can you imagine?"

"Yes, I can, and so can you. We're doing all right Lucy, you and I. And it's our Christian duty to help others, but Lord it's hard sometimes."

"You don't fool me, Suellen. You're a big softy. You whine and shake your finger at me for doling out leftovers to the Samuel's family—"

Suellen

"And the Jefferson's, and the Kimball's, and, and, and. Where does it end, Lucy?"

"Now you're preaching to me as if I'm one of your Auntie Ques. followers who needs to be taught a lesson. Who gives money to Reverend Flanders every Sunday for the Poor Folks' Relief? We both work hard as dogs for the church's Ladies' Aid Society. And who makes up those antiseptic tinctures for the hospital? And who always has me make extra cornbread, just in case, when it seems every day there's a just-in-case stopping by."

"I am not overly fond of cornbread."

"Well it's no blackberry cobbler or pecan pie," she taunted me right back, "but excuse me for failing to notice your disregard." She scratched her head "Why, I could have sworn that was you who had three pieces before lunch the other day. Pardon me, my mistake."

Lucy doesn't know that I know the secret in her recipe is a knuckle deep scoop of bacon grease. I changed the subject. "Do you want to hear what my editor at the newspaper says? He thinks there could even be a railroad strike. President Rutherford is threatening to bring in federal soldiers to keep the peace. You know both of the Jones brothers work on the line, and they barely keep a roof over their families' heads. It's a shame. Honest day's work for fair wages. Everybody wins at that."

"I expect the high and mighty rich folk who own the railroads would take exception to that," Lucy said.

"It's a shame, that's all. Most of them are proud hard-working men, and it has to be draining to not be rewarded for your efforts. You and I know, like most folks around here, desperate people do desperate things." I finished my coffee. "Let's just hope it doesn't come to that. You don't honestly think there will be a strike, do you?"

Lucy shrugged. "Still," she said. "What would it be like to travel?"

I laughed at her. "You say that word as if it were a magic spell. Travel." I wiggled my fingers. "You never wonder what it's like out there?" She looked out the window. "I mean, away from here. This small town, knowing every busybody's business. And them knowing ours."

"I reckon that's for the next generation, Lucy. We can't afford to go gallivanting off into the sunset, not knowing our destination. We're just women, after all. Sometimes, I do wish I were a man."

"Suellen! Pray tell. What would you do if you were a man?"

"I'd marry a wife, just like you, Lucy!" We laughed.

"So I could cook and clean and wash your drawers?"

"Exactly. Isn't that what most men think all women are good for? We don't need husbands, do we?"

She shook her head. "Not that there's many men left around here to even be husbands." She looked at me, not wanting to stir up old hurts.

"There's not enough to go around," I agreed. "And there's plenty of females around here who can't abide to be alone. You and I both know, Lucy, the worst thing a woman can do is to steal another woman's beau. That's no recipe for happiness."

"I know, Suellen. I'm talking about women in general, and us in specific. We're doing all right without any gentleman around, aren't we?"

"Of course. What about you, Lucy? What would you do if you were a man?"

"I'd travel. Maybe north, or maybe I'd go to California and dig for gold. Surely there's some left. I sure would like to see San Francisco. And Paris. And as soon as one of us marries a millionaire, we will, right?" Lucy raised her cup of coffee in a salute to me.

"Would you really travel, though, Suellen, if we could?"

"I'd like to think I would, even though I'm a 'fraidy cat. You are too, though."

"I am."

"Can you imagine traveling in the olden days?"

"Not on your life."

It's not wallowing in the past to realize certain forks in the road did propel an individual toward their future. Spurred by a long-ago barb from my sister, that festered in my soul, I still felt the wound from her hurtful arrow that hit its bullseye, "You were born a dour old maid and I expect you'll die one, too." I carefully tended that burning ember, fanned by a panoply of hate, and felt it flicker to welcome the dynamite of my future. Neither Lucy nor I, nor anyone in the South, was much for change or things wrenched from our control. But there is a flip side to that coin: toss it up in the air recklessly and one could be or do or say just about anything you pleased, with no censure from anyone else. In a time and place where everything matters, nothing matters very much anymore. My own low expectations conspired to cloak me in an invisibility that was breathtaking in its freedom. I took pride in being a modern woman, one who was responsible for myself. Would anyone be more surprised than I about the upheaval to come? That's a story not even my much older, bitter sister could begin to imagine.

Chapter Three

I stood in my upstairs bedroom, appraising my appearance in my mother's mirror above her old escritoire, to the critique of birds outside my window. As the overlooked middle child, it is not lost upon me that I was seen by some to resemble those watchful, far-seeing, avaricious snooping birds. Would that I could fly. I had to make do with wondering what that freedom must feel like, all the while drooping with the heaviness of my limbs planted firmly in the orange dust of the globe. If I am special, which I most certainly am not, it is that the frightening pull of gravity seems to hold me more tightly in its loathsome embrace than others. In any event, I'd rather be a bird beak than bird brain, I suppose, though that's a convenient rationale since I have no choice in the matter.

The mirror and a framed cut-out silhouette of my mother when she was seventeen, which hung on the wall near my bed, were two of my prized possessions, tying me to her. Despite what Lucy says, my bedroom isn't messy and I am most certainly not a magpie. I like being surrounded by my things: my books; two mismatched porcelain figurines of women dancing in flowing dresses, which always make me smile; a tea cup with a rare gold rim containing a few coins; ribbons for braiding my hair in the evening… Well, I could go on… There were a few more comforts strewn about my room that could seem to lose their luster in the telling.

Lucy's room, across the hall from mine, was as organized as a… Whatever is very organized? A shopkeeper's books? A physician's medicine bottles? She is as punctilious as they come, about most things. Her fabrics were all folded identically, no matter the size, one third in, one third in, folded in half, and nested atop each other, folded side out. I would take perverse pleasure in exclaiming over some pretty new material she had acquired, and unfold it, shaking it out the better to admire it, before, heavens, folding it back in half several times, in an uneven manner, just to see her eyes widen and teeth disappear. The joys of knowing someone almost as well as yourself.

Next to Lucy, my only confidant was good ol' Jasper. Even though he smelled so bad we had become inured to his stench, and he did nothing but snooze all the live long day, Lucy and I both agreed that hound dog was imbued with more

Suellen 21

common sense than any of our neighbors. And he chased after birds, fully expecting to catch one someday.

"Let's stay home today and have coffee with Jasper," I said to Lucy as we prepared for our afternoon engagement. "If I have to hear Mrs. Molloy's birthing saga one more time, it would fill me with pleasure to smack both her and her fussing infant. A genteel revisitation of a time she so dearly enjoys."

"Looks as if someone already smacked the both of them," Lucy said. She pressed her hands to either side of her face, imitating the pinched look of both mother and her child. "The woman does love her drama," she commented. Neither of us laughed, though I had to focus on buttoning my shoe to hide my smile.

"We're going calling, Suellen. How lucky we are to have boring old friends to visit with," she said. It wouldn't be a day unless one of us voiced that sentiment. "Acorn Annie's turn to host today."

I sighed. "Glory be. That woman brews the worst coffee in the County. I swear, a sip from a mud puddle would be preferable."

"Are you ready yet?" Lucy pulled a face and smoothed on her gloves. We inspected each other, bestowing the highest compliment by saying nothing.

"Shall we?" Lucy ushered me out the front door. "We have just enough time to make our purchases first." We walked arm in arm to Boswell's Mercantile first before our afternoon visit with some of our neighborhood's finest. If by finest I meant those at home and accepting visitors.

The sun was already livid as Lucy and I proceeded at our deliberate pace, one calibrated to arrive at our destination as quickly as possible but without exerting too arduous an effort as to cause an uncomfortable beading atop our lips. I will venture this ability is as natural as breathing to those born in the South, though some are more skilled than others. Lucy's face remained shine free. I felt the telltale tickle between my shoulder blades make its presence known, and lightly gave a puff of air toward my upper lip. Unpleasantries deserve to be well-hidden, just ask any southerner.

We glided into the welcome shade of the store, as I delicately brushed my gloved hand to my mouth.

The bell clanged and our footsteps marched upon the creaky floorboards, heading for unknown treasure. We walked past the front counter with its glass jars of tempting goods—penny candy, tea, spices, salt and pepper, I sniffed the air and caught a whiff of tobacco Boswell must have just unwrapped. Barrels of pickles, heads of cabbage, burlap bags of dried beans; I loved market day. But today, we were on a mission. Lucy and I had few coins in our purses to spend and had to choose wisely, but the point remains, we had coins.

Lucy reconnoitered to the left, toward the newest arrival of fabrics, and, as usual, I split off to enjoy my own experience. Tans, grays, dark browns, or, if I was feeling more optimistic, navy blue. I swear dry goods folks have some touchstone to stoke up our fevered imaginations. Try as I might, I fear I myself have been swayed to make a purchase of a brown cow-colored fabric over a more practical, and better valued, darker serge material. Now, bear with me. Of course it wasn't named Cow Brown, it simply reminded Lucy of the bovine beast we once had. And loathed. But the tag was marked "Cinnamon," and that made Lucy and myself desire it above all else. Needless to say, woe be unto the other when that dress came out of our closet. I took some solace in the fact that Lucy looked as plain in that brown dress as I did. Perhaps that image was stuck in my head as I recklessly veered as far away from the manure-colored fabrics as possible.

The smell of cotton and wool pervaded a library of textures, smooth and scratchy, slippery and stiff. "That's it, Suellen." Lucy interrupted my imagination as I dropped the corner of a cheery bolt I had unfurled.

"Not for me, Lucy," I told her, as I eyed her treasure. "Pretty," I added. I fingered it. "Won't last long. You should get a thicker weave. There was nice green back there. Emerald," I added to tempt her. She did look lovely in green colors.

"We're working now and getting paid, Suellen," she said, pleading her case. "We have jobs. We can afford a stylish look now and again, don't you think?"

"Prints are so impractical. Why, everyone would talk—'oh, I see Lucy's wearing that dress with yellow flowers again.'"

"Pfft." She waved her hands. "Everyone talks anyway. Including you and me." She laughed.

"To my dismay, I cannot disagree."

Lucy brandished a fabric she must have seen me admiring. "We deserve something nice. Something different. We need a change. We need lightness."

"We need you to stop talking right now. I swear, had circumstances been different, you would have been elected mayor of Nashville. No, you could have been governor, preacher, and auctioneer, and still have words left over."

She curtsied, and pulled out the bolt. Lucy was nearly panting in her approval and only managed to sway me by noting the price. "It's two cents cheaper a yard," she said, frowning at the scratchy navy I had been considering.

"Well, dab me in goose grease, Miss Suellen," Boswell, the proprietor said as I placed the bolt upon his counter. Boswell was an inordinately tall man with feet so large his boots could have been requisitioned during the war to run guns through the blockade. "That is a fine piece of fabric that I expect you will look mighty pretty in."

His eyes darted quickly to Lucy, and he favored her with a frown that caused his eyebrows to meet. "Miss Lucy."

Lucy widened her eyes in an innocent fashion then stared hard at the measuring tape he wielded. I had to nudge her. "Behave. He's learned his lesson."

My admonition merely served to cause her to lean her nose in closer to witness his scissors. "Dear Lord," I said in her ear. "You're making him tremble."

One time the poor man had shorted Lucy by one-eighth of a yard, and made her hopping mad. He was so affrighted by us he now recklessly cut off surplus, threw in extra ounces of rice and flour to our orders, and generally miscalculated, always in our favor. To Miss Lucy's delight.

She and I left the mercantile with an extra packet of thread and five yards of the dusty rose calico patterned with dainty sprigs of leaves that she had decided I could not live without. For herself, Lucy had also splurged and bought the cotton print with the yellow flowers. Gone were the days of billowing dresses when we used to use a full twelve yards or more of fabric for party dresses. Today's styles are more modern and practical. Plus, there aren't many parties anymore.

The fabric was a most unusual purchase for me, but for some reason, I felt most unlike myself. Upon my word, the leaves were not the usual roses or bluebells of women garbing themselves to fetch the gaze of nearby gentlemen. I sniffed. Slim pickings in that arena anyway. I had had my turn. In my youth I had beaus, and at least I can say I had married, and that I had a family. I had lost it all, and with that found the bravery that was nothing more than the curse of nothing left to lose. A most unattractive demeanor as Lucy always despaired of me, yet feeling numb was what I believed kept me with a tenuous hold on sanity, such as it was. It wasn't the war responsible for my deformity of character, it was the aftermath. And that's all I need to say about that.

My concession to the style of the day, the twining leaves printed on the material were for my vision only and better suited for a woman of my sensibilities. I thought of them as Greek laurel leaves, and my mouth hinted at a smile. Feeling victorious with my wrapped bundle, I decidedly did not think of Julius Caesar's fate. No worries. No one in that flea-bitten town would have either.

I lifted my skirt before stepping down into the dirt of the street. My daily uniform, my dark black merino, that I feared would last forever, had faded to an almost purple sheen; I should have known its blot of drabness in the dark of night with my eyes shut tight, for had I not been wearing the same for the past ever so many years?

Lucy hooked her arm through mine. "Perhaps you could donate this old dress to the railroad workers for protective garb," she said. "You scare off the rag-picker."

"I will not do you the honor of a reply."

I dropped my skirt and clutched my package tighter, thinking of the pattern I would cut.

Though I mocked any pretensions of plying womanly wiles—a glowing transformation impossible to reap with a mere utilitarian covering—perhaps I would feel a thread of connection to those around me in my new fanciful dress. I had overheard my mother once saying I was well-suited to a pink color that served my complexion well. Perhaps this cloth would brighten my features whilst I hid behind a quiet demeanor, the better to observe the charade of others.

"This will be perfect for our dinner engagement," Lucy said, referring to the invitation we'd received from Mrs. Boyer, an elderly widowed acquaintance.

"Oh joy. I had forgotten. An entry in the pristine desert of our social calendar." I clasped my hands.

"You have not forgotten."

I anticipated the occasion would be nothing noteworthy. Victuals prepared by someone other than myself or Lucy would suffice to receive my gratitude. "I will arrive, the belle of the ball, and capture the heart of a handsome gentleman who will fall prey to my not-inconsiderable charms."

"Will there be a handsome gentleman for me, do you think?"

I laughed, for it had never occurred to me, Lucy having a beau.

She stopped in her tracks. Oh, Lord, I thought. Now I've done it. Though what "it" was remained to be seen.

Chapter Four

"You honestly think I'm content to be your…" she stopped, before spitting the word. "Companion? For the rest of my days?"

"Hush. Folks are staring. And please do not stomp your foot."

She stomped. "What is wrong with the notion of wanting someone to cherish me? Desire me?"

I stiffened and at the same time tried to pat the air around her in hopes of preventing her nerves from exploding. Truth be told, I had never thought of Lucy that way.

Her eyes widened. "I don't believe it. You have never thought of me in that way, have you?"

Apparently, our complicated relationship is only on the same wavelength when it is for the amusement of the Almighty. "What is going on here?" I used the same tone as when I tried to calm Jasper.

"And don't talk to me as if I'm a dog."

"Now you've offended me." Best course of action, defense. At her silence, I hooked my arm through hers. "Oh, stop it, Lucy. One day, you will meet a handsome fellow, who will sweep you off your feet, an uxorious lover," I lowered my voice on the daring word, perhaps giving voice to my own long-buried fantasy.

"You don't believe that." She pulled away.

"Lucy LeJeune. Honestly. This is nonsense. Life has been hard. Neither of us have had the luxury of indulging in romance." I practically spat the word. "And you are…"

"I am what?" Her words were bullets. "Nothing."

"Never mind; I know what you were going to say. Nothing more and nothing less than the rest of this godforsaken world thinks."

My throat strained as though I had swallowed a pinecone sideways. "Lucy. You are as my sister. No one dearer; no one who knows me better. It's not like that at all." Though it was exactly like that. I could feel the color gather in my cheeks. "Forgive me."

"That's all I'm good for, right? Your servant sister. Someone who has to be with you, and has to like you, and put up with your infernal judgments and stiff-necked pride, because there's nothing else available." She lifted her skirts and turned and ran back toward our house, leaving me standing in the street alone. Apparently, agape.

"I hope you swallow a fly," she hollered back as she hurried down the sidewalk.

I pressed my lips together. And then, because it was irresistible, "You catch more flies with honey," I shouted.

"How would you know?" she taunted, still speaking with more excessive volume than anyone before the war would ever have thought to do. It wasn't the bombs or shelling that destroyed our hearing, it was a far worse malady, a panic that ate away at the very bedrock of our souls, leaving us floundering. Bad was good, good was bad, up was down, people were overtired children, ripped from safe naps, stripped of life's lessons to behave, be quiet, be content.

"Furthermore, I don't want any cotton-picking flies!" I replied. Oh, that I could just write out my defense, which would be much more practical, fitting and, to the point, cutting. I would lay awake that night, replaying the drama, revisiting my actions and repurposing them to a better outcome.

As you might imagine, neighbors appeared on their porches to treat themselves to our drama.

With great effort and no small amount of dignity I proceeded to our appointment, sans that shrew, Lucy.

"She has a headache," I told all who inquired about her absence. That their heads snapped back a fraction of an inch inclined me to believe that perhaps my delivery was a trifle sharp. I looked at their faces, hungry for drama. They were the ones who never wanted to invite Lucy in the first place, funny how her absence now seemed to cause a stir.

I retreated to my manners. "How is your husband, Annie?" A small, stoop-shouldered woman with a kind heart and terrible coffee, Annie was a favorite, for she generally seemed to believe the sweet words she spoke.

"He's back at the mill, and his hand is nearly healed," she answered. As I knew it would, the conversation veered into the health and scandalizing personal details of the women present, their husbands, and their children. I didn't quite gag but I'm sure my lips were pursed at the saga of Cynthia Farthington's husband and the boil she had to lance on his lower back.

The coffee was almost as bitter as my mood. I stayed merely twenty minutes longer before I left. "I must go check on Lucy."

While Lucy can talk more than any politician on a podium and used up her quota of words by her thirteenth birthday, she had an even more effective weapon. She wielded the silent treatment with a skill that would have come in handy for General Robert E. Lee, had he only known of its magical power. She found Samson's strength in silence, which brought my picayune power of refusing to apologize to its knees. To my credit, I lasted two whole days. I tried, however.

"Going to be hot today."

Lucy, who had theories of weather and its influence on everything from ones' constitution, to mood, to appetite held her silence. She was as riled as a wasp stuck in lemonade.

I did the marketing, came back and worked on my next article. I tried everything I could think of to involve her. "Mrs. Jensen gave me peaches." I sniffed at one, my skills of drama exaggerating, but not by much, the sweet smell. Her narrowed eyes didn't even deign to glance in my direction. Daggers. I put the peaches on the counter. I prepared coffee. "Funny how we like our coffee even on hot days like today." Cicadas had more to say to me than Lucy.

The good news was she flounced to the dining room table as I placed her coffee. The bad news, her lower lip remained stubbornly attached to her upper. "Good Lord, Lucy, you will have to open your mouth and talk to me sometime. How on earth will you drink your coffee?"

She settled about sewing a hem for one of her clients. "That's a mighty pretty dress you have there. Who is it for?" I clattered my cup into its saucer. "Please. Lucy. Talk to me. I am sorry, sorry, sorry. I am not to blame for the state of affairs of our lives, let alone the whole damn southern way of life. Yes, I swore. What of it?" At least she looked at me. "Oh, for heaven's sake. True ladies have an appropriate vocabulary for whatever the situation calls. Except for my mother, rest her soul."

Lucy cracked and repeated, "Rest her soul," after me. I knew she couldn't have held out for much longer. Lord how I had missed her voice. Though she wasn't through with my suffering just yet.

"Do you not see your own blindness, Suellen? Am I less than a pet dog? How exactly does the misfortune of my birth preclude the desires of my heart?"

"There's just a pecking order and that's the way it's always been. I didn't mean anything by it. And of course, I should have known you want to marry. But I thought you were happy with me."

"And for the rest of my life, being some tag-a-long afterthought? No, thank you, ma'am."

"What's gotten into you, Lucy?"

"Did you ever once, ever stop to think about my feelings? Did you never think I might be sweet on a beau?"

"I am sorry. You never talked like that before."

"Why would I? Who is there to listen? To encourage? All the times I listened to you, and your aspirations to marriage. Who held your babies before you even did?"

"Don't. Do not talk about them. I beg you."

Tears seeped from the corners of her eyes, but I would not give her the satisfaction of sharing mine. "Those children were just as much mine, and I felt their loss the same as you," she said.

"I never knew a suitable man for you, Lucy. Did you have someone you secretly burned for?" I may have emphasized the word burned a trifle much, and Lucy pounced on that.

"Of course, I had my school girl crushes, but I know what's appropriate and what's not. Unlike some."

"What is that supposed to mean?"

"You tried to make light with your sisters' beaus."

"As they did mine. What of it? We were all young, and playing roles, and no one took it seriously."

"Until they did."

I bowed my head. "You and I both know, there's a special place in hell for a woman who steals another woman's intended."

Suellen

"Suellen. They say all is fair in love and war."

"And you and I both know that is a big fat lie. Love is war. And there are cheaters and there are losers. And there are rules, and there are consequences."

"I wasn't even allowed in those games."

"No," I agreed.

"That doesn't mean I didn't want to hold a boy's hand, see him smile at the sight of me. Many did you know. But there was nothing I could do about it."

"I know. I'm sorry. It wasn't fair and right then, and it's even less fair and right now. Lucy, it's going to take so long to make things right. I will do everything in my power I can to help." "To what end, Suellen? What are you, one woman, going to do to redress more than a hundred years of hurts and wrongs?"

"I think of us as equals, friends, sisters."

"No, you don't, but thank you for saying that."

I wrinkled my forehead. Dear Lord, she was right. The ingrained injustices from an entire generation were made to be swept under the carpet. "I apologize, Lucy. I don't know what I'd do without you, and I am honored to call you my friend." I hesitated. "And to stand up with you when you marry." I reached up to dab the lone tear off my cheek that threatened to betray me after all. "And to hold your babies first, before you."

We hugged, rather tightly, more than either of us was comfortable. "Well, that was a right good boo-hoo," Lucy said, pulling away first. "Though I know for a fact your finger came off your face dry." She rubbed her thumb over my finger as I wrenched my hand away from her.

"That does not dilute the sentiment."

"Oh crack your back, Missy. I know how hard it is for you to show any emotion. But just once, I urge you to feel the cleanliness of a thorough tempestuous soul-shivering set-to." She blew her nose with undisputed pleasure.

"Your mother always told you to look for the calm after a storm," she said.

"Honey, it is the calm before the storm," I educated her.

"No matter," she said, pocketing her handkerchief. "It's best to look for the calm before, during and after those so-called storms."

"My mother also said 'patience is a virtue,' though I'm beginning to think patience is for the lazy. We need to find you a handsome husband. One who thinks the sun rises and sets upon your beauty," I clasped my hands to my heart.

Lucy snorted. "No need for handsomeness or excessive doting," she said, "though I wouldn't say no to either. However, I'd settle for good teeth and at least three of four limbs in working condition." Oh, I had missed her laugh.

"And what about you, Suellen?" Fortified with coffee, we went out back to hang our sheets on the line. "Will you marry again?"

I gave a short laugh that, strangely, felt like a cry. "Never."

"Your mother also said 'never say never.'"

"I am secure in my proclamation. Let's call it the Fourteenth Amendment to the U.S. Constitution. I hereby declare, I will never marry again. Not many men left to marry around here anyway." In a town mostly filled with women, baby boys were beginning to be born. Probably in time for the next war.

Chapter Five

Making my new dress for our dinner engagement, with help from Lucy, had absorbed my waking hours. Her nimble fingers flew in excited haste to create the latest fashion. "This cuirass bodice will be perfect for your figure, Suellen. It will fit right to your hips."

I laughed at her. "Do not think I care a fig for whether the bodice is this tight or that. Flounces and ruffles are not the measure of character."

"Good thing," Lucy replied. "You would come up sorely lacking."

Though never spoken aloud, I occasionally give thanks for my sweet Lucy. Now was not one of those occasions. Had she known my level of disturbance regarding this dress, she would have been relentless. I do not know what fire guided my own fingertips to sew the finest stitches I ever had. I worked on the hem, which Lucy begrudgingly allowed, dipping in and out of the material with a needle as if it were the very fabric of my life. Piercing through the woven strands with a wish— a prayer, if I were to be entirely honest—tugging the thread along with care, as if to show the universe or any merciful God not busy toying with the masses: I am patient, I am virtuous. I am worthy. Worthy of what, my restless soul had yet to discover.

In my younger years, it's true, I cared for fancy gowns, soft kid-leather shoes dyed pretty colors, ribbons, lace—folderols, as my father would have said, waving away their importance, from anyone but my sister, of course. I cringe at the hours I wasted, turning this way and that, dreaming up ways to fashion my hair to attract beaus. I had my fair share of gentlemanly interest, too, though some misses prevailed in hogging that spotlight. I preferred the attentions of older gentlemen, grown-up men with ideas in their heads and the sense to look past a girl and her foibles to discover her true heart and brain.

After the war, I became an old woman. Nothing mattered. I survived the best way I knew how, I suppose, just like everyone else. When your stomach is shriveled, see how strong your belief in your God or your country or your way of life tastes. Does your pride provide nourishment? When times are tough, it's the grit in our soul that either carries us up and through or leaves us to curl up and die. I would wager all survivors had bits and pieces of cracked ugliness that were used to trick fate into one more day. One more meal. One more night, and for the very lucky, one more night escaping to a sleep void of dreams. Pride, gallantry, kindness have no place in a world gone mad. I'm not excusing my behavior, merely pointing out a brief understanding of such wretched actions and a perverse sense of recognition of the very ugliness of the act of surviving. No sterling character or heroic feats to applaud, except perhaps of mothers protecting their children. One couldn't help but wonder how the reckoning would be tallied above, if intent truly did cancel out wicked means of purchase. As God is my witness, there has to be something better.

I headed downstairs and heard Lucy talking. I hesitated. Good Lord, forgive my childish behavior and certain knowledge that eavesdroppers never hear anything good of themselves. Yet we always hear something to chew upon, the devil on my shoulder decided.

"Suellen is the bravest woman I know," Lucy said. I shrugged my shoulders, true enough, I suppose, but it didn't feel like much of a tribute since pretty much everything I feared had already happened. Courage is being brave when you are scared; there wasn't much left that scared me. That's all you've got, Lucy? Come on, aren't I sweet? Smart? Good natured? Even I had to clasp my hand over my mouth over the last one. Curious. I wanted to be good natured, like Lucy? I could all but hear my sisters' evil laughter. Grumpy Skirts was a childhood nickname I never could shake. If I was brave, Lucy was kind. She had an equanimity I coveted and despaired of in equal measure.

"But along with that," I heard Lucy continue. I tilted my head toward the door, not able to crimp the small smile that had formed. "She is the most stubborn woman I have ever met. If you say a magnolia flower is a lovely shade of cream, she'll insist it's yellow. If I want to walk to the mercantile on a day other than Tuesday-walk-to-the-mercantile day, she's fit to be tied. And she holds a grudge as if it's a newborn baby that needs to be nursed." Now that was just mean.

I burst through the doorway. "And that Lucy is just the kindest, most gentle soul you'd ever meet, with nary a bad word to say about anyone." I used my most cultivated voice, my dulcet tones not fooling Lucy for a minute.

"Sorry you had to hear that, Suellen. I was just explaining to Mrs. Michael here, why we cannot attend her social supper on Thursday. As much as we'd dearly love to, I'm afraid we have plans, right Suellen?" Lucy nodded encouragingly at me.

"Yes." I composed myself. "We have plans. We sure do." Mrs. Michael was forever badgering us to head up, sit on, donate to, and plum just work like a field hand for her charity, "Our Dear Boys' Graves." Capitalization, hers. Now bear in mind, the war was long over, and, God willing, the recession was coming to an end. The world was tilting back to its proper axis, and yet that woman loved her renovation projects.

"Priorities," I actually said out loud. "We cannot thank you enough for your efforts," I told her. "We ourselves undertake to help as we can." Lucy and I found perverse pleasure in the energy surrounding young people, and people with gumption to help themselves. As a woman of a certain age, I vowed to stay out of the rocking chair as long as I could by looking toward the horizon and feeling the miracle of what man could create, instead of what those behind us had ruined. "But, thank you so much, Mrs. Michael. Maybe next time." I took her elbow to lead her out the door. "Thank you for dropping in. As Lucy said, I am set in my ways I'm afraid, and we're just two poor women trying our best to get by with only the hours the good Lord has seen fit to bless us."

Lucy closed the door behind Mrs. Michael's exit and leaned against it. She clicked the lock into place twice. She was in the habit of closing and locking doors twice, the second time was to keep out the evil spirits. We headed back to the parlor.

"She's had a hard life," Lucy said.

"And thank goodness we have not," I replied.

"You know what I mean."

"I know that no one has more hours in the day than anyone else. I know that everyone's suffering burns as badly, and I know that anything you ever love will not last."

"Grumpy Skirts," Lucy said. "Why can you never see the good in things?"

"I find it no coincidence that magic and tragic rhyme. It is the same coin that we all will spend."

"Don't doom and gloom me, Suellen. We're all trying to move on the best we can. Women like Mrs. Michael, especially."

I must confess to a bit of mockery toward other women, most notably my own kinfolk, who dared trespass into the foolishness of helpless femininity. "I have never in my life met a helpless woman. I've met women who needed help, and men who truly were helpless, and beyond help. But women?" It may not sound like a compliment because it vexes me so, but women are a brave tribe. That's why the subterfuge of women who need big, strong men to save them sits ill upon me. Who me? They might say, flapping their eyelids like a palmetto frond in a hurricane. Yes, and about as attractive. I could seldom repress an audible exhale. Any lady worth her salt knows what needs to be done. And then they do it.

I rubbed at the old scar on my hand. And once again donned the mask learnt at my mother's knee. In my mind's eye, I imagine myself a reflection of that good woman. The literal reflection before me defied that pretty picture, though I saw in my eyes some suggestion of wanting more. And having the most audacious idea that perhaps there existed more to want.

Lucy surprised me when she reached out and touched my finger. I bugged my eyes out at her.

The woman missed nothing. I pulled my hand back is if burned. "Ah, Suellen. That was surely the roughest time."

"Hush."

"I think about…"

"Hush your mouth."

"I know," she said.

I exhaled, strongly. I have the lungs of a locomotive steam engine.

"What a shame." Lucy shook her head and tsk-tsked. A sound that can entice me to violence. "She sure was a pretty little thing. No bigger than our corn husk dolls. Do you remember?"

"I swear to the heavens, Lucy. Please stop flapping your gums." The woman was surely a horsefly in a past life.

"Suellen," she said gently.

Dear God above, would that I were a train as I would surely have run her down.

"Your scar is nicely healed." I held my hand away from her. "Why, when I saw the ragged tear, clean through to your finger bone, as you dug that hole, it shattered my heart all over again. You do believe she's with the angels now, right? Along with the others?"

I slid my thumb alongside the scar that lined the curve of my right index finger. I wore my gloves most of the time, covering the angry explosion of stretched skin. My steam engine had collapsed. "What do you want me to say, Lucy? These things are best not spoken of." I had no air left in my voice. My skin flushed hotly, as if tears were trying to spill out of my pores. I gave a little cough. So why were her eyes filling with tears?

"Your inside scars need to heal," she said.

I gave into her hug but kept the salty acid of my tears inside, where it could better burn a hole in my soul.

Chapter Six

I sat on the faded milky blue counterpane covering my bed, comforted by its worn familiar cotton, threadbare in places, the cost of hard-earned dreams and unwelcome nightmares. Last Christmas, Lucy had presented me with a new quilt she had sewn, though I used it only during the long, cold nights of winter as I couldn't bear to give up my ragged blanket from my past life. A poor talisman, I suppose, but it had warmed the bodies of my children, and had accompanied me several times near death. Not near enough, however.

Lucy entered my room with her creation to help me dress for our dinner party, excited as a cricket. She herself was wearing a pale green, newly-finished afternoon gown that I could not wait to borrow one day soon.

"We need this, Suellen," Lucy said, twirling with a hop to show me her angles.

"You are childish."

"Better than being an old grandma," she returned. She shook out my dress and laid it upon the bed. "Stand up, Suellen. You are about to be magicked into a princess."

Imagine my surprise as I donned my finery. I thought childish feelings about fripperies and fancies had long passed. My fingers glided over the bodice I had professed to have no concerns for, then tugged at the tight waist. I smoothed down the skirt which was gathered on either side. I twisted my wrists. "I am enamored with these flaring sleeves," I told her. The rose color was indeed flattering, and the embroidery of golden threads, which Lucy had added, created a finery beyond comparison. I lifted my eyes to observe the fit from my dear mother's mirror. My hands cupped my bosom and my breath retreated to the back of my throat. Something very strange was happening to me. I was not sure I did not like it.

"You look lovely, Suellen." Lucy dimpled at me and curtsied. "As do you." I nodded my head.

We went downstairs, the tips of our shoes tapping lightly on the steps. We joined arms and went out to meet our horse and carriage. "Thank you, Jaffrey," Lucy called out to the boy from Hansen's Livery Service. "We won't be too late."

I smiled my appreciation and gave him a penny as we both lifted our skirts and prepared to climb into the driver seat.

"Scoot on over, Lucy. You know I drive better than you."

"You think you drive better than I do just because of that one time."

"That one time you nearly got us killed when the back wheel went off the bridge by the Henderson place?"

"It wasn't my fault," Lucy said. "It was absolutely your fault."

"That is not very kind."

"That is very accurate."

"Your unkindness?"

"Your uncoordinated efforts at steering the back end of a horse," I told her. "Sit," I said, gaining the seat. She sank down next to me and we both smoothed our dresses. The horse neighed, as if in approval.

"Now I'm taking orders from a horse?"

"If the shoe fits," Lucy said, then laughed her loud musical laugh. I clicked my tongue and the carriage lurched forward. She jumped on the hard seat we shared and clung to the side. "I fear my spine will not deliver me the full size as when we started."

"Hush."

Lucy has been by my side as long as I can remember. We fight like sisters, of course, but truth be told I have more kindly feelings toward her than any living relative I care to claim. We don't talk of these things, but I prefer to think it is not my imagination she feels the same way. She often jests it is our opposite natures that fit together so well. Only a few days separate our birthdays, though mine comes first, and I always make it a point to share a small token with her as I have no recollection of ever celebrating Lucy's day. Though I hazily remember my father presenting her a candy on her special day, or a ribbon. The myopia of my selfish youth, I suppose. Though we are of a similar shape and size, she is softer, from the inside out. I have oftentimes told her she is filled with more emotion than I. She can love like a heartsick heroine in a novel, though her hatred can far outpace that. She is one of those fidgety persons who needs less sleep than others, who finds the pattern in an uneven rhythm of society. I myself thrive on rituals and routine. It distracted me to no end her wispy notions that come upon her at all times of the day, unannounced, unexpected and unappreciated, by me. I tried to tell her the benefits of having an orderly mind: "If we know we do the laundry every Monday morning, that's one less thing we have to think about."

"If you are bound and determined to be married to your Monday morning wash, your Tuesday evening fried chicken, and your Wednesday morning dusting, when is there any time left over for inspiration? Can you spell spontaneous, Suellen? Of course you can't."

It was because of her dig that we were headed out to dinner in the first place. I had accepted this invitation on a spur of the moment, which might as well be the cliché for lapse of judgment. I wanted to show her I could enjoy a little variety in our lives. Every now and then. Just a small crumb at a time, of course. Wouldn't want to take up too festive a lifestyle.

For some reason, my stomach was filled with butterflies, but my new ensemble gave me courage. Lucy can wear my dresses and I hers, and, though hers are always a little looser on me, we make do to stretch our wardrobe. Her skin is flawless and isn't prone to the splotchy red creep which phantoms my neck upon the slightest agitation. Which I was just about to feel.

Lucy nudged my skirt with her knee.

"I see her," I said. I slowed the horse to a stop.

"That woman," Lucy shook her head. "She sets my teeth on edge."

"Yoohoo!" It was Miss Bouchard. Pray, never ask her the time, she'd as soon tell you how a watch is made. "Suellen, Lucy." Her hand was waving hard. "Off to supper?" She didn't even wait for our answer. "I'm just back with a fresh baked pie from Mrs. Perrin. Mr. Harris is coming over this evening." She giggled and dipped her gaze. I could see the tips of her boots toe in toward each other. "There may be plans," she admitted, "and that's all I am going to say."

"Sounds serious," Lucy said. "You look mighty fine."

"Well, it's all thanks to you." Miss Bouchard swirled her skirt. "Mr. Harris loves this dress. And, so, I was wondering if you had any remnants of leftover fabric? Do you think you could sew a matching bonnet for my little Scruffy Muffin?"

"Your dog?" I asked.

Lucy cut me off. "Of course, honey. I'm sure I can come up with something. But, we must be on our way lest we are late."

Suellen 39

After what seemed an eternity of infernal southern goodbyes, we were off. "Hyah," I clicked my tongue and the horse started.

"She means well, I suppose," I told Lucy. "And your fine dresses do nothing but help her.

She does look quite *soigné*."

"Pretty from afar but far from pretty."

As we rolled over a rut in the road, I allowed my shoulder to bump companionably into Lucy's. I was inordinately fond of this woman.

We neared Mrs. Boyer's house a ways outside of town past the church. "Slow down, Suellen," Lucy begged me. "You do everything too fast." She grabbed onto the sideboard. "And, you are also too sudden to judgment," she chastised me, as my own mother used to. "We should be kinder." That pronouncement, heard all my life, had the power to cut deeply. Would that I could harness the heat throbbing with the strength of ten horses pulsing through my veins.

"It's not my fault fools abound," I replied. "And you know you agree with me."

"Pride may goeth before a fall," Lucy said, "but Lord knows it's smugness that always precedes Armageddon."

I should have heeded her warning.

Chapter Seven

I did not begrudge Mr. Harris (or the dog who would soon be sporting a bonnet), to Miss Bouchard. Perhaps I begrudged the thought of a happily-ever-after not mine.

I clutched the still-warm cornbread wrapped in a dish towel that Lucy had made for us to offer up to our hostess. Mrs. Boyer fussed over it as if it were a bottle of champagne, of which neither Lucy nor I had ever tasted.

Mrs. Boyer directed the choir at our church, the mayor at his official business, and any of the townspeople it occurred to her that needed directing. As a busybody of the first degree, she had an imposing stature, encouraged by her enjoyment of food and libation alike. She practiced her feminine wiles by wearing dresses two sizes too small—honest truth, as Lucy had sewed several of them for her. She was wearing one of the gowns that evening, a celadon satin dress that Lucy swore she'd had to stitch the seams twice to make sure they would hold. Mrs. Boyer was a widow with suspiciously dark hair (no one could guess her age), and had the energy of a roomful of misbehaving toddlers. That, combined with an appetite for socializing, should have made her bear the brunt of a town full of disapproval, but her outlandish opinions were meant with such obvious kindness toward positive outcomes, no one could take offense. That her dictates oftentimes worked out, to the surprise of her victims, only added to her power. Pity our generals had had no acquaintance of her.

I thanked Mrs. Boyer for her kind invitation, and tried to bargain with the good Lord above. Such a state I was in for some odd reason, my thoughts got jumbled up and I basically vowed to be on my best behavior, and if it was in His Almighty's plans, perhaps a suitor could spark some excitement, of the good kind, in our lives.

"Dear, dear, Suellen!" For Mrs. Boyer always, yet always, spoke with exclamation points. She looked me up and down twice. She reached her hands around either side of my ribcage and shifted my corset. "You'll do." She nodded her head and turned to Lucy. "And the lovely Lucy!" She wagged a finger at her. "I shall be calling upon you very soon. I've ordered the most delightful taffeta for summer soirees!"

"I will be honored," Lucy replied.

"Join me! I have someone special," she sang out, "I want you to meet!"

We walked into the front parlor, one of the most handsome in town with its maroon velvet draperies and two floral-patterned settees. Ferns on pedestals framed the settee near the windows. I would have ferns in my house one day. I felt my heart interrupt its steadfast widow's rhythm.

Apparently, my shadow noticed. "What is the matter with you?" Lucy asked me. "Shh."

Mrs. Boyer led us to meet her other dinner guest who stood as we approached. My bosom, newly plumped thanks to a layer of ruffles and a tighter than ordinary tug on corset strings, tingled in a not unpleasant manner. To my chagrin, the hand I held out to meet Dr. Kincaid's, trembled.

"Please, ma'am," the timbre of his voice struck such a chord in my ears, I may have jutted my jaw to clear incipient congestion, "call me Theodore."

Theodore Kincaid. A more euphonious name I have never heard.

"Hit the floor, Theodore," Lucy whispered. "Let him have it, Suellen."

A frown as fast and furious as buckshot was carefully aimed between her eyes, to no avail. While I have never been a woman ever suspected of light virtue, my bank account apparently draped my shortcomings in a gauzy veil of desire. Talk of religion, politics, and how much money one does or does not have is as welcome as a bellyache. While I hold no stock in the first two, as for my "fortune," it's not much, but perhaps more than others. I had given the what-for to far better male specimens than Theodore, thus engendering Lucy's silly admonition. She folded her arms and tilted her mouth down in a most unbecoming fashion.

"Theodore," I nodded, peeking up at him, aghast to discovery my eyelashes fluttering like palmetto fronds, not in a hurricane, but perhaps with warning of an oncoming storm. His own eyes, a velvety cornflower blue if you must know, sparkled back at me through his smudged spectacles. His hair was a bit overlong, and endearingly tangled.

I don't recall what I ate, or how I ate it. I do know very little comestibles passed through my lips as my throat seemed to have some blockage. I hoped I was not falling ill.

I spoke little, and it could not have been the small sips of sherry that imbued the whole table with such a bright glow. Besides, Lucy, sitting to my right, had replaced her empty glass with mine, twice. The witty give and take of shared ideas between Mrs. Boyer at one end of the table and Theodore at the other had my head turning.

Lucy propped her elbow on the table to cast an aside. "You look as if you're watching poor ol' Jasper chasing a rabbit."

"Thank you, as that was my intent." I whispered to her, then cleared my throat. "You disagree with the president, sir?" I was showing off; however, the rest of my brilliant repartee had an audience of one, inside my own skull, as I found myself too timid to speak. Pity. President Rutherford, or as many in the South referred to him, Rutherfraud, had to make concessions to appease many of my ignorant countrymen. I glanced at Lucy, knowing she agreed with my thoughts. Perhaps more vehemently than I.

The cadence of Theodore's voice coupled with his eloquence was captivating. He smiled at me, since I appeared nearly incapable of speech. "The president talks a fine-sounding game," he said. "Working to get the South to accept racial equality and fighting for civil rights may look perfection personified on paper, but our good president will fail in his lofty endeavors."

Lucy puffed out her cheeks, curled out her lower lip, and flared her nostrils in her best imitation of a simpleton. "Stop it," I whispered as the doctor engaged in answering a question from Mrs. Boyer. I pivoted the heel of my new black lace up shoe and found Lucy's foot under the table. With precision I pressed the outer edge of my foot atop of hers. She was fond of her precious new boots, and with an audible exhalation conformed her face back to repose. She straightened in her chair.

"Behave," I told her.

"You behave. Are you ill?" She whispered back.

"Everything all right, dears?" Mrs. Boyer had heard Lucy.

"I'm fine," I assured the table, before peering sideways at the good doctor.

An awkward silence descended after dishes had been cleared, until the scrape of Mrs. Boyer's chair announced time was up. I yearned for the night to end, so strangely did I feel, yet I was devastated when it did. Lucy and I both refused coffee, as I knew that's not what would be keeping me up that night.

"Goodbye! Thank you all! Lovely! Lovely!" Mrs. Boyer called out to us. She clapped her hands as if the night had been some sort of performance.

Dr. Kincaid, Theodore, insisted on escorting us home. He would return the horse and carriage for us, which was the most gentlemanly offer Lucy and I had had in many years. Irritations at those little life's maintenances, like arranging transportation, fixing that smoking chimney, or repairing the rotted wainscoting in the parlor, underscored how bereft we were of manly attentions.

When Theodore helped me step down from the wagon bench, I deliberately went weak at the knee. The better to lean in to him. I inhaled deeply, as if trying to smell the gentleman; can you imagine? Was it my imagination, or had he puffed out his chest, the better to rub against my arm?

"Come along, Suellen," Lucy said, dragging me by my arm. Sometimes I hate her.

"I'd be obliged if you ladies would come to my house next Sunday for supper," Theodore said, including Lucy in his invitation.

"We'd love to," I said. "We'd be delighted," I added, trying out that most strange adjective I was sure I had never uttered before in my life.

"Oh, good Lord." Lucy was obviously confused at my genteel manners as well.

"Hush," I said not turning my head. "I'll see you inside." I shooed her away. And dear God, I may have tittered. A word I despise, a mannerism I detest. A reaction I do not understand.

He tipped his hat. "Miss Lucy, Miss Suellen." He stared a second longer at me, the stars serving to illuminate our very important unspoken conversation. I could only hope they chose not to highlight the dewy perspiration that appeared on my face, as if I were a field hand hoeing the red clay soil after a drought.

"It was Jaffrey's carriage light, not the stars," Lucy told me later when I tried to recapture the night's details. I decided to keep to myself how the tone of his very voice upon the three syllables of my name, struck a chord—had any sonata ever sounded sweeter?

Instead of chattering anymore Lucy and I retired to our bedrooms as I mused at how tall Dr. Kincaid, Theodore, was. In his high-collared white shirt and fitted vest, both in need of pressing, he appeared quite broad of shoulder. I am ashamed to admit I wondered if his chest had brown curls to match his fine soft hair.

I shut my door, protecting my reveries, and disinviting Lucy and her infernal tongue from the lashing she was obviously dying to give. Theodore had tipped his hat and said he would see us both next Sunday afternoon at two. "I'm sure my children will love you."

"Children?" Lucy had said, far too immediate for the etiquette required to protect the man's ears. I only hope the horse's hooves drowned out her indignation. "Upon my word, that man has children? How many? And what, pray tell, does he want with you?" She nodded her head looking like a sage of Delphi. "What is wrong with you? Perhaps you need spectacles to see what's going on." She had tried to reach for my forehead then. "Are you taken with a fever? I thought you appeared peckish at dinner." I jerked my head from her reach, though my ears were not as lucky as she was not even close to being finished with her interrogation.

I embraced immaturity with a light-heartedness I had never been afforded before, during or after the war and merely smiled at the woman.

"Rub those eyes of yours, dear Suellen," she told me. "He wants you to be wiping behinds, cooking dinner, and washing out his drawers."

"Hush. No need to be vulgar." I felt like my mother, who had indeed uttered that very admonishment many times. I was a grown up at last. A grown-up lady. Why then did my thoughts stall upon Theodore's underclothes?

Chapter Eight

Funny how laundry day shows up right quick, too soon most times, but if you are looking forward to a special day or event, my stars, how time toys with us. Sunday took a month to arrive.

Lucy drove the buggy, though I was a much better horsewoman. I didn't much care for horses—truth be told they scared me—but driving a buggy? Well now, that was an exhilaration. Lucy and I usually took turns, though she could see better than I under the stars.

"Sit down," Lucy snapped, flicking her wrist as she tugged on the reins. "You drive too fast on your way to a funeral; heaven knows you'd kill us trying to get to this engagement."

I had taken special care with my appearance and, though she didn't want to, Lucy helped.

She fashioned my hair and insisted upon allowing me to wear her favorite lavender dress, which was the most frilly gown we owned between us.

"Dear Lord, what are you wearing?" I had not had the presence of mind to notice until we were in the carriage and her shawl slipped off her shoulder. "You choose today, of all days, to unearth that bovine abomination?"

"Don't I look nice?" Lucy asked as if I had complimented her and her choice of the cow-brown "cinnamon" dress we usually only wore when we were in one of our "moods," or incapacitated.

"Well, no."

"Thank you." She could not keep the devil of a smile off her face. She clicked her tongue.

The horse jerked the wagon forward.

"I cannot believe you wore that brown dress. Pick your battles wisely, Lucy."

She merely took one hand off the reins and tugged at the collar of her drab dress. I set my own shawl aside and said nothing more.

The June afternoon was unseasonably warm, and I had worried all week for nothing. I was quite sure my anxious thoughts staved off any rain showers which would have led us to cancel our dinner invitation. I fidgeted in my seat, fussed with my hair, and may have sighed a time or two.

"I don't like this, Suellen. You're acting like a child." Lucy said.

"And you're acting like old Orson," I snapped. He had been an overseer fired years before the war for whipping slaves for the slightest infraction.

"Take that back," she said.

"Oh, Lord." The last thing I wanted was Lucy in a mood. "I didn't mean it. I'm just nervous."

"Nervous about what? That man is not for you; don't go getting all starry-eyed."

I made a disgruntled noise. "I am not starry-eyed. How dare you? I was just thinking. Maybe we're too hard on people, Lucy. Maybe, life isn't a war after all. It's just a series of battles. I'm trying to hope maybe there is happiness left. Maybe there are second chances."

"Well, shut my mouth. Have we met before? Where is Grumpy Skirts? I like her better. Don't let some dandy turn your head, Suellen."

I clutched her arm to hang on as she drove over a rut.

"You did that on purpose," I told her. "What's gotten into you? You've been sulking all week."

"And you've been flitting around all week, like a simpleton. You don't hear me half the time; you burned the chicken last night, yet you ate it as if it was meringue."

I laughed. "What on earth are you talking about?" Lucy knew me too well. I hummed a song to prevent any further conversation.

"Stop humming that sappy 'Oh! Susanna' song. The second you start whistling is the second I toss you out of this wagon, Missy, and I am not fooling." She grumbled some more. "Humming and whistling. god-awful noises made by fools. How come the only people who enjoy whistling are the ones blowing?"

"What would I ever do without you?" I asked her peaceably. Though she had a sharp tongue, Lucy always looked as if something good was hidden around the corner, for no perfectly good reason. While it was one of the things I loved most about her, it could also prove to be most tiresome. That's why her stubborn taking against the doctor was so baffling and hurtful.

Then she began to sing.

"Oh, Suellen, don't you cry for me.

We're going to this supper and a fellow for to see.

I saw you with your rosary beads, the weather it is dry.

You prayed all night 'bout all your needs, Suellen, don't you cry."

"Are you quite through?" I asked her, holding on to my seat.

Lucy merely snapped the reins.

I ignored her too, and stared at the chestnut horse which made me think of my father. He had been overly fond of spirits. Outside of my family, neighbors and friends claimed to find him charming and delightfully outspoken. A word to the wise, "outspoken" by its very definition is neither a delightful nor charming trait. No one cares to hear contrary or ludicrous opines unless it is to chew upon for entertainment at a later, less public venue.

My father never paid me much mind, and that's not a bid for sympathy, as I returned his regard in full measure. Only one time that I remember, his eyes lit up as I walked into the stable, the sun hard behind me. I could still feel that girlish flush of pleasure, *Why, he does care for me.* When I continued toward him, stepping into the cool of the barn and out of the spotlight of the sun shining through motes beaming across the hay and the strong odor of horses, dogs, sweat and leather, I entered a shadow that focused my poor features. "Where's your sister?" he had demanded.

I was my mother's favorite. We had only to share a glance to commune about the very things that offended our sensibilities. Loud noises, or rude earthy things that smelled like wallowing pigs, of which I was very afraid. Like my mother, I preferred the sweet, gentle ornaments of God's grace, like flowers and paintings, and making a parlor feel cozy. Imagine my dismay during the war after Mother passed away, and the cruel discovery that the very maintenance of living itself is diametrically opposed to those accoutrements. There's no time to pick flowers when your blistered hands were occupied preparing yet another meal.

While my bank account should be qualified to care for me and Lucy in the years to come, there is an age-old question of how much is ever enough. Since everyone's definition of "enough" is as varied as one's preference for pecan pie or

48 Dee DeTarsio

sleeping in longer than seemly, my enough had become wrapped up in working my fingers to the bone to never feel the crushing embarrassment of being poor, like we were during and after the war. On that one point, I shall give my sister a pass. I never agreed with her methods, but she never even knew I had any plans of my own. I wasn't afraid of hard work; I was afraid of hard work not being enough.

And now that I had some small leisure, I sometimes felt I was rotting on the vine, looking toward the sunset and not only not fearing death, but eagerly courting it. I never was one to put off until tomorrow what needed to be attended to today. By working hard every day, I thought I would have time to spend with my children, and their children, and truthfully believed I would eventually mellow into a kindly, sage mother, satisfied that my efforts would reap rewards. I would, one day, not be so short-tempered and impatient. I would be able to set down my burdens before it was too late.

Unfortunately, too late came too soon. My children and husband were gone. My very dearest children, the two I had held and tucked in at night, and felt impatience with upon their misdeeds, and the one I had held nothing but grand dreams for. They all slept beneath the cedar trees. I had wondered but once to the unanswerable question of why the anguish felt so much worse for that unknown baby. My savage grief had been my penance, though sometimes I was glad she wouldn't have to suffer. I polished the stone that had been my heart into a sparkling diamond, tended with rage. With all expectations extinguished, my bitterness took on a characteristic I felt I had been born with. I am sometimes surprised when I feel a warm breeze upon my face, or savor the juice of a sticky peach nearly overripe, to find myself offering thanks to a God I no longer care for.

I glanced over at Lucy. Though she and I both professed we would rather be bored out of our gourd than scared to death as we were after the war, a certain restlessness had captured our souls. I knew Lucy felt it, too.

"We've shared some rough times, Lucy."

"So, you're going with melancholy?"

"You know what I mean," I told her. "Maybe our luck is changing." She spared a glance at me. "Something is changing."

"I am secure in the knowledge that I did my best," I told her.

Suellen

"That's a highfaluting way of saying 'you could have been worse,'" Lucy reminded me. She sighed. "Just because you suffered in silence doesn't mean no one heard you, honey."

I frowned. "Sometimes it pays no quarter to have a friend who inhales your exhales and believes your business is theirs. You don't know everything there is to know about me."

Lucy's stubborn chin dipped as she looked up at me. Those green eyes of hers held no mercy. "Suellen, nothing you do can surprise me."

I would prove her wrong.

Chapter Nine

"Inky, Stinky, and Pink Eye," Lucy whispered to me as we alit from the carriage in front of Dr. Kincaid's house. Two of his three children stood side by side and stared at us, as did the baby, who was being held by Theodore, rather awkwardly.

Lucy liked children better than I, and I sincerely hoped this brood would prove no exception, that Theodore and I might have opportunity to talk. Theodore and I. How many times have I worked that equation into conversations this past week, both aloud to Lucy and in my own private thoughts? I had done my research and Mrs. Boyer had done the rest. She filled in the personal history that Theodore's wife had died in childbirth a year back. That must have been with Stinky, I thought, as Theodore handed me the baby bearing as loaded a diaper as I've ever felt.

"Mercy." Lucy gasped and stepped away from us. I jostled the baby, looking for hints of Theodore in his buggy little eyes. The motion must have smeared an uncomfortable amount of refuse into the child's behind as he began to wail. I handed him off to Lucy. "You're so good with the little ones," I said.

Theodore introduced us to his nine-year-old daughter, Ila Rose, who stood with her arms folded in front of her, though I could still see fingernails so black she could have carved out the detritus and used it as ink to copy a prayerbook. Next to her stood little Vaughn, age approximately four years, who promptly hurtled his body, face first, led by crusted over blood-red eyes, headlong into my skirt. Why is it always the mangy cats that want to be petted?

Dinner was a stew that Theodore charmingly admitted came from his kind neighbor woman. That my soup bowl had a chip and Lucy's was less than clean only served to heighten my desire to help this poor man and his family.

As the doctor told stories about medicine, saving this person and that, he talked about his new position. Was it my imagination that he stared at me a split second longer than warranted? I responded, but was unsure of what that response was, and, more importantly, what it was supposed to be. It is funny how we assume we are being understood, when that misapprehension must provide nothing but amusement for the heavens.

Suellen

"And what is your new position?" I asked, trying to look like a woman of some thought and substance.

"It's in Oberlin, in Ohio. They have a college of renown, where I will be teaching classes, as time permits from treating patients," he told us. "They are a quite progressive lot there. They have provided me with a house. For myself and the children," he paused. Again with the probing look, doctor? "We will be heading to Ohio before long."

"Oh. Such a shame."

"Suellen," Lucy said.

"I mean, we have just met, and I'm sure our fair city could use a doctor such as yourself."

When the doctor laughed, I was entranced. Caught up in a fairytale. Hook, line and sinker, as the romance novels say.

"Thank you. That is so kind. It is a lovely town, though my wife was very happy here, near her people."

Pause. Pause again for more respect. Then Lucy and I at the same time stumbled over each other, "Sorry, so sorry for your loss."

"She was a good woman, and the children miss her terribly."

"They are fortunate to have you for their father, sir," Lucy said.

Chapter Ten

A few evenings later at supper together in our own home, Lucy and I were strangely quiet. Heaven knows what got her goat, but I had my head in the clouds. I tossed Jasper the leftover ham hock bone from the soup Lucy had made.

Even Lucy smiled along with me at his pure joy in setting about the business of sucking out every last morsel of flavor. "Jasper Three has it all figured out," I told her. "We should all be so lucky to have a wag left in our tail when we get old."

"Funny how he can't hear a dang-blasted thing, especially when we call him, but catch a waft of my green bean soup, and his snout gets all wiggly." Lucy passed her hand before her face.

"He does smell as if he's rolled around in the cavity of a rabid possum."

"And then bathed in the hot sun with slobber on his fur to gild that lily," Lucy added.

He barely noticed as I bent to rub his ears, so content was he with that bone. "And yet, I find great comfort in his odor." Lucy herself just sniffed for effect and took her plate into the kitchen.

The next morning, thoughts of Theodore continued from a most pleasant dream. I headed downstairs to prepare our breakfast of oatmeal and coffee, and to let Jasper outside.

I found him curled up in the kitchen, just like every other morning. I took note to remember this old hound. And our rituals. And his comforting presence. And his loyalty. And his particular odor that didn't bother me, or Lucy, in the least. He waited for me. I would be sure to spoil him with extra pieces of ham. When he didn't get up, I crouched down to chide him. "Come along, Jasper. It's time."

Funny how those words can have different meanings. I patted his head. His drooping eyes opened then, and through his rheumy wet gaze he looked at me. He panted something fierce. "What is it?" I asked him. I knelt beside him then, a sickening flush rising up from my ribcage. I am not one for looking for signs or pretending animals offer intelligence and wisdom where none exists, but that dog looked clean through to my very soul. Lord knows, he had seen me at my rock bottom very worst, and had been with me through every deprivation known after that ac- cursed war. He was both the blanket of a missing mother's approval, as well as the bolster to my own children. He was painfully grateful for every careless crumb—literal and metaphorical—I had ever tossed his way. My eyes felt as cloudy as his looked as I struggled to understand what he was trying to tell me.

"Good Jasper," was all I could manage to whisper. I ran my hands over his head and scooped my fingers down and under his floppy ears. Just like I always did, not even thinking about it. He licked my hand. I nodded. "Please accept my immeasurable gratitude for your loyalty. Well done, Jasper."

"Goodness, Suellen, who are you talking to?" Lucy found me there, next to him, rocking on my knees.

"I'll go get the doctor," she said, meaning Theodore, as she hiccupped on her own sob. "He'll help us bury him."

How I cried over that dumb dog. All I could remember was that his dripping foul tongue had once licked the skin of my children. How he had come every time my husband called his name. In my grief, I couldn't help but wonder for what purpose I was left behind. What great sin had I committed to be punished with this continued existence? What kind of world did I live in where missing that dog would leave a larger hole than that of most of my friends?

Theodore arrived shortly thereafter and his embrace gave me comfort. What a relief to be held in that fine man's arms. I was honored to be the focus of his attention. He must be a very good doctor. I put a plaster on my aching heart and couldn't help but leapfrog into the future, my future, perhaps with this handsome, God-fearing man.

The rest of the days of the week passed, as they do, and we rerouted our routines without Jasper. While Lucy had thoughtfully pushed aside her chair to cover the spot where Jasper used to lie, the indents from the chair legs left in the carpet broke my heart anew every time I chanced upon those grooves. When they faded, would my heartache?

I felt as if I in some way betrayed that dog when my guilty heart would flicker with joy upon my meetings with the doctor.

"I am aggrieved," I told Lucy. "I miss Jasper, I'm restless for a change, and have come to decipher that there is more to this life than we are currently living. Don't you think certain folks come into our lives when we need them most?"

"I think you think that, as infatuated you are with the good doctor. I am very sure, however, you would have crisp words for a helpless female going on and on about a man like you do."

"I don't like your tone."

"I don't like your judgment."

"I don't like your temper."

"I can assure you I certainly don't care much for yours."

Doors were slammed to make way for the silence. I spent hours away from home and took refuge in Theodore's attentions, subdued though they were, as befitted a confident man of his stature.

I used to wear my pain like a well-mended shawl, knitted in the old country and passed down from grandmother to granddaughter. See this rend? That hole? A gaping wound puckered and marred the entire line of the shrug, an outline of my disfigured shadow. Two babies and an unborn dream snuffed out like my bedtime candle; some days the darkness could tolerate no light, but of course I imagine many folks feel that way. I had hunched my shoulders with humility against the next blow from above, but surely, I had thought, that would be my admittance fee to heaven.

But with Theodore, I could stand up straight. I had no need for the security of an old woman's shawl. I was made whole again.

I said "yes."

Chapter Eleven

"Please tell me you did not accept that man's marriage proposal," Lucy said.

"Yes. I did. And that's that." He loves me, I wanted to sing. I kept quiet, but had I looked in a mirror I'm sure I would have seen a smile so smug I should have been frightened. I defied the fiddler of the universe, or whomever it is that trolls for unwarranted happiness. For once I was unafraid that I would be zeroed in on *tout de suite*, as my mother would have said. A lady seeks no attention, she had believed; a great lady even hides from the Lord above.

"We are moving to Oberlin. It's in Ohio, where he is contracted to be the town doctor."

"Yes. I remember he's about to leave town. You better not be including me in that arrangement, because I am going nowhere. I'm staying put, and that's that." Lucy pouted. "If you hope to saddle that man like a bucking horse, that's your business. Funny business." Lucy added.

"Watch your tongue, Madam. We are in love." There. I said it. I pinched my lips together feeling unused muscles fight to smile.

"Suellen. You are the smartest woman I know. Please reconsider. He wants a nursemaid for those brats. You are unencumbered, a charitable word for all alone. You have a tidy sum of money, too."

"Tread lightly, Lucy."

"I heard he proposed to one of the Loughton sisters, but she refused to move away from her family."

"He's wonderful," I said. "He's kind and smart, and I can talk to him about anything. You know how tough times are here for folks. There's already two other doctors here. Theodore says he can treat patients and earn a good living in Oberlin. Theodore says it's beautiful there. Theodore says we'll be very happy. I'll be part of his family. Besides," I nearly twirled on my toes, I was so full of jubilation, "Theodore says it's not a risk if you have nothing left to lose."

Lucy put her hands over her ears. "Theodore says this; Theodore says that. If Theodore told you to moo like a cow, I'd bet you'd do it. Theodore sure does say a lot of things."

I pulled her hands down. "Lucy. Of course, you're coming with me. We need you. Theodore and his family need you." I wanted to die with my happiness at the prospect of tidying up that forsaken family; starching Theodore's shirts; baking him rhubarb pie, which he had confided to me was also his very favorite!

"Liking the same kind of pie does not make for a happy marriage." For of course I had mentioned this remarkable coincidence to Lucy. "You just met him. What's the rush?"

"Why wait until tomorrow?" I beseeched her. "The only thing sleeping on decisions has ever gotten me was a crick in my neck. Life is too short. Wishy-washy isn't my way. I hesitated before over this path or that, whether I should say something or naught. I have many regrets, Lucy, as you well know. I'm not being reckless for marrying the doctor. Nothing has ever felt more right."

She bit her lip as if chomping down on words we both knew would taste sour. "Who threw the dog bone in the punch bowl, Lucy? Be happy for me."

"It's not just that, Suellen." "Then what?"

Words failed her.

"Change is hard, honey. But suffering is worse. We'll be so much happier, you just wait and see."

Her tears began to fall with such wrath I feared she hadn't heard me.

***

Our marriage was to take place in three short weeks. As we had both been married before, and I was *une femme d'un certain âge*, it hardly mattered to me. Matrons could whisper behind their fat fingers for all I cared. "They can go hang," I told Lucy. I had never been happier. Except…

Lucy disliked Theodore. "You don't dislike anyone," I cajoled her. "You even make allowances for Mr. Murphy, even though he squeezes where he shouldn't and can't keep his spit inside his own mouth."

"You're not marrying Mr. Murphy," Lucy said in a sullen voice. "I like Dr. Kincaid well enough, Suellen. I just don't like how fast all of this is happening."

Suellen 57

"You just feel left out, honey," I said, and gave her a hug and pulled her close. "Nothing's going to change. You will be with me, we'll take care of each other, just like always. And now, we'll have a family, a real family."

She either was so overcome with her emotions, she couldn't answer me, or she was giving me that infernal silent treatment once again.

Meanwhile, I deliberately tried to think of anything but my impending wedding night—with my husband. Hard to do, seeing's how it was all my thoughts pursued down that railway track in my mind. I, who had vowed never to marry again, had fully expected to live out my days with Lucy by my side and find some measure of peace and contentment, when the unthinkable happened. Love had been lost to me for so many years; disappointment upon hardship multiplied by misery subtracted by my own strident personality equaled an acceptance that such was my lot in life. I had no hope for anything better, and felt, if not content, at least resigned to plod heavily along, one gravity filled boot at a time, until the angel of death would mercifully take pity upon my soul.

I scoffed at romantic novels and the girlish chatter of friends about me who had disclaimed "love at first sight," as if that were such a thing. The cosmos was having a laugh at me, as the very second I met Theodore, our eyes exchanged a secret message, some complicated code that I still cannot decipher, but one of such exquisite complicity I cannot ignore. I gave thanks upon every waking moment for experiencing—at risk of sounding like a lovesick schoolgirl—a rapturous gladdening of my heart which I never thought possible.

Lucy's cornbread had never tasted more satisfying, her fried chicken more savory; yet, it was my tongue that was the sweetest with a patience I have never been accused of owning. "So this must be how the rest of the world feels," I said in a whisper as I nestled my head on my pillow at night. I was finally invited to that special party that all of the people I had ever admired attended. A great, glamorous gala of goodwill, laughter, and ease. I sent my acceptance posthaste, and even volunteered to arrive early to help with set up.

Every morning my head would spin with thoughts of me as the good doctor's wife, blossoming into a person of importance, nurtured by the proud smile Theodore would wear. The people I would help, the woman I would become.

Lucy's churlishness did not surprise me. I knew she was scared to leave it all behind. "Lucy, I am scared too, but we have nothing to lose." I had grabbed her arm. "You, more than anyone, should know whatever we face, we face it together.

The North has to be less hate-filled than our own backyard has become. The war hasn't solved much of anything, except to widen the divide between black and white folks, marking off boundaries that I imagine will not be crossed for generations, if ever."

As it was Monday afternoon, Lucy and I retrieved our sheets drying on the line in the sun. As we met in the middle to match the corners, she couldn't help her smart mouth. "You and he are nothing alike. He is reserved, quiet, set in his ways."

"That's just the way he is," I told her. "He is so smart, he reads all the time. Oh, the discussions we will have, when we know each other a bit better. He is simply the most intelligent man I believe I have ever met."

"If you and he are so smart, then why the need to rush this whole business?"

"I think the question should be, why ever should we wait?" I smiled at her sweetly and carried my share of the laundry inside.

***

Upon notifying my editor of my impending nuptials, he responded more favorably than I had hoped. "Lucy," I bustled into the parlor where she was pouring our coffee. "My column is being dispatched to several newspaper outlets across the country. I will be paid extra for each one that runs it. Even though I will be married, I shan't forget how to write. It's going to appear in the *Columbus Evening Dispatch* and in our new hometown newspaper, the *Oberlin Weekly News.*"

"I should be able to keep up with my sewing, too, don't you think Suellen?"

"Of course." I was thrilled beyond words she was thinking of her future. I handed her the newspaper. "I don't believe you've seen my latest."

"Dear Auntie," she read.

"A dear person of my acquaintance is set to marry a man so unsuitable I feel as if I have no recourse but to heed your wisdom. My friend is so smitten, she, who under normal circumstances prides herself on her very unshakable opinion of right and wrong and proper, cannot see straight. While the gentleman in question appears to be an upstanding citizen, I fear his motives are simply to obtain a nursemaid for his children and housekeeper for himself.

"Please help me convince my friend to reconsider her actions, and know that an unsuitable alliance is a recipe for disaster and far worse than remaining true to herself, even if that entails being alone.

"Sincerely,

"A True Friend."

When Lucy looked over at me with a wary tilt to her head her suspicion was matched by my own. I nodded at her to keep reading. She handed me the paper instead.

"Dear True Friend," I read in a sarcastic tone.

"How lovely this world can be with friends such as yourself. I always like to start with a positive 'thank you very much' for your good intentions," I told Lucy.

"Before you let them have it?" Lucy asked.

I rattled the paper to continue. Lucy became absorbed in a hanging thread on the sleeve of her light blue calico dress. "However, the love between a man and a woman is oftentimes woven of so fine a gossamer thread as to be invisible to those outside its magical embrace. Love, in its very many forms, is too precious a gift to be tarnished by the unwarranted analysis of prying eyes."

Lucy reached for the paper and took it from me. "What on earth? Your editor let you print this?" She scanned for the column, running her finger down the page. "Are you talking about yourself, here, Suellen? You and Dr. Kincaid? Theodore?"

"Why?" I asked her. "Because this letter could have been written by you? It highlights some of your very same concerns."

"Why, I never," Lucy sputtered.

"You never were a very good liar. Actually, scratch that. You are a very good liar. Did you write this letter? Are you referring to me?"

"Suellen. Please. There are many, many folks who could have written this letter. The aftermath of the war has made for some mighty strange marriages."

"And what, exactly, is strange about the marriage between Theodore and myself? Tread lightly. Honey."

"No. You know how I feel, Suellen. I have nothing to hide. We don't know him that well, and I don't want to see you get hurt. And it's a huge undertaking to be moving, and all the way up North. I'm scared, and you should be too."

I sniffed. "While I have no idea if you submitted this letter or not, nor do I particularly care," I said, as Lucy folded her arms and plucked a thundercloud from the sky to plaster atop her cheeks, "please continue reading my words, and my feelings on the subject, to put this matter to rest, once and for all."

She read. "And know this: it is the fragile, broken heart, Dear Reader, which loves best, for has it not already felt the scourge of great emotions? Has it not been broken, mended, repaired, imperfectly, but mended just enough to risk being broken again? Why would you deny a damaged vessel the chance to feel whole again?

"Perhaps you would do better to question your own motives for dictating this request. What are your own sad eyes looking for that you cannot see? Without the threat of loss there would be no true love, for that's what love is."

She cleared her throat. "Therefore I protest, it is not fear for your dear friend, but rather a jealous whisper from your own lonely heart." Lucy's voice rose as she repeated the words. "Jealous whisper?"

"Pretty good," I said. I smoothed down my hair. "My editor loved that line."

"I beg of you to reach for love wherever and however you find it, and welcome it into your heart with the tender care and respect it deserves. While I do believe you have true concerns for your Dear One, rest assured, I recognize your plight and bestow upon you this advice: I dare you to take a chance in your own life." Lucy scoffed. "For Pete's sake, Suellen. Why didn't you just tell her to live happily ever after?"

"Oh, Lucy. You are happy for me, aren't you?"

"Yes. I am. I just want to make sure you are happy. And doing the right thing." She glanced at me and set the paper aside.

"Ladies."

My reply to Lucy was interrupted by my betrothed's voice at our screen door.

"Theodore, we didn't hear you arrive." I rushed to the door. "What a pleasant surprise. Come in." I chanced a quick look at Lucy, embarrassed for the both of us at our squabbling words.

"I can't stay," he said. "I was heading home and thought I would stop by and propose a picnic tomorrow. The weather should be fine." He held his hat in front of him, fingering the brim. His shirtsleeves were rolled up, wrinkled, and none too clean. I yearned to smooth down his hair.

Suellen 61

And then rumple it all up again. "I have a confession," he added. "I couldn't help but overhear your set-to."

"There was no set-to," I said. "Lucy and I were reading my column. It was just published." Perhaps I was bragging. Lucy remained stubbornly in her chair, not disagreeing mind you, but not agreeing, either.

"Well, no worries about that," Theodore said. "Once we're married you won't have time for your scribbles."

Lucy spoke first. "Suellen, if eyebrows were flags marching into battle, yours would be leading the charge." She stood up and put her hand on my arm. "I'm sure the doctor won't mind you continuing with your journalism once you are married. Sir, her editor just informed her that even more newspapers would be printing her advice. Isn't that wonderful?"

"Oh," Theodore said. "Fine." He had the grace to apologize. "I beg your pardon. I haven't really had time to read them, much. Of course, you must do what you see fit. I'll see you tomorrow, then?"

The screen door hadn't even latched shut at his exit. "He couldn't get out of here fast enough," Lucy said.

I didn't thank her for her defense. She didn't welcome a continuation of our disagreement.

We were even.

Chapter Twelve

Lucy had an appointment for alterations with Miss Hopkins, the daughter of one of our neighbors we got our eggs from, and I was that excited to have private time with Theodore. "I'll bring everything," I had told him. I knew my eyes were shiny. Had anyone seen me in the kitchen that day making preparations for our picnic, I would have directed attention to the precise slicing of my perfect loaf of bread. Lucy had chastised me for my continual checking as it baked. "All the heat is going to escape and it will be doughy in the middle."

"Pshaw," I told her right back. I firmly believed the love and, indeed, gladness behind my every motion would infuse this picnic with deliciousness beyond compare.

The exactitude of my cutting, and the symmetry of the very angle at which I sliced the thick ham sandwiches was sheer artistry. I hummed along, pouring my very heart into the ingredients of the rhubarb pie I made. I even splurged and added strawberries.

I carefully packed a wicker hamper and hitched a ride with my neighbors who were headed to town and offered to drop me off. Theodore would see me home.

"Where are the children?" I asked as he greeted me.

"The boys are playing out back and I just sent Ila Rose to her room for her inconsiderate tongue."

I raised my eyebrows. "Are you all right?" I paused, then he paused, then I added. "Would you like me to go talk to her—" He didn't even let me finish my sentence.

"Would you? Please, talk some sense into that child. I know she misses her mother, but her drama causes nothing but grief in this household. I don't know what to tell her or how to get her to stop using such a mean voice. Gus is scared of her and, quite frankly, sometimes, I am, too."

I smoothed my skirt and stood straighter. Dear Lord, I wish Lucy was here. She was the soothing one. What in the world was I supposed to tell a nine-year-old girl who stared at me as if she were plotting how best to finagle her hair ribbon

Suellen 63

tightly around my throat. "Of course, dear," I added, enjoying playing at engaged couple. I marched off to her bedroom, desperately trying to assume the air of a concerned mother, one who had the exact right words in her arsenal.

I knocked on the door. "Ila Rose?"

"Go away," she smart-mouthed me.

"Please. I just need a moment of your time." The sounds of her crying continued, and I would have had to have been a hard-hearted ogre to not feel a twinge of sympathy. I don't know that I would have been happy to greet someone like myself as a stepmother. The thought gave me pause before I gently opened her door. I walked into a disaster. She was flung upon her bed which wasn't even made up. A dirty nightdress, apron and ripped stockings littered the floor, as did a cracked dish of, dear Lord, was that hardened oatmeal? I gingerly made my way to a small stool next to her bed and, after I removed the book upon it, sat down.

"Ila Rose. Can you tell me why you're crying?" Though I had a pretty good idea.

"It's my father," she said, sitting up and looking at me. Her eyes were narrowed as if I were the culprit, which I supposed I was.

"What has he done?" I asked calmly.

"He's marrying you." Cue fresh onslaught of wailing.

"Hush. Yes, child, he is." I made the mistake of patting her knee. She kicked my hand off. "Don't touch me."

"Ila Rose, can we talk, girl to girl?"

"You're an old lady."

"And you're a sassy mouth."

"You can't call me that. You're not my mother."

"I know that. But I'd like to be part of this family. I'd never replace your mother, but sometimes a family is made up of people who may not be related by blood, but by people who care about each other, nevertheless." I wanted to pat myself on the back for that sentiment. I tried to remember the exact phrasing to tell Lucy later on. "And I'd like very much to care for you and your brothers."

Was my smile a touch too arch, causing the fresh set of howls? "I hate you and I will always hate you! And I will never care for you and my brothers will never care for you and you think my father cares for you but you are wrong. W-R-O-N-

64

Dee DeTarsio

G, wrong. We hate you and just wish you would die. My father loves me better than you, so there." And then she stuck her tongue out at me.

My hand itched to slap her impertinent little cheek. The nerve. "You're just like my sister," I shouted back at her. Yes, I raised my voice. I'm not proud of it, but sometimes you need to do what must be done to gain the attention of imps. I was sure it wouldn't be the last time I would have to partake in such drastic measures. "You think the sun rises and sets upon you and your spoiled wishes. Let me tell you something, missy, it does not. And the sooner you learn to respect those around you, especially your elders, the happier it will go for you. I know it's hard for you right now," I was finally able to modulate my voice. "But it will get better." Say something solicitous, I warned myself.

"I don't belong in this family," the poor girl lamented. "My father only loves the boys. The boys, the boys, the boys. And his stupid patients."

And all at once, I was back in my own nine-year-old painfully thin body, all wobbly elbows and knees. Grumpy Skirts. How I understood that poor child's sentiment. I blinked and recalculated.

"I never felt as if I belonged in my family either," I said in a voice so low she had to stop her yowling to hear me. But what could I say to make her feel better? My father's so-called wisdom popped into my head. He could turn from charming to mad faster than anyone I had ever seen. "You'll get nothing and you'll like it!" he used to say, to slaves and us girls alike, whomever was badgering him about something. I suppose there was unity to be found among us as we dodged his rages.

"You didn't feel like anyone noticed you either?"

"No. Sometimes it's like that in families. You fuss and fight, and try to get your fair share of attention."

She sniffed. "Everybody thinks Gus is so cute."

"He is, and he's just a baby, so I think he needs a little more attention than a big grown-up girl like you. When you were little like that, I'm sure your parents spoiled you to pieces."

She nodded. "My mom used to sing me songs at night." I smiled at her.

"I sing them to Gus and Vaughn some nights. And try to help them remember her."

"Ila Rose. Those boys are so lucky to have you as their big sister. I imagine it's not easy being the only girl. And I suppose your father relies upon you quite a bit."

She bit her lip. "He's so busy he doesn't even know how hard I try and help with those boys. They are always hungry."

"Do you remember when we first met?"

"You mean when you came to supper at our house less than a month ago and now my father is marrying you?"

Lord give me patience. "That would be it. May I continue?"

She wiped the back of her hands across her tears so hard her eyeballs squished. "When your father introduced me to you children, he started with you. The look he bestowed upon you, his firstborn, and only daughter, was such a look of pride and love. It must have been truly special because I made note of it, and thought what a wondrous daughter he has."

"Honest? He looked at me special?"

"Perhaps I am not all that you would wish in a stepmother. I am finding it difficult right now to know how to comfort you; therefore, I have decided that I may speak plainly to you with just the truth." She swung her legs off the bed. "Sometimes, even grown-ups like your father can have a hard time and may need a little understanding from time to time. But never forget how much he loves you." She pushed herself off the bed as I inclined to receive her hug. But she pulled a face and recoiled without touching me, and then raced from the room yelling for her father.

I let them have a few moments together, and stared out the window. Vaughn was running for no apparent reason and little Gus was just starting to toddle, wishing with all his might to follow after his big brother. I absentmindedly began to fold Ila Rose's clothes, and pulled up the sheet and blanket on her bed. I tucked the edges in ever so tight, just as my mother had taught me. "No matter how bad the day," her voice had said with purpose, "falling into repose at night into a neatly made bed shows that order in our world will prevail." If only it were that easy. The hogwash adults tell children. Do they really believe their own nonsense? I believed my mother did; therefore, I believed her. Oh Lord, I had been so woefully unprepared for being a mother the first time around. How on earth would I manage this time? The things my mother never taught me could fill a library.

I walked back to the kitchen, espying marks upon the wall. Ila Rose, aged three, marked by a little line just above my knee. Lines near her name went up six more times, and Vaughn's line was marked below hers, aged three. He needed his fourth year documented, and Gus wasn't even noted. I will do right by you children, I vowed. I looked away from their mother's framed picture that hung in the parlor. She had truly been lovely.

I knew Theodore still mourned his wife. I felt a sting of jealousy burn down my throat, shamed at what a vile creature I was. I swallowed that jealousy with a cup of resolve. I would nurture him and make him forget he had ever had another love. After all, he found me. But I would nobly honor her place as the children's mother. I brushed my hands together with confidence.

"Theodore, dear?" I called out. I followed the trail of excited voices outdoors. Vaughn had tied the checkered tablecloth I had packed in the picnic basket around his neck like a cape. Both boys' faces showed evidence of the massacre of my strawberry rhubarb pie. Ila Rose chewed on such a mouthful of sandwich her cheeks bulged like a squirrel's as she threw her crusts of bread at the boys. I could have cheerfully boxed all their ears.

"Thank you for the picnic, Suellen," said my beloved. "It is perfection." "Yes," I said. "Just perfect."

Chapter Thirteen

"Suellen, are you ailing? What's wrong?" I hastily put the lid on my box of face powder and set it back on the dresser. Lucy came to my side and stared at me in the mirror. "It's not too late to call the wedding off," she reminded me. "You don't need to marry him. We will be fine." She patted my cheeks, rather rougher than warranted. "You do look peaked."

Dear God in heaven, I thought, stepping away from Lucy's administrations. My comportment of bliss exhibited the exact opposite of my heart's desire? I pray there be no light upon my wedding night.

"You don't understand," I told her, filled with an unusual generosity, tinged with a touch of pity for Lucy's single state. "I'm so excited about marrying Theodore I can hardly sleep." I sighed. "I'm afraid something will happen to prevent the wedding."

"We don't have that kind of luck," she sassed.

"Hush," I smiled fondly, filled with the good mood of love.

My attention had been solely upon my beloved. I find it odd that most folks are nothing out of the ordinary, myself included. We disdain those who clamor for attention and superiority—I had a sister just like that—yet, when it comes down to it, how surprised we are to discover that we do think our own selves special, and worthy. Worthy of what remained to be seen.

The shockingly short engagement period of three weeks, which even that timeframe I had bemoaned, fearing something would occur to prevent our marriage, was flying by in spite of my impatience. With mere days until we were to be wed, I was now counting the hours and minutes. "A watched pot never boils," Lucy reminded me, throwing my own advice back to me.

"Hurry. He's here." I skipped down the steps at the knock on the door. I paused, patted down my hair, as I had seen my sister do countless times before. I pinched my cheeks and had no need to feign my smile. I opened the door.

How my heart gladdened as our eyes met and our souls recognized each other. He knew me.

As I knew him. He saw right through me and deciphered what was hidden from others. "Do come in," I said, wondering where on earth that breathless voice had come from. We went into the front parlor, and I nearly swooned when he sat next to me on the sofa. I offered him a drink of sherry, with trembling hands.

Lucy came down and together we served the meal. Thick slabs of ham, Lucy's fine cornbread, a savory succotash, along with the smoothest mashed potatoes, with nary a lump thanks to my fine administrations, smothered in butter. "Dear Lord, Suellen," Lucy had told me. "He's not going to throw you over if he finds a lump in his potatoes."

The pouring wine from the decanter sounded like a song to me. "Suellen must really like you," Lucy told Theodore. "She's eating lima beans."

"Lucy."

"It's all right, ma'am, Suellen," Theodore said. "Do I have to eat mine?" Oh, how we laughed.

"And this ham is my favorite," he said, "it just melts in your mouth." He didn't notice as Lucy lowered her head, suddenly shy. "That and this cornbread are all a man needs."

"And the potatoes are so creamy," Lucy added. She took such a big spoonful her cheeks bulged.

"I've never particularly cared for potatoes," he said. His fork had pushed them to the side of his plate. To make room for yet another piece of Lucy's ham.

"They are bland, aren't they?" I said brightly, quashing my hurt feelings. Honestly, what did it matter he didn't like my potatoes? I dabbed at my mouth with my napkin and changed the subject. I couldn't wait to hear his ideas on how best our country could be put back together.

"Upon my word, Theodore," I began. "President Rutherford does have some good ideas to help the South get back to work." He raised his eyebrows at me which I took as an encouraging sign. "And perhaps he can help those poor railroaders."

"Now, Miss Suellen, I think politics make for a dreary subject." He patted my hand which rested lightly on the tablecloth. The warmth provided a balm which made me forget what I wanted to ask him.

But still, I couldn't help myself. "Would that we study politics and war that our children have the liberty to study mathematics, philosophy and painting." I

Suellen 69

stopped as Theodore looked at me with surprise. "John Adams," I said with a shrug. "A hundred years ago. I paraphrase, since he referred to his sons, yet I prefer to think this is important for our daughters as well. I do love history, don't you?" Then I laughed. "We have much to discover of one another, Theodore," I dared to say.

"That we do," he said agreeably, finishing his wine. "But the poor president has too much upon his plate to make much of a difference anywhere. Do you know he has been fooling around with a fellow who has some sort of a talking machine?"

"Tell us more," I said. "Lucy and I thank our lucky stars at all the newfangled things coming about in this world. We can't imagine how hard life must have been a hundred years ago. What does the talking machine do?"

"I'm sure it's an amazing invention," Theodore said, "but who would ever want to use one? We have the telegraph to send our communiques if we need to, we have letters delivered by the U.S. Mail on some of the finest trains in the world, and we have newspapers. What more does man need?"

My imagination was lit, as was Lucy's. We laughed, and not only in charming deference to our male caller.

"But what does it do?" Lucy interrupted.

Theodore held up a hand to his ear and jutted his neck forward. "Apparently it's a newfangled device, a box of some sort, that you talk into, and then you hear another person, from somewhere else, talk back to you."

"Oh, my. Imagine."

Theodore smiled at me approvingly. "I believe it's called a telephone or some such nonsense.

You and Miss Lucy seem to talk enough to each other, why would you need a machine to do that?"

I smiled so widely my stays felt constrictive. "Lucy and I don't need any machine," I agreed. "Why we can practically telephone," I practiced the new word, "our thoughts to each other." I glanced at Lucy. She usually loved gossip and all the latest news. Why, every night we took turns reading to each other, and sharing any new found information. Unfortunately, she was in no mood to celebrate our current state of affairs. That's a poor stab at a double entendre—she had no patience for what she saw in her future, either in general in the world, or in particular by my side. If I had a speaking machine nearby, I would have dearly loved to holler right into Lucy's ear, "Grumpy Skirts."

"Oh, what a fine time to be alive," I said. I reached across the table for Lucy's hand and squeezed. I know we are settled and safe, but for the love of God, Lucy, I tried to "telephone" her: We're still searching. You and me. Searching for what, we were about to find out.

I turned my attention back to Theodore. "Don't you find at least an uneasy truce is beginning to spread? Things are getting better for the freed people?" I asked hopefully but couldn't hide my reservations, for Lucy and I had seen firsthand the tribulations visited upon them. "How are they ever supposed to get a fair shake?"

The doctor shrugged. "It's been an ugly decade following the ruinous war. There are still three miserable factions, us versus freed slaves versus the federal soldiers. Thank the Lord, the president has finally seen fit to understand the so-called Reconstruction is nothing but a farce and is pulling out the troops. Now maybe the South can rest easy again and get back to the business of running its own affairs."

"And yet you are moving North," I ventured to say.

"I don't have time for politicking; I have people up there, and I quite find that I am looking forward to a cessation of the miseries found down here. Let those who clamored for fight and might and freedom pick up the pieces. I expect to make a good living up there." He paused and looked at me. "For my family."

My hand fluttered at my throat before I realized what a simpering female I must look. "There are so many people still suffering," I murmured. "The president promised to support honest and peaceful local self-government in the South, as well as reform the Civil Service. You don't think he'll succeed?"

Theodore snorted. "Let's talk of something more pleasant, shall we? This is the finest meal I can recollect ever having, and I look forward to many more. Thank you, my dear."

I wanted to expire of happiness right then and there. Even though Lucy had prepared the parts he liked best.

While I understood Lucy's reluctance, the only fly in my ointment was her disregard for the doctor. "He speaks highly of you," I would rebut her ceaseless arguments. He did, too. He would oftentimes include her in our carriage rides during all-too-seldom opportunities to visit. I cannot say I was happy, preferring some time alone with my beau, yet I did want to prove to Lucy that he was a good man. Our times when it was just the two of us were rare; remember his three children. He loves those little ones and expected me to have the same instantaneous fervor for their well-being. In a haze of sentiment not my usual forte, I understood, and ventured to accommodate. So while he was busy encouraging his offspring to take to me, I worked on my side of the fence to help Lucy see the light of his truly good heart.

"Lucy, tell Theodore about the mayor's wife ordering her dress from you."

"The mayor's wife ordered her dress from me."

Theodore smiled. "I hear you are a fine seamstress."

"And the wedding dress is simply divine," I added. Theodore had insisted on paying for the fabric for my gown. Lucy chewed on her lip. I knew she was dying to rip into something, I just didn't know what. "Isn't it, Lucy?"

"Yes, ma'am."

"Theodore, tell Lucy about what Vaughn said yesterday."

Theodore wiped his mouth with his napkin, he was so elegant, and allowed me to pour his coffee. "Lucy, pass over the cream."

She complied as Theodore thanked her. I sighed in contentment. This would work. We would be a fine family.

"Vaughn said 'Miss Lucy is as pretty as a princess,'" Theodore said.

"Isn't that sweet?" I interjected.

Lucy, not looking at Theodore, nodded. "He's a good boy."

He wasn't, but that was beside the point. He was a spoiled stinker, but the dear little motherless one needed some love and care and discipline. Lucy and I would see to it that he got it.

"Lucy, why don't you make Theodore some of your leftovers?" She and I crossed paths back and forth as I cleared the dishes, taking them into the kitchen. She wrapped up some cornbread for him to take to the children. Thank heaven for Theodore's neighbor woman who was watching them so we could have a quiet meal. I hummed as I made quick work cleaning the dishes and stacked them loudly, giving the two people I love most in the world time together to discover what I knew about each of them.

My darling Theodore. I giggled. Yes, giggled. To say that the word darling had ever crossed my lips was an impossibility. I was physically incapable of emitting that word through my vocal cords. And yet. Yet in my thoughts, it was how I thought of Theodore. He rescued me with a power of love that cast the world into a heretofore unimaginable place of serenity, security, and sensuous enjoyment. My mind was not in the gutter. I am using sensuous to describe how soft the cotton dish towel felt in my hands, how warm and soothing the dishwater was, how the clang of the silverware as Lucy gathered up the utensils in the dining room was a wind chime melody, serenading the very birds.

I cocked my head, thinking back. Growing up, one of our helpers had strung some old forks together, along with a broken tea cup and rusted tin, and hung them in a tree over our garden to scare the crows away. My father used to complain it also scared his sleep away; for once, I had agreed with him. My memories swooped back to some fifteen years ago, trying to sleep in my bed, my skin sticky with a sweat that smelled just like my sisters', the vinegary brine of pickles. Unbidden, an image of my sister pushing me, with her dainty hand that she loved to flutter helplessly in front of gentleman. Instead of the unsettling feeling I got in my stomach at the thought of her ways, I could see that same hand pushing my shoulder down, forcing me to sit on the padded bench at her vanity.

"For heaven's sake, Suellen," she had scolded me, "you are growing up, and you better stop acting like a big baby. Here. I'll show you. Once." She took her brush in one hand, and roughly undid my braid with her fingers, making sure to catch on every tangle. I kept one suspicious eye on her from the mirror and jerked my head with each merciless tug she made. "There. Your hair's not that bad. Pity about the color though, Mouse." She said, using a long-forgotten nickname. "Sit up straight." She brushed my hair which reached down my back. At least I had a bit of a curl at the ends of my drab mane, which I knew sat ill upon her precious shoulders.

"I can't have people pitying me for having an ugly sister, now, can I?" Just as I was about to tattle, loudly, I caught her look in the mirror. Whilst we would never be friends, perhaps she did care for me, in her selfish, self-centered shriveled soul. "I'll lend you my pins, you Ninny, but be sure they are back on my table before bed." She proceeded to put my hair up, for the first time, in a sophisticated style high atop the nape of my neck. She nodded at her handiwork and told me to pinch my cheeks. "Not like that," she shoved my hands away and gleefully took the opportunity to do it herself. Before we could venture into fisticuffs, she told me I looked pretty. "Pretty enough," she added. "Now wait up here with me for another minute, I hear Pa yelling. If we go down too soon Mother will put you back in braids quicker than you can say jackrabbit." Even though she ignored me at the barbecue we had attended, and thus all the boys followed her lead, I felt a ghost of the smile that had crossed my face that day.

I wiped my hands on the towel and picked up the peach cobbler I had made for Theodore. Every slice from every peach had been filled with a ferocious wish, as if I could infuse the very sweetness of the cobbler with my love. I carried it into the dining room.

I walked in to see my beloved comforting Lucy. His hand dropped from her arm as I entered.

I placed the cobbler on the table and clasped my hands under my heart; ah, friends at the last. "Whatever are you two conspiring about?" I nearly sang, I was so happy my two favorite people in the world had found a way toward each other.

Lucy jumped up from the table and hurried from the room. Theodore cleared his throat and sat down again at his seat at the head of the table. "Miss Lucy is a right good girl."

"I think so, too." I beamed at him.

After dessert, as I saw him to the front door, he even went out of his way to call "Good night" to Lucy and thank her for the fine meal. He was so well-mannered. I clasped my hands, anxious to receive my farewell. I lifted my cheek toward him, and smiled at the thought that he did seem to like my peach cobbler. He settled his hat on his head, gave a quick tug on the brim, and headed out into evening, home to his children. Poor dear, he had so much on his mind.

Later that night, it was more than the extra cup of coffee I had enjoyed, lingering with Theodore after dinner, which loosened my tongue. I sat on Lucy's bed as she pointedly plumped her pillow and closed her eyes.

"Silly goose." I pushed on her shoulder. "Talk to me. Tell me how much you like Theodore." Lucy opened her eyes.

"Suellen. We'll talk in the morning. I'm tuckered out."

"I know, I should be, too, but I'm not. I'm wide awake. Lucy. He's wonderful. He's going to give us a good life. You see that, right? You like him?"

Lucy couldn't help her smart mouth. "You have nothing in common with that man."

"He is as good on the inside as he is handsome on the outside." I told her. "We are attuned to each other. I can sense his compassion, his caring. He is so gentle and soft-spoken. He has impeccable manners. Did you notice the way he drinks his wine?" I help my hand aloft gracefully.

Lucy pretended to snore.

"So help me Lucy, if you spit on my good fortune I will hate you forever."

"Suellen, I'm not going to tantrum over anything, and I see your mind is made up. I just think you may be rushing things. Why not wait a while? Get to know him; get to know his children?"

"There is no time as you darn well know. He has to move, why in less than a week. He needs to be in Ohio to start his new position. And neither of us are getting any younger." I patted her counterpane. "Lucy. Seriously. We are in love. You are coming with us, you will be with me and we will care for each other, as always."

"I don't think I can come along, Suellen."

I straightened my spine, my neck stretching as if to give me an inch more space for wisdom to deal with this calamity. My hand reached out and smacked Lucy right on her cheek. So much for wisdom. My fingers tingled with heat from the force of my effort, and I am downright ashamed of how lovely it felt. I leaned down to force her eyes to meet mine. My finger pointed in her face so close she could have bit it had she had the desire. I may have withdrawn an inch or two, but I channeled my not inconsiderable temper with a voracious trumpet from my own vocal cords. "How dare you? After all I've done for you. Treating you as my own sister after all this time."

Her eyes darkened, with that unrecognizable flicker. "You will come with me, and you will be my family."

"Give it more time, and then maybe."

"There is no time. We have decided." Oh, what confidence the small word "we" bestows. I turned from her and stomped across the hall to my bedroom. Lucy's exasperated sigh stopped me cold.

"You must put aside this misery," I called to her. "Aren't you one smidgeon curious about life up North? It could be so much better for both of us."

Her muffled voice came back at me. I almost couldn't hear her. "As I've never belonged here nor there, I doubt I shall feel at home anywhere."

I went back into her room and was about to turn down the lamp on her night table. Let her stew in her own juices, as my mother would have said.

"What about me?" Lucy said, her tone church quiet, when I didn't respond. She always was one for flair. If I hollered, she whispered lower. If I quieted in repose, she would wave her hands dramatically. If I refused to see humor, she would pick at me as if removing a wrong stitch in a seam I had sewn, until at the very least I would finally smile.

"What about you? I just told you, you are coming with us." I brushed the front of my skirt, relieved to be finished with her nonsense. Poor dear, she was worried I would forget all about her with the doctor to dote upon. As always, the mere thought of my future husband caused my heart to flutter and my breath to quicken.

"Suellen, weren't we happy here? Just the two of us? We are good together. Please, I beg of you. Just don't rush into a decision you might regret."

"Why, pray tell, might I regret it?"

"How do you know he's the right man for you? What if there's another, better man, just waiting? One who will come along and not force you into something neither of us are ready for."

"Force me? What has gotten into you?"

"It's just not right. I don't know about all this. It doesn't feel right. Something's off. What if he's not who you think he is?"

"Sometimes you just know." Lord, how I patronized that girl.

"What if..." She sat up, I could see her shining eyes, pleading with me to understand. "What if I wanted to marry?"

"Excuse me?" I said, though I had heard her perfectly clearly.

"What about me?"

"I just told you. You will come with us."

She stilled, then bowed her head. "But what about what I want?"

"What do you want, then?"

"Do you honestly not know? I am a woman, too, Suellen. I want romance. I want courtship. I want a good man to lie with."

My hand flew to my mouth, causing Lucy to smile. "Why do you find that so hard to believe?"

"No need to dip in the gutter."

"Suellen. I want to know love, I want marriage…"

I had automatically interrupted her, to my everlasting shame. "But you're a sl—" She returned the favor and quickly cut me off. But it was too late.

Her nostrils flared and this time it was she who leaned in uncomfortably close to my face.

Thank the good Lord her venom had no bullets or I would be slain. "I'm a sl—?" She mimicked me. "A sly pickaninny? A sleeve off your dress?" She pinched my arm, plucking at the material of my dress. "A slatternly creature who deserves no love, no man, no husband, no babies of her own?" She took a breath. "Don't you dare ever, ever, ever, say that to me. I am as free a woman, no, freer, than you will ever be," she said. "Did you never consider I might want the same as you? A man's arms to hold me tight? A man's voice to comfort me in the night?"

I covered my ears.

"A man's shoulders to share my burden?" She looked at me in disbelief. "You didn't, did you? I can't believe it. I had no idea you cared so little for me." Her shoulders slumped.

"No. Forgive me, my dear. Of course you would want those things. How selfish I have been."

My hand went to my throat, my fingers nervously rubbing lace for comfort. "I didn't think. I had no idea. Dear Lord, have you met someone?"

"Shut up. Shut up. Shut up, Suellen. You never think, do you? No. I have not met anyone.

Who would I have met here anyway, and without you and the rest of this town knowing about it? But why wouldn't I want the same as you? Why wouldn't I want a man to love and to love me back? Why wouldn't I want a home and family to call my own?"

"I thought I was your family. I thought I was enough."

"You thought I wasn't good enough, you mean."

"No, that's not true." I could feel the burning redness marking me guilty as charged, it was true. I was a hypocrite.

Lucy pushed back the covers and grabbed at her nightgown, raised as she prepared to flounce out of the room.

"I suppose I'll get the silent treatment now," I taunted.

"I won't hold my tongue this time. This marriage is doomed. It will be the worst thing in the world, mark my words."

"There's nothing but a whisper between what you fear and what you secretly desire."

"Are you talking about you or me?" Lucy asked me. As she left the room posthaste, I don't believe she knew the answer to that, either.

I may have taught Lucy how to read, but it was she who taught me how to read the situation.

Chapter Fourteen

Lucy and I spoke to each other, but only when necessary, and only in short, terse sentences. "Please remember the eggs from Mrs. Hopkins."

"Please pass the gravy."

"Would you please try on your gown for the final fitting?" I complied, and took solace from her strong hands, smoothing a tuck here, pulling up a seam there.

I needed someone to tell me how to feel. Who could explain this upheaval of emotions that I experienced? I teeter-tottered between elation and despair. I reminded myself the doctor had chosen me, he must have feelings for me, a devotion as deep as mine surely had repercussion of the desired kind. I banished whatever reservations I had and thought not to look for trouble where none existed. Like a love-sick ninny, I perversely relished the blood beating in my veins and I cosseted every action of this new romance. I was convinced it was more than a business transaction to procure a housekeeper for himself and his children that prompted Theodore's proposal, and as soon as we had some small privacy in our new home, I would prove to him I was the helpmeet and wife of his dreams. I patted my cheeks and smoothed my hair. Lord, I was a grown woman and shouldn't be so lighthearted. I went up on my toes and rocked back, seemingly incapable of staying still. I sighed, until Lucy, dear Lucy, threatened to scream. "Stay still." She was pinning the hem of my gown.

Was it infatuation, as Lucy insinuated? Or love? Who cares? All I knew was that I grabbed at the miracle before me, compelled by the very measure of righteousness in my soul.

I am not superstitious. However, two things happened in the final few days leading up to my wedding day.

The first may have gone unnoticed, had not Lucy, in her usual dramatic fashion, gone on and on about it.

"Bad things come in threes," Lucy predicted ominously.

"Nonsense." I told her. "What are you talking about? So do good things." I wagged my head.

Suellen 79

Lucy and I had exchanged roles, and I wasn't sure I didn't like it just fine.

"It's a sign," she continued, dogmatically. "Suellen, you have to stop this wedding. We'll just stay put, you and me. Like always. We're doing fine." I merely put my hands on my hips and smiled at the poor child. I wasn't going to indulge her silly whims by asking what ominous "sign" she had encountered.

"Suellen," she warned me, "I'm telling you. This is very bad. It's as if the universe itself is conspiring against this whole venture you're forcing us into. Look at this." She held out her arm and pushed back her sleeve.

"You gave yourself goosebumps, you silly goose. You need to calm down."

"I shudder to think what will happen." She ran from the room, expecting me to follow her. I sighed and got up to go after her. She had flopped down on her bed. "Lucy. Calm down.

Now what? What superstitious folderol has got you so strung up?"

"It's just a feeling I have. And you know my feelings are always right."

"I know no such thing. Is there a storm coming?" I glanced out the window. She was petrified of storms and I have never seen a woman get as riled by wind as Lucy. She would become practically psychic and could predict hours in advance when a storm was threatening. Her hair would crackle or some such nonsense, though she was always correct and we made sure to close our windows and prepare. Sunbeams streamed through the old magnolia tree outside her window, its leaves rustled in the soft breeze.

"Why it's hardly windy out there. Do take a breath. Take a nap. Take whatever you want, just be happy for me. For us. Stop this superstitious nonsense. That's all it is. Nonsense."

"You're the superstitious one," she told me. She sat up and clutched a pillow. I sat next to her. Her room, though completely different from mine, was lovely, in a sparse, sterile way. I liked to hang onto things, broken things mostly, like my mother's old china figurine, one that I'd always fancied was a beautiful version of myself, minus a left foot and holding chipped pastel flowers, but still pretty enough if you liked that sort of thing. Lucy's one incongruous pleasure, folded neatly at the end of her bed, all four corners lined up, was her quilt, a labor of love made from scraps of material she had saved for years. Just ask her and she'd be happy to tell you the history of each piece. "This came from your pa's jacket," she would say, rubbing a rough brown tweed piece of material that I personally thought was

80   *Dee DeTarsio*

ridiculous to use for bedding, but it wasn't me kept warm by memories I preferred not to visit.

"I will miss this place," I said. The sentiment was true enough, but I was trying to distract Lucy from her imagined calamity. "But we'll have so much fun decorating our new house."

"That's just it, Suellen. I don't want to. This is all too sudden; it just doesn't feel right. Mark my words, this will not end well. Guess what happened?" She clasped her hands in prayer.

I tapped my finger on my lip, as if contemplating. "Did a spider cross your pillow this morning? Did you step on a crack? Oh, I know, a black cat ran clean in front of you and as you ran to get out of its way, it stopped and looked you right in the eye and spoke. Lucy," I tried to hiss like a kitty cat. "Don't move to Ohio. Don't get on that train. Don't wander around a room full of rocking chairs." I permitted myself a smile. "There's a mouse in your future."

"Stop it, Suellen."

"You are going to let superstition dictate how you and I live our lives?" I looked at her and knew what she was going to say.

"You saw Voodoo Valene, didn't you?" I asked her.

"I had to. And it's not good." She sat closer to me.

I crossed my arms to signal I wouldn't believe one word of what was about to spill from her mouth. "Go on."

"She said, 'All is not as it seems. Beware the false man.'" Lucy covered her face.

"Stop shivering. You're being ridiculous. That's it?" She didn't answer. "What else? Did she say you were going on a long trip, too? Why, the whole town knows that."

"She's trying to warn us, Suellen. We should stay put."

"Thanks to Mrs. Boyer, everyone here knows I am engaged and that we are uprooting ourselves to head up to the heathen North," I said sarcastically. "Why are you believing that woman over me? Who knows you better than anyone?"

"She has the sight, Suellen. She knows things." Lucy tapped her temple. "She knew Mr. O'Conner was sick before anyone else, right before he passed. She predicted you would have a new beau, before year's end." Her posture slumped. "And me, too."

Suellen

81

"See there? You can't pick and choose the prognostications that work in your favor, miss. Now dry your eyes. Her soothsaying doesn't rule out us leaving here with Theodore. It will all work out. Trust me."

Lucy sighed. "I want to be happy for you, Suellen. For both of our sakes."

I stood up then and brushed my hands on my skirt, as if clearing away the bad omens that did feel now omnipresent in that room. I had met that meddling Valene once before. She was nothing but a bombastic pretender, as if the louder she opined the more joy she received scaring God-fearing Christians. She did have a presence though, being perhaps one of the largest women I have ever met. Pound per pound, her predictions carried no more weight than the rest of our longings, but her convictions tipped the scales heavy through her ebony skin, leaving no room for doubt among her clientele. My introduction to her though had been nothing but a poor dead chicken and wasted five cents, to say nothing of an afternoon.

"Lucy. Have you ever stopped to consider that even the universe and Good Lord above don't quite know what's going to happen next? I do not believe there is a checklist for every sorry soul down here. Well," I mimed reading a paper in my hands, "Suellen needs one more kick in the teeth and an unfair happenstance before she can have a few moments of happiness. It says here," I continued, "Lucy is a good enough sort and deserves a beau, but she needs to have two more comeuppances."

"Stop it, Suellen. You don't want to rail against the fates. Do be quiet."

"Well, shut my mouth." I sassed. "We make our own mistakes. We make our own retributions. We make our way as best we can."

Funny how an idea, once planted, can shoot its roots clean through ones' brain and into the heart. I had stopped praying about fifteen years ago, when things were very bad. The Good Lord and I weren't quite on speaking terms anymore. There was nothing left to pray for, anyway. I was emotional about my marriage, and I had to finish packing. Lucy reached for my wrist.

She gasped. "You have goosebumps, too. Suellen. Look."

I rubbed at my arm, the skin speckled as a naked chicken. "I refuse to meander down that dark path," I told her. "We are moving forward."

"We don't have to," she said. "That's just it. Let's stay, Suellen. We have a roof over our heads. We have friends, we have a place here. Your newspaper writing is going well, and you don't need to rush things; no good will come of it, you'll see." Her voice had risen.

"I suspect hindsight gives everyone a magnifying glass to see where they went wrong. Unfortunately, it doesn't work in the reverse." I held up my hand to stifle her protest. "You are plenty prophetic, it's true. It's just that your accuracy flies far and wide."

A few moments later I heard her slam her bedroom door, clatter down the steps, and, for good measure, bang shut the front door on her way out. In case I misunderstood her misapprehensions. I smiled. Her unease made it easier for me to parcel my own concerns. Lucy was headed for the church, unless I was mistaken, to make penance for her visit to Valene. I forget who it was who said we are a sum of our parts—part Christian, part culture, part voodoo, part vanity.

Lucy was a farrago of contradictions. Even when I hated her, I couldn't help but love her, and if that's not what a family is I'll eat my hat.

I packed up a box of mementos that I wouldn't be taking with us. I didn't expect to see them ever again, or want to, for that matter, but couldn't quite bear to let them go. Mrs. Boyer knew a family who would be moving into our place next month and renting it, though I supposed someday, I would consider selling it.

A crack of thunder coincided with the clasp of my valise. I jumped. "Ah, that's what Lucy was so worked up about," I said aloud. The rain pelted the house, and more thunder presaged the lighting by only a split second as I worried about her being caught in the storm. I went downstairs to wait for her in the gloomy light of the parlor, missing her amid the storm's fury. She arrived shortly thereafter, soaking wet, but delivered safe and sound thanks to the kind ministrations of my fiancé.

"Get in here, quick. Theodore. Thank you so much."

"My pleasure, Suellen. I saw Lucy here darting out of the church, trying to make a run for it.

I insisted upon giving her a ride. We waited it out a spell and escaped the worst."

My heart swelled. I felt a tingle all the way clean to the tips of my hair. "Thank you." I tried to convey my feelings to my beloved. "Come in, won't you?"

"No, ma'am," he said. "I need to get home. We have a couple of busy days ahead of us." And with that, he took my hand and kissed my fingers.

"I declare," I whispered so softly no one heard me. "Come on, Lucy. Let's get you dried off." As I helped her towel her hair, she hugged me, tight.

"Sorry, Suellen," she said, "for everything." The woman does hate to apologize. Thank the dear Lord she had come to her senses and decided to accept our fate.

"Well, that takes the cake," I told her, giving her a quick hug in return. We are not an affectionate people, but I was that pleased. I may have even thought, "aha," as if at long last my life had turned out to be the pleasant surprise I had always wished for. I beseech you, never, ever, allow the word "aha" to take up residence in your heart. Mark my words, it will not end well.

***

We were to be married two days hence, the day after the Fourth of July. Lucy, the doctor and I, and his children, spent the holiday gathered as a family at the park. The mayor's speech, as boring as could be expected, was cut short by Mrs. Boyer, who made the whole town stand up and bid us farewell.

"Dear, dear, girls," she boomed. "Fremont will never be the same. We will miss you both, terribly. Your good works, your good hearts, and your great, good charm."

"I wonder of whom she is speaking?" Lucy whispered out of the side of her mouth to me. "Hush."

"Our doors will always be open for you and yours," she finally concluded. She signaled to the pokey band, if one can call a trio of wizened old soldiers charged with beating on a drum, spitting into a harmonica, and tootling last gasps of breath into a trumpet, a band. My mouth contorted and I coughed into my hand lest I start to cry. What on earth?

We were assailed by our friends and neighbors, who wished us well. Mrs. Perrin was overcome with the excitement of the day, and no doubt her pesky grandchildren, and it was with no small pride I saw the Doctor slip over to her side and lead her to a shady tree. He cared so about all of his patients.

What with the smell of summer grass beneath my feet that made my eyes suspiciously itchy, and that bright blue sky puffed with cotton clouds that made me squint, Lucy looked as lachrymose as I felt. Fortunately, before things declined into too deep a well of sentimentality, the children, especially Gus, became fractious. They ate too much ice cream, took too much sun, ran around like hooligans, and were sound asleep by the time the fireworks were over. My heart exploded at the look Theodore and I exchanged over the baby's head which rested on my shoulder. We were to be married the very next day. I could hardly believe my good fortune.

Chapter Fifteen

It was an uncharacteristic risk on my part, accepting the doctor's proposal and moving three states away, which I suppose, depending upon the outcome, will make me very lucky, or very stupid. No sense waiting around to see what tomorrow would bring; tomorrow was never a friend of mine.

My journey began the second I said "yes." I do not go for lovey-dovey touches and such nonsense, especially for a second marriage. Nor does the doctor. He is a man of great intellect and sense, a man of science. Though he holds the dear Lord above all, as is proper, he is skeptical of everything. As he should be. Oh, the conversations we would have. The things he could teach me. I blushed as an immodest thought tried to burrow its way into my mind. I relished learning more about medicine, and healing. He thought mine and Lucy's herb collection "quaint," though we had seemed to cure Vaughn's pink eye with our poultice of eucalyptus leaves. Though Theodore wasn't impressed, saying only that by making the poor baby cry like that, his tears were a natural emulsion leading to healing. He could think what he wanted. Lucy and I had shared a look.

Lucy and I had helped each other pack. My new valise, or portmanteau as Lucy insisted on calling it (have I mentioned it was a wedding gift from the Doctor?), made me feel so worldly. He was so kind, he even purchased the same for Lucy.

It contained my nightclothes, underthings, and two new dresses. I pictured myself in them all, an incomplete portrait in my mind, fuzzy with details that nevertheless glowed. My hairbrush would fit on top. I was ready. My set of sheets, towels and a few household items, were packed in trunks, already headed to the train station.

I closed the case and barked at Lucy. "Honey," I said, as if the endearment would forgive my tone, "enough. You need to finish packing." In her room, I found her rearranging the contents of her bag. "And lock up your hound dog countenance while you're at it." I pulled a face at her. "What is it? Are you ill?" I pressed the back of my palm against her forehead. She grabbed my wrist.

"Suellen. I think you're making a grave mistake. We don't belong in the North. Everything we know is here. Our people…"

"Lucy. Need I remind you, we're the only people we have? You are as a dearest sister to me. Dearer than the ones I was burdened with, at any rate."

Again, she gave me that guarded look that occasionally flits across her face. The one I cannot stand as I cannot understand it, nor can I make heads nor tails of its purpose. "Dry your eyes. This will be our life's grandest adventure. I, for one, cannot wait to turn my back on the hellish memories of this place. The same grind of our neighbors and townspeople griping about the good ol' days. We were there. It wasn't that good." I pulled her up off the bed. "We have nothing here for us, Lucy. And nothing left to lose."

She squeezed my hands.

"Say it," I told her. "Whatever it is, God knows no one knows each other better than us two. However, I cannot read your mind or your puppy dog eyes begging me to intuit some secret message. Whatever is it?"

"Nothing, Suellen. You're right. I'm just scared. Scared of traveling. We've never been on a train. Or out of the South for that matter. And to travel all the way up North? We could freeze to death."

"Oh, Lucy. It's normal to be scared. But wasn't it you who was the one craving travel, and riding in a train clean across the country? What happened to that dream? We were rotting in this town, Lucy. We would have been dogging our same dusty steps 'til both of us passed." I smiled at her. Was fate waiting to smite me for the supercilious smile I gave her?

"We have been given this miracle. Theodore. The doctor." I clasped my hands at my heart as Lucy cast her eyes down. "Oh, I know I'm being silly. But he's so wonderful, and offering us this new life. He will take care of us, Lucy. And we'll still be together, just like always." In an unexpected show of emotion, Lucy hugged me close. I inhaled her comforting essence, an indescribable odor of her salty skin served as a sweet balm that was as familiar to me as my own scent.

I had no doubts about turning my back upon all that I had ever known. "There will be such a freedom in saying goodbye to all this," I spread my arms encompassing the house and town surrounding it. Jettisoning thirty years of never being good enough, rich enough, pretty enough, never being simply enough. "Goodbye, ugly dirt road. Goodbye, door that sticks for no reason, causing us to wrench our arms countless times a day. Goodbye, Miss Bouchard and your dog in a bonnet."

Suellen   87

Lucy laughed. I silently added a prayer so Lucy would not hear me. I wish you all well while I pray to God for a kind reception of us in the North.

"Goodbye, graves," Lucy added softly.

"We said goodbye to those a long time ago." I left her there in her room.

My kinfolk hadn't much opportunity, nor rhyme nor reason to pack their own bags to embark upon a faraway future. Most folks settled around here three or four generations ago, and were proud of it, as if the mere fact of doing nothing, by virtue of their very birth, earned them some special status. Well, my high-and-mighty neighbors, even the pine tree can lay claim to that dumb argument. You can barely stop those pines from spreading into fertile farmland, just like those ignorant crackers who seem to have litters of babies. I shook my head. Staying put in the same miserable plot of ground only makes you wooden headed enough to grow right where you are planted. No observable effort required.

I picked up the box of items we were to donate to the church. Lucy had been there after me I saw, cherry-picking sentimental hogwash. A cracked porcelain vase that had once belonged to my mother, that Lucy used to fill with brown-eyed Susans to try to curry favor with my mother, was missing. I presumed it to be rolled among Lucy's clothes in one of the crates we were sending on ahead. I dug deeper in that box and smiled, knowing that if she hadn't retrieved our family bible, I would have. There was a hodgepodge of household goods, accumulated over the years. I was proud of myself for donating all the little figurines. Lucy used to tease me about setting them up on the mantle as if they were the front line of Stonewall Jackson. I straightened a few chipped plates to fit better underneath some old candle holders. I slid my finger through the circular handle as I must have done hundreds of times before. I waved my left hand in a protective cup against an invisible flame but before I could open the door of any nighttime memories growing up, I deliberately blew into my hand, extinguishing the past.

I did have to hand it to my forebears who had to come from somewhere to allow me to stand upon my own precipice. I suspect the ones who did work up the gumption to hit the road usually had a shadowy reason, as if they had no other option but to leave. Probably very quickly. Did wanderlust arrive from necessity, or was an adventurous soul programmed into one's very bones?

Had their homeland become too oppressive, the horrible day-to-day realities too odious to bear, that the unknown became the brass ring? Imagine, pushed to an uncertain welcome via a treacherous crossing atop a fearsome ocean, and believing that as a last chance lifeline. More likely, as I always suspected in my father's case, criminal deeds had conspired to propel ill-suited travelers, an unsavory population, and the poorest of the poor, to hightail it out of the land of their forefathers. Fear, thy name is the unknown.

As someone who preferred many times to hide in my bedroom with what my sisters had called "my sharp pointy nose" buried in a book, instead of visiting with neighbors or taking tea, I was the least likely suspect to embark upon a journey into the unknown. Real life adventures were certainly not my forte. My sisters, wherever they were, would unite for once and collapse in giggles if they could see me now, all my belongings packed up and ready, my foot tapping, impatient to go.

I didn't know I had a desire to travel until it became a possibility, and then I wanted it more than I had ever wanted anything. Time was running out and I knew as I had never known before, this was my last chance. Last chance to make amends for whatever sins I had committed. Last chance for any semblance of the peace I so greatly craved. Notice happiness is not what I sought.

Thank the Good Lord for modern times, efficient travel, and the United States railroad. I couldn't imagine the hardships that befell medieval travelers. Would I have been so brave to hoist my life, such as it was, and board a ship for the other side of the world? What reason could pry me to escape the confines of my current misery?

My mother's mother always said, "Better the demon you know than the one you don't." Lucy had given that sentiment a big "Amen."

Lucy, more than myself, tried to pray about our adventures. We had witnessed, and were about to experience for ourselves, the leap of faith required to embark upon a journey with the other two in that fateful trilogy: love and hope. Lucy joined me at the foot of the stairs with her luggage. She held up the bible she had rescued from the donations.

"Who knew our destiny would be found in the slapdash of twisted threads spelling out faith, love and hope, as featured in the very first sampler I had ever embroidered?" I asked her.

"The greatest, as the Good Book says may be love," Lucy said, "but for heaven's sake, do not minimize that oft overlooked kernel of hope which has seen us through unbearable times, far more than so-called love." I nodded at her approvingly. She always was a resilient soul. When she wasn't being so gosh-darned stubborn.

I agreed with my faithful companion, "Because you can always hope for love."

Chapter Sixteen

I could dismiss the words of Voodoo Valene, and the fight with Lucy that I had rather expected would have been more spectacular than those Fourth of July fireworks. But, perhaps there was another sign that I chose to ignore. The third event, according to Lucy and depending upon how one calculated, occurred on the very day of my marriage, and actually gave me pause. In my eagerness to marry my beloved, I laughed away any foreshadowing of Lucy's nonsense.

Lucy had sewed me as fine a wedding dress as that Podunk town had ever seen. She copied it off the reception gown worn by our new president's own wife, Lucy Rutherford. She was a woman I had most admired; she even had a college degree. Lucy, I supposed, was simply rather partial to her name. In any event, we had admired a photograph of the dress in the newspaper.

My Lucy was able to adapt the gown with flair. My gown was simpler of course, and she talked me into a luscious and daring dark amber-colored satin, that worked well with my coloring. As well as could be expected, that is. The hem had no train like the president's First Lady, of course, for what need of that here in these dusty rural parts? I pity the woman who engages in the pretension of a formal train, she might well end up with one of her neighbor's pecking hens looking for grain under there. It was the most gorgeous garment I had ever, or expect will ever, wear.

The day of our wedding Theodore surprised me, canceling all my unspoken fears over his aloofness and quiet courting. He had secured the services of an actual photographer. We were to have a wedding photo. I was so excited with this most generous and sentimental gesture. He was such a fine man. He knew me, and knew that this picture—that I already imagined, framed, and me looking upon it every day for the rest of my life—would be my joy. How sweet and kind and perspicacious of my love. We were still getting to know each other, and had some minor misunderstandings, but his thoughtfulness put everything to rights.

Lucy would continue her stoic suffering, but our standoff was about to come to an end. Try as she might to ignore me and treat me coldly, Lucy paused at my door. She looked into my face and shrieked. "What have you done?" She took a step closer.

Suellen

My eyes nearly crossed as I saw her zero in on my misfortune. My fingertip felt the telltale bump. My desire that perhaps no one would notice was dashed by the look of horror she gave.

"Is it that noticeable?"

"Lord above, Suellen. This is a disgrace. You look wounded. You look like a poor confederate soldier who took a minie ball dead center through his forehead. I've seen pictures of carnage look more peaceful." She shuddered. "You look like a nightmare I once had after you read me that story about a Cyclops. You look…"

I interrupted her tirade. "I believe I understand." I hung my head. The most important day of my entire life loomed, and it took all of my energy to not see the blemish as a betrayal, an omen. And about to be captured in all its glory in a photograph, preserved for future generations.

"Bad luck, bad luck."

Maybe Lucy was right. First Voodoo Valene, then the storm, and, Lord, I was so sick and tired of fighting with Lucy. Maybe this was another sign.

"I know what you're thinking. Stop. Let me see." Lucy pushed me to my bed and inspected the damage. "How in the world are you still fussing with such a dismal complexion?" She clucked her tongue like a chicken.

"How would you like me to answer that?"

She peered closer. "You are getting married today. You are having your first photograph ever taken. Do you really want to stare at that thing for the rest of your life? You will be grumpy until eternity. Folks down the road will stare at this years from now and wonder what on earth happened to you. 'Is it some disease?' they will marvel."

"I'm going to wear a hat," I told her.

"Throughout the ceremony? Throughout dinner?" She made a face. "And what about your wedding night? Besides, no hat is going to sit atop your head, wearing my dress."

"In the grand scheme of things, Lucy, this is such a small indignity that I would presume to hazard a guess that my betrothed may not even notice. He is a professional medical man, after all."

"I'm not calling into question his doctoring skills, friend, but the man does have eyeballs." She pushed me down onto the bed. "Stay here." She fled the room and returned with her sewing basket.

"You're going to embroider a blemish cozy?" I pictured a dainty piece of cotton with a bright red rose in full bloom, attempting to hide my imperfection.

"Hush." She lifted her sharpest scissors from the basket as I held up my hand.

"What do you think you are doing? You are not performing surgery upon this blemish. Like it or not, I will survive and I don't expect most people to expire at the sight of me. Especially Theodore. He's a doctor."

"It's for Theodore I am doing this," she scolded. The back of her left hand abraded the angry red pustule situated dead center on my forehead. My mother always claimed ladylike thoughts produced a pure complexion. As my thoughts had been far from ladylike, I was fixing to agree with her.

"Sweet words, soft skin," Lucy said, quoting another piece of my mother's infernal wisdom. "Stop smiling," she said. "You have nothing to smile about."

"If you pierce my very skull with those razor-sharp scissors, neither of us will face a happy fate."

"You always were prettier than your sister," Lucy said, as she fussed with my hair. No need to divine which sister she was referring to. I sniffed, the only agreement necessary. Lucy continued. "Pity, no one could ever see that since she was too busy sucking all the joy out of the room. It was as maddening as your uncle who gnawed on those leftover dinner bones meant for Jasper One, remember?" Lucy imitated his atrocious manners, baring her teeth. "And before you knew it, he could practically whittle a toothpick to use for his after dinner digestif the way he vacuumed out those poor bones. I swear they were so bone dry they whistled while he chewed upon them."

"Enough. I was there, too, remember?" Though I choose to forget. I never belonged with the family to which I was born. Perhaps that's why I rejoiced at the thought of entering a new one. I'm sure Theodore's children and I would grow to care for each other.

Lucy then pulled the hairs from either side of my temples and before I could protest, took those silver scissors that glinted in the sunlight and snipped my hair clean off. She fussed, clipped little bits and pieces here and there, and pulled those newly shortened locks so hard I was immobilized. I ran for the mirror. "I cannot believe you just cut my hair." I now had a fringe of short hair covering my forehead.

"Look."

Suellen 93

And I did. "A drastic solution to a rather temporary problem, don't you think?"

Lucy stood beside me. "This style looks so pretty with your heart-shaped face." She reached up to pat the curve of my cheek."

I yanked away from her touch. "You mean my pointy chin?"

"Sit," she told me. She unraveled my disheveled braid. She wound it into a chignon and fitted it into a snood at the base of my neck. The fringe covered my forehead and the offensive eruption, but created a softer look. It was a little ragged, but to prevent the eyes of my beloved, to say nothing of the photographer, from snagging upon my 'war wound', was well worth the risk. Inexplicably, my head, shorn of a few inches of weightlessness, did somehow feel lighter.

"I'm not finished. Stay put." Lucy escaped out the doorway and returned a few moments later. Bearing arms.

"What in the world?"

"Relax. This won't hurt a bit."

"Put that thing down." I held up my forearm to my face and leaned away from her. "You've gone mad. You want to kill me?"

"Though sometimes I do, my dear, this isn't one of those occasions. You've got to help me now. Sit." I sat back on my bed.

Lucy held the rifle by its end, gripping the wooden handle. "If I can't stop you, if you are really going through with this marriage, then I vow I will help you the best way I can."

"By killing me?" I looked at her, and the gun, curiously. We had found it in our cottage when we had moved in and kept it in the corner of our kitchen. Whilst we would never shoot it—heck, we had no bullets—the suggestion of its authority made both of us women feel a little more secure in our home. "We could always bat an interloper over his head if needs be," I had decided, persuading Lucy to allow us to keep the firearm within reach.

"Close your mouth and help me. Take this." "Help you what. Knock me out?"

"Stay still. Hold this end." She shoved the wooden stock I into my hands. Because of its unwieldy length and the fact that she was brandishing it parallel to my very eyes, I was most uncomfortable.

"It's hot. What have you done?"

She lifted her dress to protect her right hand and held up high on the neck of the barrel. Its heat threatened to scorch my already much maligned forehead. She grabbed my new short fringe of hair and placed it over the warmth of the barrel. She tugged along the length of shorn wisps and I could feel her curl the hairs over the rifle. "What in tarnation?"

I screamed and pulled back as the length of the gun flashed on my skin. "That's hot. You burned me. Stop."

"Be still. I'm almost finished." She stepped back to admire her handiwork. At the same time as she dropped her hand from the barrel, I went to thrust the rifle back to her. Before it could fall to the floor, we both reached for it, and in the tussle, the old rusty trigger was jiggered. We heard the click and before I could even think, I wrenched my arm to the right. As both of us had seen the damage first hand of what guns, rifles and the degradation of war could do to a person, we each screamed and covered our ears. The gun clattered to the floor. Long forgotten buckshot ricocheted and screamed out of the barrel. It missed both of us, thank goodness but blasted a ragged hole in the small cameo of my mother that hung on the opposite wall. Lucy had caught me "worshipping at her shrine" as she had called it, many a dark day.

Panic mirrored in each of our faces and rendered us unable to move or speak after our initial shriek. Finally, Lucy said, "Dear Lord, Suellen. What a shot." She moved to the tatters of the paper, lifting the frame from the wall, displaying scattered plaster behind.

"I'm so dizzy," I finally managed.

"You don't think it's a sign, do you? Your mother, God rest her soul." Lucy, that hypocrite, made the sign of the cross, as did I. "She would not approve of this marriage, Suellen." Lucy held up the cameo and peered at me through the hole. She let out a nervous giggle.

"Why are you laughing? We could have been killed. What possessed you to use this gun to curl my hair?"

Lucy stood there breathing heavily. "Necessity is the mother of invention," she finally said. "But, Suellen, you could be a gunslinger. A sheriff's deputy." She poked her finger 'round the remnants of my mother's missing face. "And not only that. Look. You blew her forehead clean away. It's almost as if…"

"Don't you say one more word," I cautioned her.

"'Tis not superstition, Suellen, but my goodness. What are the odds? Here you are, battling with a wound of your own," she nodded toward my now thankfully disguised misfortune of a blemish, "and you save our lives, and manage to target the exact same area on a cut-out piece of paper on the other side of the room. That is some kind of coincidence." She came and sat next to me on the bed. "That is the most bullseye shot I have ever seen. Think about it. Your mother is trying to send you a message."

"One would hope messages from beyond would present themselves through loftier pursuits than hair grooming and smoothing one's complexion."

"It is a sign, don't you see? We should stay here. We shouldn't move up North, Suellen. We belong here. Maybe your mother is trying to prevent you from making the biggest mistake of your life."

"As I live and breathe, Lucy. I would need another pair of hands to mark off all of the 'biggest mistakes of my life,'" I said. "If you're so sure it's a sign, have you considered perhaps it is her blessing, and maybe a sign of encouragement." Even I had to laugh at that. My mother had not been what one would call an encouraging soul. And her blessings were doled out as carefully as a miser believing there was a hole in his bag of gold. Why, then did I miss her? Was I falling into sentimentality because it was my wedding day?

Lucy in that way she has, read my mind. "I know you miss her. And I know she would be proud of you, though a team of horses wouldn't have been able to drag those words from her mouth. We all miss those days when our biggest worry was a scolding for sassing, but we still knew there was fresh churned butter to go on our cornbread for supper and that our featherbed would cradle our dreams every night." Lucy sighed. "I'm just scared, Suellen."

"I know you are, honey. But, again, I am telling you. We have nothing to lose. This is our one chance to go somewhere, do something. Ride on that train you were so twitchy about. See the country. Meet new people. For once I have the courage." I ended.

"Thanks to Theodore," Lucy interrupted in a sarcastic voice.

"Yes, we owe much to Theodore. He is a fine man. And I love him." I challenged her.

She lowered her eyes. "I know you do. I guess I'd rather stay right here with the troubles I know, than go on and look for new worries."

"Love makes us brave, Lucy. We're going to have a fine life with Theodore, just you wait and see." I didn't say it aloud, I had my pride, but my voice quivered with an unspoken plea. Please be happy for me. For us.

As we sat on my bed together for the last time in my old room, I could feel the beat of Lucy's pulse, and I assumed she could feel mine. We both gave a weak laugh and I saw that neither of us were going to apologize, for the gun, the gunshot, or our differences that were finally beginning to feel resolved. At the very least, the countdown of time marched us toward an unspoken agreement. I was the grudge holder in this tableau and I knew Lucy would eventually come around. Lucy nudged me and nodded toward the mirror.

"I knew you would look beautiful with your hair that way."

Chapter Seventeen

Lucy pulled out a flannel rag and picked up her sewing scissors again and sliced and diced at my fingernails until I wanted to scream.

"You're going to make me bleed," I told her, pulling my hand back sharply.

"Stay still." She concentrated at the task at hand, my hand that is. "Your fingers look as if they came from ten different sweet potato farmers."

"Need I remind you, these fingers do the work of ten men, friend. As do yours."

She finally ditched those sharp pointy scissors and rubbed lemon oil into my nails, polishing them with the flannel.

"Feels nice."

"Looks better." She finally released my hands.

We both stood and looked in the mirror, somehow finding it easier to meet the other's reflected gaze, as if the bounce softened the harder edges of our emotions. Dear Lord, I loved my hair. I lightly touched the fringe at my forehead.

"You, my sweet Lucy, made a mountain out of a mole hill." We turned to head downstairs, as Lucy made a few final tugs and adjustments to my gown.

"I am not the one sporting a mole hill upon her forehead," she said, unperturbed. "I love your fringe. You look younger, and very stylish."

The explosion of the gun had somehow served to calm my nerves—as in I had none leftover to worry about the ceremony, or our train travel, or indeed the whole upending of my entire life. "Did you just giggle?" Lucy asked me.

"Hush."

The photographer was out in the front yard setting up his equipment. He had on plaid pants tucked into his boots, and a shirt creased from the fruit of his labors; his jacket was draped over an assortment of cases. "Good day, happy wedding," he called out as Lucy and I made our way toward him.

"You are a vision," he said as he kissed his fingertips. "And your hair. Tres moderne." Lucy nudged me. I was suddenly shy, not used to being the center of attention. "Mrs. Kincaid?" He smiled. Dear me, how I loved the sound of that.

98   *Dee DeTarsio*

Not quite yet but soon enough, I thought, so I didn't bother to correct him on that score. "I am Mr. Roth from the renowned Roth Photography Studio all the way from Atlanta, Georgia." He executed a deep bow. I'm sure I was blushing.

"I fear he will curtsy next," Lucy whispered.

"Hush."

"And you must be the sister of the bride," he said to Lucy. Neither of us had time nor inclination to correct him on that either, before he continued on. *"Enchante.* Would you lovely ladies like to take a look through my lens?"

"My bride-to-be does enjoy the new inventions," Theodore said. I had heard his carriage pull up a few minutes earlier, thankfully after the discharge of the gun. We had planned to take the photograph in front of my house, and then load up the last of our cases. We were to wed that afternoon at Theodore's house and spend the night there, before embarking upon our journey. I bit my lip and crossed my fingers, afraid someone or something would snatch this fairytale from my hands.

"You both are pretty as a picture," Theodore said, doffing his hat to myself and Lucy. I shyly patted at my stylish new fringe of hair and awaited his remarks.

"I'll go gather the children," he told us. "Where's Gus?" He called to Ila Rose, where she and Vaughn were chasing each other in the side yard. He was such a good father. And such a busy man.

"You do look pretty, Lucy," I told her. She was wearing her best dress, a watered silk pale green gown. I loved that dress and would have been happy enough wearing that to my wedding, but she and Theodore, in rare agreement, insisted on something new.

"It's your day." She held my elbows, scrutinized my face then fussed again at my dress. "This gown is your masterpiece. I thank you from the bottom of my heart, dear sister," I told her. She had that inscrutable look in her eyes. As I believe I've mentioned, we are not one for flowery words and high-strung emotions.

Mr. Roth settled a funny black cloth carefully over my hair and allowed me to look inside a small glass lens. The front of our shabby little house gained a measure of importance when viewed through the glass, a framed solemnness in a perspective I had never noticed before. With a pang I realized it had been a happy little house for us. "Lucy, it's a marvel." I let her peek next.

"Of course, you won't see the house in the photograph of your cabinet card," Mr. Roth told us. "I have this backdrop." And with that, he fussed with a painted canvas featuring Greek columns with ivy, thrown over a line stretched between two poles. "And in two weeks' time, I will develop the negatives from my glass frame," he explained, going on about some sort of chemical reaction. "And of course, I do artistic touching up of the photos, erasing any bugaboos or blemishes."

"I still like your hair," Lucy said.

"I even use a most soft hand with some tinting," he said, brushing at his cheek as if confiding a most grave secret. "This will be a keepsake for the ages. You will love it. My cabinet cards are truly masterpieces."

It was a blessedly beautiful day, and I was proud to sit for my portrait with Theodore.

Theodore sat in the chair and I stood behind him in my finery, my hand upon his shoulder. I will admit to excitement, and could hardly wait for the time I would spend staring at that picture forever. The other photograph included the children of course. And then Theodore graciously suggested one with Lucy and myself. She and I stood side by side, still as we could be. I felt a momentous marking of time at the flash of the photographer's light and knew I would remember this moment forever.

"Talk of telephones, our very own photograph, and a train trip halfway around the country. Aren't we quite the modern family?" I joked. Though Mr. Roth cautioned us all to stay still, I feel quite sure my sedate smile was the beamingest of the bunch. Truth be told, I had to think about poor dead Jasper to keep my smile from becoming unseemly.

Theodore gathered us all into the buggy to ride out to his house for the ceremony and party to follow. I had never been happier. I clutched his arm possessively and breathed in the fabric of his coat sleeve. I was audacious enough to think the word 'mine.'

We would spend the night at his home, before embarking upon our journey in the morning. A hot blush blossomed over my cheeks; I could not wait for my wedding night.

Chapter Eighteen

Though Lucy had tightened my stays with a vengeance, it wasn't that which caused my shortness of breath. I had never, in my girlish crushes, been so aware of a man before. I peered out the side of my eye, noticing a few whiskers he had missed on his newly shaven cheek. The brush of his mustache upon my fingers at our greeting had been nearly unbearable and I was dismayed to wonder what that would feel like pressed upon the skin of my belly. I drew a deeper breath. Lucy looked at me. "Do you feel hot?" she pressed the back of her hand upon my forehead. I shook her off, unable to stop the demons loosened in my veins. My lips themselves already felt swollen with kisses to come. I shifted in my chair and wanted to swoon. The silk of my pantaloons chafed against the starched cotton of my petticoat, which rutched against the back of my dress as I sat next to my beloved. The very backs of my legs were tensed atop the cushioned chair in an unbearable ecstasy. I hesitated to move as a most welcome embarrassment left me both content and fuming, with what I could not fathom.

The ceremony itself had taken seconds, the dinner that followed mere minutes, yet both felt an eternity. We were a small group; Lucy, myself and Theodore, his children, the minister, and of course, Mrs. Boyer, the woman responsible for it all. Two more couples, friends of Theodore's joined us. Mr. and Mrs. Gladstone sat across the table from us. They were the kindly neighbors who lived next door to Theodore, and helped with the children. They spoke with gusto and, as I noted, topped off their wine glasses more than once. I like to think they were joyous upon our nuptials and Theodore's finding of a suitable bride, but the thought did occur to me perhaps they were gladdened that the children would be moving. I dabbed at my mouth with my linen napkin. Shame on me. I accepted their toast, once again, with good grace.

The other couple was Doc Faison and his wife, Clara. Theodore had worked with Dr. Faison and respected him mightily. But it was because of Dr. Faison and his encouragement Theodore had accepted the position up North. I didn't know whether to thank him, or wish he had enjoined Theodore to stay here in town. Dr. Faison was a few years older than Theodore, but had many more years of

Suellen 101

tending to patients left to him. I always felt under the microscope with the man, who, in spite of his abstract air of not paying attention, never missed a thing. His wife, Clara, was a pleasant surprise. Confident enough to interrupt her husband to voice her own opinions, and I felt chagrined that we could have been friends had we not been moving away.

I imperceptibly leaned to my left to tease the hairs upon my arm with a brush against the fabric of Theodore's shirt. He had removed his jacket after the ceremony. What a gentleman, I thought as he pulled away with a nod at me. The candles on the table burned brighter than any I had ever seen, and as I saw him stare at the flame before us, its heat matching a blurred ripple of distortion of my dreams. I knew he felt our connection. My senses were so enchanted I believed I could even hear the flame as it consumed its wick.

"Love is smoke raised with the fume of sighs," I whispered daringly as the rest of the table conversed. His smile was reward enough. My Romeo. He understood I was quoting Shakespeare. Oh, the days and precious nights I had envisioned. Long talks about poetry, politics, literature, and books we would read together, I imagined, all while lying in his arms, his strong hands resting beneath my bosom.

"Suellen. What is wrong with you?"

"Let be, Lucy." Lucy and the doctor glanced at each other and continued eating. When would those two ever become friends? I sipped at my wine.

Theodore cleared his throat and stood up, offering a toast. He thanked Mrs. Boyer for organizing the service and our dinner. "And I would be remiss if I didn't also convey my gratitude for the introduction to my bride," he said to her as our guests around our table clinked glasses and laughed approvingly. I had never felt more beautiful.

After dinner, Mr. Gladstone played merry tunes on his fiddle, while the children linked arms and danced in the parlor. His numerous cups of wine served to replace whatever practice he may have required as his confidence in his talent was exceeded only by his enthusiasm.

At long last, Theodore was as eager as I, he gently folded his long elegant fingers upon the inside of my arm. My elbow a willing accomplice pulled tighter into my frame. I loathed the barrier of my stays and heard my own laughter as never before, high, girlish, apropos of nothing. I felt the breath part the doctor's lips, an intoxi-

102   *Dee DeTarsio*

cating waft of port, and his own special potion. I was finally getting what I deserved. I could wait no longer. Our guests departed, Lucy put the children to bed and went to sleep herself, sharing the bed with Ila Rose.

The doctor, bless his heart, so solicitous, offered me privacy to prepare and left for one last celebratory nightcap. I trembled as I put on the fine white lace chemise that Lucy had lovingly sewn for me. In the mirror on Theodore's bureau, I pinched my cheeks then unwound my hair, smoothing the strands on either side of my face. My fringe of hair looked very stylish above my widened eyes, the fading light showed darkened pupils portraying my joy. The clock ticked. I fancied each second an approbation from the universe at this momentous occasion marking the second half of my life. I could not believe the kindness of this good man, my husband, as he graciously gave me all the time in the world. I prepared our bed and rolled back the sheets. I pointed my toes as I slid between the sheets, allowing my nightgown to daringly rise to my knees. I plumped two pillows beneath my back, which arched of its own accord, painting what I hoped was a most pleasing picture, never mind the shame, of a new bride eager to receive her groom.

My breath caused me to gyrate, I was in such a state of nerves, before I heard the soft tap upon our bedroom door.

He opened it slowly. His blue eyes glinted as he raised the candle before him. "May I enter?"

"Yes," was the only word I could manage. He came in to make his preparations and sadly blew out the flame.

The rustle of his arrival in our marriage bed is a sound I will remember all my life. I was giddy, I was innocent; I forgot to be ashamed as I turned to greet the rest of my life. I felt his lips, beneath the soft scratch of his mustache, upon my forehead. I pressed my chest toward him and inhaled. I was no trembling virgin, of course, and yet I trembled.

"You must be so tired," he said, his soothing tones a solace to my starving soul.

I smiled in the dark. Loving man. "I've been waiting for you," I whispered. My whole life, it seemed.

"It went well today, do you think?"

"Yes," I whispered, agreeing with him.

Suellen 103

"The children did fine. And, Lucy," he paused, and I waited, holding my breath that he did not make a disparaging remark about her. "Lucy does well with the children."

"She does," I replied eagerly, anxious to promote goodwill. "She is a good woman."

"Yes. A good woman." His voice had slowed.

"And you are a good man, husband." I smiled up at him, willing him to look at me, and my nightgown, as I waited for more.

"Thank you." He paused a beat, "Wife." The awkwardness between us was sheer ecstasy. I loved the newness of us, the patterns of our dance together that was still to be discovered, the certainty that our shared moments would be wondrous gifts. One of the things I loved best about him was his kind regard and care for me.

"You should get some sleep." Then the dear man squeezed my hand, his fingers happening upon my new wedding ring, upon which he gave a slight turn. You are mine, I imagined him feeling. I am yours, I wholeheartedly agreed without needing to say a word. Our union was meant to be and I would not be so ungrateful as to not embrace this love and life and family and shelter from the storm. I was so unlike myself. Maybe this is who I was, who I was meant to be, and the good doctor had come along and healed me. The philosophers were right, a loving heart is the truest wisdom.

"Goodnight," he said, turning on his side.

I timidly patted his shoulder. Hoping my touch would be viewed as the invitation it was.

Though I had no idea how much he had had to drink, I did wonder how anyone could fall asleep that quickly, especially on a wedding night. His snores were a manly reminder that he was my husband, my husband, my husband, and I settled my shoulder next to his broad back, exploring this new intimacy.

I hesitate to include what happened next. While I lay there and pretended to be content, the snores of my husband, the Doctor, receded into a hypnotic pattern. My very own hands betrayed me. They cupped my breasts and I pretended it was Theodore. I could not get comfortable. I turned on my side and slid my hands between my knees and squeezed. I rubbed my cheek against my husband's back. An innocent gesture, one I planned to repeat every night for the rest of my life.

My left hand bearing its new ring flew out to smooth that long, tired torso of his. He worked so hard. It was a privilege he had chosen me, an honor I will spend eternity working to deserve. My hand continued its caress. It moved over his ribs down to his waist. I spread my fingers at the expanse of his hip. I sniffed his night shirt that smelled of freshly laundered cotton, hung in the Tennessee sun to dry. My lips parted to brush over his shoulder, and met the seam of his garment next to his skin, a taste that left me wanting more.

Far enough, I warned myself. I let the weight of my palm settle in a proprietary gesture on his flank. I began to rock myself back and forth to usher in my own sweet dreams. My eyelids became heavy, but I fear not with the somnolence I desired. Oh, my stars.

As if playing the chorus of "Li'l Liza Jane," my fingers hit upon a lower register, and I slowed to trick myself into dropping into a deep sleep. My fingers drifted lower. I encountered my husband's anatomy. I shifted in our marriage bed, a little closer, my forearm now was atop his hip. I pressed into his back, and cuddled close for warmth. I let my hand go limp in a natural hold that rested on him. I matched my breathing with his as he grew hard in my hand. My fingers couldn't help but explore and I squeezed, as hard as I sometimes wished he would venture upon my person.

The throbbing in my ears became nearly unbearable as I was sure he was roused to wakefulness. I stopped my furtive movement and strained my ears to listen. And then I heard the baby cry.

An hour later, after I had to rewash my face and hands from dealing with that snotty child, I crawled back into my cold bed. "Love is patient, love is kind." I sighed.

Chapter Nineteen

The next morning, we had to move quickly. We were boarding the train that would take us to Oberlin, a journey of two days. Imagine! Perilous distances, which early pioneers had taken weeks and months to traverse on horseback, aboard buggies, and even on foot. A silent nod of gratitude to those brave explorers, and a hurrah to modern times. Three states away, up through Tennessee, Kentucky, and into the North in Ohio. For Lucy's sake, I readdressed my nerves as excitement for the coming train travel.

"The railroad workers are threatening to strike," she told me, as we struggled to get the children dressed. "We could be abandoned in the middle of the country."

"I know you don't want to move, Lucy. But trust me, this will be good, for both of us. I'm married now." I caressed my most precious wedding band. "See? No bad luck, no misfortune coming in threes." I could well afford my gentleness. "Most people don't get a chance to change, so maybe just this once, you can change how you look at it, for me." I imitated a smile my mother used to wear. "Why, look at me. Haven't I changed? I have more tolerance for fools these days."

"Well, I believe calling folks 'fools' cancels out the tolerance part."

We laughed together. "Folks aren't that bad, Lucy, if we just give them a chance. I do have no small regrets about my stiff-necked pride that may have cost me heartache. And don't bother to snort like that, honey; it's so unattractive. But Theodore's taught me what it means to be confident. I can leave my insecurities behind me, and with him by my side I can be the best version of myself."

"You don't need the doctor to make you a better person, Suellen. You're fine just the way you are. Prickly pear and all." She folded her arms.

"Well how fortuitous that I am finally the sweet miss my mother had always dreamed I could be. What's that, Lucy? You'll give what a week?"

***

106   *Dee DeeTarsio*

With the children dressed and fed, we departed for the train station, the children waving one last goodbye to their home. Lucy and I tried to act sophisticated as we embarked upon our journey, but it was our first time riding in a railcar. Garbed in our finest attire (mine, a lovely lilac-colored dress, patterned with a daring black and mint plaid, and Lucy, her good luck green with scattered purple violets near the hem, neck and wrists, which she had embroidered), we donned our gloves and pinned on our hats. We felt smart with our new portmanteaus, the perfect bridal gift to the both of us from the doctor. We arrived at the train depot with plenty of time to spare, or so we thought. "Lordy, I thought we would never get out of that house. How can three small children cause so much disruption? Ila Rose, stay near."

The tips of Theodore's ears were a bright red under the brim of his hat, the color leeching down onto his cheeks, a sure sign of displeasure as I was learning.

His irritation was mine of course, for while we managed to finally wrangle the children at our agreed upon time of nine o'clock in the morning for our ten-thirty departure, our timing was somehow off by more than twenty minutes.

"Railroad time," said the clerk behind the grill.

"Each railroad claims its own time," Theodore turned his head to tell me. "There's some in Congress pushing for a uniform time throughout the country. As more folks travel, sure would be nice." He snapped shut his timepiece and slipped it back into the pocket in his vest.

At last. Leaving the South, which for better or worse, mostly worse, had betrayed me and millions of others. My butterflies I put down to excitement, and lack of sleep. And perhaps a dash of worry. I frowned at Ila Rose who was peckish this morning. Those children.

"Stop fidgeting, Ila Rose." I retied her hair bow for what must have been the tenth time.

The smell of the smoke mixed with the press of bodies—a very pastiche of humanity—felt as if we were a pickled experiment stewed in fear; overriding excitement offered up a stink overpowering in its very action. Lest my eyeballs should look like Lucy's, pivoting in her head like a child's pinwheel, I closed my lids seeking solace.

Screaming children, peevish, already hungry, tired, and needing a nap, (yes I am referring to you, Vaughn), presented a crying cacophony in concert, as if nerves

Suellen

107

were contagious. An obnoxious infant, obviously ignored by its mother kicked at my dress. Dear Lord, it was Augustus. "Stop that now, child." I handed Lucy my pocketbook and took a squalling Augustus from her arms. I rocked him to try to hush the little banshee and even pressed my mouth to the top of his head. The doctor was too busy arguing with the clerk to notice my tender administrations to his child. Unfortunately, Augustus noticed and screamed so loudly it induced a flatulent eruption that did not seem able to come from one so small. I turned my head to notice an elderly gentleman behind me take a step back, but not before he winked at me. The surprised look on his face mirrored mine.

I nearly expired with embarrassment. How does a lady handle such a situation? Gone were the days when ladies rarely left their homes, and then only for close family sojourns. I was completely uneducated on how to deal with this modern world, ignorant of customs and travel mores. I clamped down on the urge to grab Lucy's hand and run back to our old, safe shack, where we would find comfort in our familiar chairs—she in the faded green, me in the brown—the outlines of our forms as settled as if they had been manufactured exactly to our measurements. As Augustus increased his volume of shrieking—notice how amplification only serves to benefit the giver, certainly not the receiver—I reverted to the very etiquette of my mother in a situation she surely never envisioned. I pretended the whole thing never happened. The drizzle of perspiration down the centerline of my corset did not receive that telegram.

The burly grey-haired gentleman behind me, in his fancy clothes and brocade vest, which should never have been seen in the bright sunshine of a weekday morn, magnified exactly what was wrong with public travel. That man, who had had the audacity to wink at me with his one good eye, had no manners whatsoever. I didn't know where to look, I didn't want to seem insensitive to his deficiency; his eyes were an unmatched pair, in that they were not a pair at all, most likely from a war wound that marred the left side of his face with a thick, red raised scar that nearly closed his eyelid and ran halfway to his mouth. My ring finger found comfort in the heaviness of my new golden band. My thoughts tumbled, quicker than the glance that insufferable stranger and I had shared, the thoughts in his noggin sparking out of his one good eye as if he knew all about me. Please. I find public displays crass. Public gatherings suspect. I yearned for the solitude of my own cozy nest, with my husband. And Lucy. My arms throbbed with the unwieldy weight of the wiggliest child. And the children, my new family, I added quickly before the good Lord above noticed any hesitation. I rocked baby Gus back and forth.

And-may-we-all-be-happy-together, I prayed in an unfamiliar prayer that I hoped was received with the purest intentions with which it was fervently sent.

The baby, struggling in my arms, sneezed over my shoulder. Good. I rather hoped he had aimed in the direction of that infernal stranger standing behind me. My uncharitable thoughts merely resulted in the little stinker rubbing the residue over his pink-cheeked face with his little baby dimpled fists. Of the three children, perhaps I had the softest feeling for him, for he was a miniature version of Theodore, with fairer hair that promised to become a bright shining brown, sparkling blue eyes, and the fact that at least he usually responded well to me. But he was working himself into a full-on tantrum, varnishing bubbles of mucus across his face. "There, there, little man," I crooned. He pressed his face to my bosom and wiped his head back and forth. The child needed a nap. And I needed to bathe.

"Dr. Kincaid," I began. He held up a hand, still in negotiations over our tickets. He pulled out a few coins and handed them to a porter who gathered up our luggage. He grabbed my elbow, not very gently, and bade me and Lucy and the children to follow him. I spared a glance at Lucy who trod my heels, holding on for dear life to Ila Rose and Vaughn.

Chapter Twenty

The train engines were billowing smoke and sharp whistles were inciting an already overanxious group of ill-prepared and infrequent travelers, myself included, to near apoplexy as one and all surged for the step up to our railroad car.

"Hurry up," Theodore barked. I would forgive his tone, I thought virtuously, though the push he bestowed upon me was excessive. I was glad to see he was gentle with Lucy, handing her up the step to join me. He picked up Vaughn, boarded the train, and led the way to our seats.

Dear Lord. Now that we were well underway it was exciting. Off to the unknown, but traveling there in the finest and safest of conveyances. It had its good points, I must admit. I settled into the slippery leather of the seat. The doctor had purveyed us a private seating situation for our little family. I must admit, I was becoming fond of the notion of our family. Kin. And then Ila Rose kicked Vaughn, who retaliated by pulling her hair. Two days in these close quarters? My nostrils flared as Lucy sprang into action. "Vaughn, sit by me here, at the window. Ila Rose, come. Now, stop. You can change seats in little while, once we're on our way. Look, Ila Rose. How many other children can you count?"

"Bless your heart, Lucy," I whispered. I swiveled my head for a look. "Dear Lord, there are a lot of children on this train. Why, where in the world is everyone going?"

Theodore, obviously retaining his equanimity, answered kindly, happy to share his experience. "Not everyone is going through to Oberlin as we are, Suellen." Would I ever get over the joy of my name on his tongue? "Though some are going all the way to Chicago."

"Chicago," I said. "And we'll sleep right here tonight?"

"Yes, ma'am," he answered. "The porter will pull out these seats and they become beds.

Though of course, we'll have a chance at several of the longer stops to get up and stretch our legs a bit." He sat back looking satisfied. "We're going to have quite an adventure. And you will like the house they have set aside for us in Oberlin."

His look of satisfaction did my heart good. His use of the word "we" never failed to charm me. And his mention of our house together just about made me burst.

"Imagine. We'll be through three states of the country before Sunday night. I feel so very modern."

Theodore laughed, a delightful sound that melted with the noises of the train making ready to embark. A whistle tooted, a sound we had heard from afar, jarring in its intimacy; doors slid shut; engines were being stoked up. Our porter in his fine navy uniform and polished brass buttons spared a kindly smile at me, and I was reassured this would be a memorable trip. I put my hand upon Theodore's arm and squeezed in appreciation.

The train slowly inched its way out of the station, and we all looked out the window, amazed as the trees began to lose focus and blurred into the background.

Vaughn's "How fast are we going, Daddy?" competed with Ila Rose's, "When will we be there?"

My own equanimity, as is usually the case, was short lived. Vaughn screamed until Lucy opened the window, which caused a cinder to blow into Ila Rose's eye. Her father, the physician, took an abominably lengthy time to deign to examine it. By that time, I had snapped at Lucy to close the window and my image of myself as a worldly traveler, making memories, had deflated. Squabbles and discomfort have no place in one's memory book, I've discovered. Mundane inconveniences, the mostly true reflection of travel, would not make for an adventurous recounting of a so-called journey, so I was beginning to suspect most travelers see fit to omit the very true hazards.

An ill-balanced spring poked through my seat to bedevil me as I suffered through not wanting to importune another in my family by suggesting a seat change. I deliberately smoothed both my forehead and the thought that dwelt there upon Vaughn's incessant whining. The magic of the green countryside with russet tilled fields walking by in long-legged exaggeration as our train passed, ceased to amaze the baby in a very short period of time. Lucy passed around ham sandwiches, which I must admit…there was something about eating in public, on a train, traveling at very high speeds…it was exhilarating. For most of us. Ila Rose developed a belly ache and requested at frequent intervals as to the time of arrival. Lucy lowered the window and bade her tuck her fingers in the crack to help with her indigestion. How my husband could sleep through it all was beyond my comprehension.

After Ila Rose and Vaughn engaged in a lively game of who kicked whom first, they slouched in their seats, blessedly offering a respite from their shenanigans. Baby Gus had finally fallen asleep, and took my arm, cradling his heavy head, with him. I shifted carefully so as not to wake him, but pins and needles coursed through my shoulder. The side-to-side sway of our car, clacking pattern of the wheels over rails, set up a soothing hypnotizing trance. The train slowed as the conductor announced our next stop.

"Imagine, Lucy," I whispered over Gus's head. "Soon we will be halfway through the state of Tennessee."

"I am comforted by your smile, Suellen. Though, I wish I could say the same about my legs. Would you care to change seats?"

We laughed, as she had witnessed my discomfort as I shifted position. "I could not do that to you." Gus whimpered and popped open his eyes.

"Dear Lord, Suellen, what is that smell?" The doctor, looking aggrieved again, woke up and waved his hands in front of his face. As it was emanating from his own year-old child, I assumed the question was rhetorical.

"He needs a diaper," I said, and bit my tongue back on the word 'obviously.'

"Did you not bring a change?" He asked.

"You had the porter take our things," I reminded him.

"It's a long trip," he said slowly, as if that made him seem patient.

"And it's our first time traveling by railway," I responded even more slowly. "I was not aware our baggage would be separated from us."

"They have a baggage car," he said. Ila Rose and Vaughn began to whine yet again, and with the lurch of the train threw themselves across the aisle to gain their father's lap. Lucy scooted next to me and helped soothe Gus, who was working up a very red face.

"Thank you, sir. Now I know there's a baggage car. Pray, is it far and can we procure our belongings?" My tone belied my words as I wished for him to take charge.

"Suellen, I'll go get what we need. I'll ask the porter for help," Lucy said as she stood up. "Allow me," I said to Lucy. I handed Augustus into her arms. A whistle blew nearly piercing my composure as I timidly went to explore. My expedition was fueled with guilt that I had gotten the better end of the deal. The conductor pointed the way as I traversed through two more passenger cars. Lordy, the people I saw. Farmers, many of them; poor country souls, eyes wide with fright; and harried mothers, busy quieting clusters of children, filled with questions and energy.

Oh, the energy. Voices, loud—some filled with joy and others screeching with the nagging drain of relentless demands for attention. My own heart beat faster as I forgot my worries in the contemplation of theirs. Perhaps I was meant to be a traveler after all. I could see it now, I would become a gracious woman of experience. I would accompany Theodore on trips to explore the country. We would learn together, and he would teach me, oh, so many things. My pace quickened as my confidence engaged. I smiled gently at a woman biting her lips fearfully, her hands folded in prayer. "Poor thing," I said, patting her shoulder as I passed by. "It will be fine." I took my virtue and proceeded toward the baggage car.

"All aboard!" Hollered the conductor. "Take your seats," he cried out. I saw the cluttered baggage car straight ahead, as the train gave a jerk and began to move. I was amazed at the loudness and the slight rocking of the floor beneath me. I quickly altered my step left and right to gain access to the baggage car, which also carried the U.S. Mail. Imagine, hundreds of letters written and sent, to be couriered to relatives far, far away.

Through a window, I could see the tail end of the depot disappear and I reached my hand out to hold onto a rack. I stepped inside the car and looked around.

As luck would have it, I quickly espied my valise, situated right next to Lucy's. I unstrapped Lucy's first, as I believe she had had the foresight to place a few folded diapers and some rags within easy reach. My fingers found a folded piece of paper. I opened it and read the contents.

My face flushed as I recognized the very fine hand, written by my husband.

Fremont, Tennessee July 5, 1877

My Dear Heart, the note read. I find it necessary to put pen to paper in an attempt to assemble some order to my tumultuous thoughts. I am beguiled by your beauty and grace. No matter what happens in the future, know that I will hold you always

Suellen 113

in my very greatest esteem and will never dishonor the feelings we have shared. It is my belief that I am the luckiest of men to have encountered a singular love such as ours.

Yours affectionately and forever, and then signed by my beloved, Theodore Kincaid, M.D.

I smoothed the paper. Oh, the dear man, I thought. My heart was infused with grace, and gratitude. In his haste to write me this love letter, exquisitely expressing feelings he had heretofore been unable to share, he had mistakenly slipped it into Lucy's case. I closed my eyes and folded the paper, placed a gentle kiss upon it, and stuck it into the pocket of my dress. I bowed my head. "I am so very blessed."

The thud of a heavy-sounding package from the back of the car, and the very rumbling beneath my feet interrupted my rosy glow. I took a few steps before I stumbled and bumped right into the very same cretin who had been standing behind us in the ticket line.

"What are you doing?"

"Ah," he said straightening his stance. He had been crouching low in front of a big green box that was in the far-left corner.

"Is that a safe?" My voice shrilled so high it hurt my own ears. "What do you think you are doing?" I couldn't believe it when he merely smiled and shrugged. At that, three things happened at once.

The train shrieked a head-splitting whistle so loud it made the baggage car shudder. The man wrapped his hand around my mouth, lifted me against his person then lurched our bodies tightly against the opposite wall of the car. His chin dug into my shoulder as my face was pressed into an unforgiving canvas bag of the U.S. mail. Before I could scream, an explosion ripped through that tin can contraption, and, in my confusion, I thought it had propelled the train into faster motion.

Three more things happened. The oaf released me. Then he grabbed the handle of the door to the safe and removed a great deal of money that, obviously, did not belong to him. He had the audacity to tip his hat at a man hog-tied on the inside corner of the car near the doorway, whom I had not noticed before.

Oh, Lord, why do bad things come in three? The bandit, yes bandit, shoved his ill-gotten gains in a leather satchel, and reached for me. By this time, I knew I had been deafened for the rest of my life, and my vision wobbled with great black holes. He lifted me up and carried me right out of the door, down a step as the train began to accelerate. My screams were swallowed by the very velocity of the whooshing air.

"Hang on." I heard his orders but my stunned senses could no more obey than a newborn baby being told to stop crying. No matter, he had the strength of a maniac and held me aloft so my feet merely brushed the edge of the step, hovering above fast-disappearing, rocky ground. I started to kick my feet and struggle against him. He jerked me hard. "Here we go."

He jumped, taking me with him. Let's be factual; he pushed me in front of him and we were airborne for nearly three seconds, which seemed to take three years. Damn that number three. I remembered my three babies, my dear Lucy's laugh, and Theodore's sweet kiss at my wedding, where I fully expected to finally have three decades of joy.

We hit a grassy ditch and the savage force turned our limbs so we rolled as a child's sideways summersault, together down the incline. The impact knocked the very breath from my lungs, twisting my corset all askew. I sat up slowly as the train's caboose disappeared from my vision. My hands held my head and squeezed as if preventing leaking brain cells from escaping the assault I had somehow managed to live through.

We were barely past the depot and as my injuries had not yet caught up with my broken body, I opened my mouth. My scream was only rivaled by the great whistle of the train as its chugga-chugga pistons faded. Pity no one heard me. The man's fleshy hand reached up and covered my face. Of course, I bit and kicked and writhed and moaned. But, he was a lucky thief, as our dispersal in the valley next to the tracks was low enough and curved from any vantage point that most likely anyone, had they even known where or why to look our way, would have missed us entirely.

Chapter Twenty-One

Funny how many times over the course of my life I had said, "I thought I was going to die." "I want to die." "I wish I were dead." I actively sought out the Grim Reaper. Until I was actually faced with the very real prospect. I backpedaled so fast, and to my amazement found myself praying, "No thank you, sir; not just yet, please."

"What did you do that for?" I screamed my head off. "Who are you? I cannot believe this. Help! Help!"

"Sh, sh," that vermin had the nerve to tell me. "Calm down, ma'am. Please. I'm not going to hurt you." Rage defeated death's shadow. He had no idea who he was dealing with. I was no longer petrified. I was furious.

I got in a good kick to his midsection which nearly laid him low. He wrastled his arm about my neck until I felt a very bad tingle. I stilled and he whistled. And can you believe it, out of nowhere from behind a copse of trees, a black horse, saddle and all, appeared from over another set of tracks.

I shook my head, things looked blurry. I could see no one else. The carpetbagger, for what else could this misanthrope be, threw me up and over the saddle. My stomach collided with the pommel and knocked my breath loose. Helpless female, my eye. I turned my body and vomited upon his vest.

The horse shied and for a moment I thought I would be thrown and manage to escape. The wretch vaulted himself up and beside me. "Hyah." He held the reins in his right hand and leaned his left elbow onto my back, pinning me in place.

And then I was scared.

He rode so hard and fast I thought I would break in two. After about thirty minutes by my reckoning, though time is inversely proportional to one's enjoyment of it and therefore difficult to judge, he slowed and I could see we were in a forest. It makes no difference where, as I did not make a habit of traversing local wooded areas. All I knew was I had to outsmart this rogue and make my way back to that train depot, and the authorities. And help, and my husband. Oh, Theodore. He must be worried out of his mind. Forgive me, Lucy, I prayed. All will be well.

I felt the horse stop. "Ma'am, ma'am," he said. I felt him slide off the horse and reach up to touch my face. "Stop playing possum." I remained still. He walked under the horse's big head to gather me from the other side. I squinted, but had to rely on instinct. As I felt his hands reach up for me, I went limp and he pulled me from my perch. Gauging the time, I kicked with all my might, thanking Lucy for recommending my sturdy leather traveling boots.

"Oof. Son of a…" The horse danced but I managed to slide off the rest of the way and the second my feet touched the ground I began to run as if my life depended on it. I would like to report that I outdistanced that no-good, shiftless varmint, but, truth be told, I only dented his sizable nose, superseded only by his ego, and he was upon me in fewer steps than would make a reasonably good tale. His boot stamped down upon the hem at the back of my dress.

My hands merely cushioned the blow to my face as my knees hit the ground. A light rain had been falling, and the ground had become dampened to muddy my fall. I rolled to my back quicker than anything, but he was upon me. I believe by that point anger had kicked that worm of fear in its hind section. I apologize for my vulgarity, but when you have been kidnapped, tortured, and ripped from the bosom of your family, one makes allowances.

"Ma'am. Please." He crouched beside me to help me into a sitting position. I jerked away from him. "I'm not going to hurt you."

"I am mortally wounded." I rubbed my bruised ribs.

He smiled. "Are you hurt bad?"

"Take that shiny-tooth pole cat grin and…"

Once again, his big hand covered my mouth. I bit his palm and clawed at his hand. He wrenched his hand away. "I don't want to gag you or tie you up. Please. Let me explain."

"Let me explain? Fool! Do you know who I am? Do you?" He shook his head.

"I am Mrs. Doctor Theodore Kincaid. Does that name mean anything to you?"
"No, ma'am."

"We were just married."

Suellen 117

"Congratulations." He inclined his head. "Pardon me for not removing my hat." His damp hair seemed noticeably darker. Before I could give thought, he continued his interrogation.

"Were you on your honeymoon?" He look properly chastised. "With all those children?" I exhaled.

"We are moving to Oberlin, Ohio. Where my husband—"

"The doctor," he helped.

"…the doctor, has a new practice to run. He will even be teaching at the very prestigious Oberlin College. Why, I am sure right now they have deputies out looking for me. You will be caught. You will be tried." I tried to catch my breath. "You might even be hanged."

"Calm down. And please accept my apology. But dang it all, what in the world were you doing in that baggage car? I couldn't take a chance that you would alert everyone about what I was up to. That's why I had to make a split-second decision and bring you along. You weren't supposed to be there. No one was supposed to be there."

"Except for the gentleman you thoughtfully tied up?"

He looked sheepish. "I hated to do that, but I had to." I broke through his laconic reserve. "Ol' Ronnie didn't mind. He'll be all right. They'll discover him at the next stop." He paused. "Well, if they go looking for you, I expect he's already been untied. Even so… I needed time to get away before they sounded the alarms. I was hoping they would be well into Kentucky before they noticed. But now, I'm sure they will have a posse on me within the hour. No matter. I'll make sure we don't get discovered. And, again, please accept my apologies. You do understand I had no choice but to take you? I said I was sorry. I will keep you safe." He had the nerve to tip his hat at me.

"What were you thinking? You are a robber. You are a thief. You are no gentleman."

"I can explain. If you'll stop talking long enough for me to get a word or two in our conversation."

"I have no need of conversation with one such as you."

"Ma'am, you seem to be a bright, intelligent young lady."

"Sir, though you do not deserve that salutation, raising your eyebrows and offering false complimentary words will do nothing to help you out of this pickle." I flared my nostrils and raised my head.

"Your expression signifies your distress over this most distressing situation, I agree."

"Then don't you dare shut your eyes because I will take your gun and feel no remorse at permanently shutting them for you." I had a moment of misgiving, since he apparently could only shut one eye on command.

"I see good manners have no merit here, and I will simply tell my tale, and hope for a kernel of understanding."

"Good manners? Good manners? Are you any smarter than a horse? You kidnapped me. You harmed me. I demand you take me back to my home, right this instant."

"Ma'am, don't blow my hat off. I apologize a thousand times. I cannot release you. It wouldn't be safe. It is unfortunate you came upon me at that most disadvantageous point in time, but such is fate."

I made a scoffing noise in the back of my throat. "*Tu es bête comme tes pieds.*" Lucy and I were the only children in my family to study French, and we had taken great delight in crafting insults that no one else could understand.

"I assure you, I am smarter than the bottoms of my feet," he said, cocking his head. I tried to make a break again and turned to crawl, but he was on top of me like a stink bug before I could heroically leap to my feet as I had imagined doing but seconds before. Perhaps I had read one too many romance novels for I sadly realized the hero of this story was missing; heading on a train in the opposite direction. Oh, Theodore.

"Don't be afraid."

I panted in my extreme distress.

"I am a good man…"

"Horrid creature."

"Who was placed in an untenable situation…"

"Preying on innocent women and children."

"And needed to access money…"

"Money that does not belong to you. Thief! Cheat! Liar!"

Suellen 119

"From robber barons who are threatening our very way of life."

"You're the only robber I see."

"You do know about the impending railroad strike? Even you cannot be that unaware."

"Even I? Even I? I am a journalist. I know more about current affairs than our own poky mayor. Who do you think you are?"

"Don't go blistering my ears," he said. "Then surely you know how the railroad workers are being jiggered out of fair wages. They can't even raise their families. Why, it's worse than it was during the worst of the war."

"Where are you from, exactly?" I narrowed my eyes at him. He had a slight accent, but one I couldn't place.

"I am from a farm, up north, in Ohio, not unfamiliar with your final destination. But I was working for the U.S. Government on Reconstruction. And witnessed more thievery than you could even imagine."

"I imagine it takes a thief to recognize one of their own."

He paused. "I can't tell you anymore."

"I see. You've run out of excuses. Protesteth too much. You're guilty. Sinner. For shame." I folded my arms, as we were both still seated on the ground.

"The president is withdrawing federal troops from the South. Have you ever asked yourself why the U.S. Army was in Dixie so long, twelve years after the war? To safeguard the rights of black citizens. But tell me, has that happened?"

"Of course not! Those people suffer. But it hasn't even been a generation yet."

"How long is it supposed to take? To earn dignity, to work, to provide for your family?"

"Some folks are doing fine," my voice trailed. "It's not my fault."

He gave me a rather kind smile that I wanted to punch right off his mealy-mouthed face. "Nevertheless, man's capacity for evil never ceases to surprise me," he said. "Let's just say I work for the underdog."

I interrupted whatever he was about to carry on with. "You are the evil one. You are a dog. You kidnapped me. Tore me from the bosom of my family. I am in pain, sir, and probably have broken bones, bruises, injuries I can't even imagine." My breath deepened in my very real and great distress. "You sit here conversing with me about the fairness or unfairness of life. It's all been a long, hard road.

For everyone. Why, I'll have you know…" I said, my voice raising. "What are you doing? Why are you folding up that handkerchief?"

"It's a bandana," he told me. I unfortunately opened my mouth again, just enough for him to tie that scrap of sweaty-tasting fabric around my head. Before I could even raise my hands to pull it off, he had managed to tie them in front of me. I'm sure my eyes were popping from their sockets and if they had only one ounce of the power behind the savage hatred I was feeling, he would surely have been burnt to a crisp as if struck by a lightning bolt sent from above. As it was, the scar crossing his cheek and eye began to curl off of his face. His left hand lifted to pat at it.

"Now, ma'am. Please, be still. I just need to explain. Has anyone ever told you your mouth could get you in a heap of trouble?"

I stamped my feet. It wasn't a proper stomp because of my unladylike position there on that hard ground.

"All I ask, is that you listen. Two minutes." He held up two fingers. "And then, I will remove your bindings. Nod your head like a good girl."

I shook my head no, and squealed like a pig.

He sighed. "Well. You might as well listen to my tale on the ride we have ahead of us." He helped me up, but my legs nearly buckled. I crouched to make it harder on him.

"If it is any consolation, I believe I hate having you here that much more than you hate being here." With that, he lifted me back on the horse, and heaved himself up behind me. I barely fit on that horse with his large stomach, though it did serve to cushion my spine.

Chapter Twenty-Two

"What are you? A con man? A bandit? Are you in a gang?" I began my tirade the second he showed pity and removed my gag. We had stopped as the sun set. Somewhere in the course of our arduous journey, his scar had worked itself right off of his face, leaving a smooth countenance and whole eye. He escorted me to a fallen log and seated me like the gentleman he was not. I held out my hands and though he sighed, he undid the knot. I made a grandiose production rubbing my wrists and rolling my shoulders. I was only half exaggerating, riding on a horse for hours on end is not something I recommend. I stretched out my legs before me.

"Well?" I continued. "What's your game?"

"Never you mind."

"What kind of masquerade are you playing at?"

He had made quick work of gathering some twigs and set about building a fire. He placed rocks in a circle to create a crude fire pit. He threw sticks and struck a spark on a flint to light the flame. Darkness makes everything feel colder. And lonelier. The flame caught easily and before the sun entirely faded from that dismal day, I studied him. "Your hair is quite dark. You had powdered it to look like an old man. Why?"

He sat back on his heels, feeding twigs into the fire. "How old did you think I was?"

"I thought you were buffoon years old."

He laughed. "If we had met under different circumstances," he told me, "I would have been honored to call you friend."

"I regret the pity I actually felt for you because it appears you do have two healthy, perfectly good eyes." He looked nothing like the one-eyed elderly coot in line behind me who had winked. He was broad shouldered, though not as tall as the doctor, with thick muscular legs that wouldn't have been out of place amidst a herd of pagan Apache Indians, riding their horses bareback, guiding them with their knees, set to terrify honest citizens.

"Though I beg a million pardons, ma'am, at the subterfuge, I am that pleased my disguise worked." He rubbed his hair and beard, which again darkened with his ministrations. He pulled out padding from beneath his shirt front, and my eyes nearly popped out of my head.

My breath had finally slowed, though I feared my insides would never be the same. "Why did you take me with you, anyway? You could have left me."

"I fear that is a question I will ask myself until the end of days. I rue my ill-advised response and your abduction, and again, ma'am, I will not hurt you, and I will return you to your family, as soon as my mission is completed."

"Mission." I scoffed. "You don't need me for any so-called mission. I demand you release me."

"Now, I can't do that. You would go running your mouth off to the authorities and your family, and rightfully so. That's what I would do," he said as I began to deny it. "Let's try to make this at least as civilized as possible. My name is Manford Fitzpatrick. Please, call me Manford."

"I'd as soon call you the devil."

"As you wish." He smiled at me.

"Mr. Fitzpatrick." I sniffed. "If that's your real name?"

"It is my real name, though I do admit to having others as the occasion warrants."

"Shyster."

"I am sorry, you know, Mrs. Kincaid." He lowered his head sheepishly, as if admitting to a prank. "I made a split-second decision back there on that train in the mail car. You weren't supposed to be there. No one was. Well, except for Ronnie, and he knew the score, so to speak, and went along with it. But when you showed up, I couldn't risk you hollering to the conductor and engineer. I would have been captured quicker than anything. I needed time. The odds were better to take you with me."

"Take me with you? You act as if you invited me along to a garden party. Don't talk to me. And don't act as if you've done nothing wrong. It doesn't get much worse than this."

"It gets plenty worse, and I'd imagine a fine lady like you knows that. I am sorry for how things have turned out. I apologize for the miscalculation on my part." His voice was raised, but he continued in a more modified tone. "My first mistake was taking you off that train with me, but my thoughts were a little jumbled, as you can imagine, and I believed that leaving you behind would see me arrested sooner rather than later. Surely you can understand that?"

I was more petrified of the surrounding woods, ghoulish in the flickering shadows cast from the campfire, which did little to dissipate the mosquitos, than I was of the bandit.

"So here we are." I said.

"Here we are," he agreed. He had prepared a bedroll for me.

"This smells," I opined as I curled into the horse blanket he had graciously provided.

"It's warmer than my jacket."

I kicked my foot, to which he had tied a rope that led to his wrist. He jerked his arm back and pushed his hat brim over his eyes to settle into sleep. I stared up at the moon, so long and so hard, and wondered if my beloved was gazing up at the same. I prayed, if by praying I mean yearned that Theodore could feel my entreaty. I am safe, husband, and will be reunited with you soon, serves as prayer in my book.

I could not get comfortable. "I am a newly wed bride, held captive against my will, by an outlaw."

"When you say it like that it sounds like a romance novel."

"I hate you and I will see you hang." Even I shivered at my words, though he appeared unaffected.

"I see a pusillanimous godless creature, a spineless ne'er-do-well who preys on women and the less fortunate." My fingers itched to slap his smile, which I could barely make out in the firelight, right off of his face.

"You know what I saw, back at the railroad station?"

I folded my arms and turned on my side away from that monster, making sure to pull hard on the tether that joined us.

"I saw a desperately unhappy woman, pretending to be happy."

Chapter Twenty-Three

The next day was even worse than the one prior, but not as bad as the third day. Don't think I didn't imagine Lucy's wide-eyed head bobbing righteousness of her dire prognostications. She was right. She did have the sight. We should have stayed put.

"I am supposed to be on that train, with my people, headed to Ohio. There's a college there of some renown, and even people of color are welcomed. My friend Lucy, well she's like my sister, we've been together forever." I bit my lip, missing her with a pang knowing she was left to deal with poor smelly, screaming Augustus, and would be stricken with panic over my abduction. I couldn't bear to think of her shattered nerves. And Theodore's. He will find me. He will rescue me. "Oh, why did you kidnap me? How dare you take me like this? I won't stand for it."

"Desperate times call for dangerous maneuvers," my captor said, not sounding much happier than myself. "The woman at the station, holding the hands of those children, that must have been Lucy?" he said. "She looks like you. In fact, you two could be sisters."

"We grew up together," I said. "I expect we have similar habits. But, we are closer than siblings. You said you have sisters? They are not all they are purported to be. Lucy is better than a sister." My face stretched in a crumpled smile that threatened to make me weep. Shoulders back, chin up. We both fell silent until I could take no more.

"You ruined everything, you know. For the first time in my life, I was on the right course. Things were turning out the way they were supposed to. I'll never forgive you for this." I looked down at my hands, clinging to the horn of the saddle. "I'm getting sunburnt."

Although I suffered mightily, the weather was lovely. The clouds were my favorite, patterned rows of wispy cotton. Bright yellow flowers flirted with birds. I smelled like a stevedore. I couldn't decide which hurt worse, my headache or scraped knuckles. My legs threatened to crack like a wishbone.

Suellen 125

We had been on that dang blasted horse for hours, a jolting back-breaking experience that compounded the pains already suffered by my bruised form. Suffice it to say I was capable of continuing my discourse from the day before. "I cannot sleep on the ground one more night. I am a grown, married woman. The last time I slept outdoors was when I was a child. And that was a lark. And we had featherbeds. And I only lasted until ten o'clock."

"You are most cantankerous," he finally interrupted me. I was only surprised he had managed to hold his tongue that long as I was finding my own self quite tedious. When one is held against their will, one can only maintain a level of terror for what seems to be an amazingly short period of time. He had lost the upper hand.

"I've a good mind to leave you," he said in a loud voice. I yawned. "But I fear the very animals of the woods would unite to propel you back into my path and out of their wilderness. I have never met a more contrary person."

"As I have no dog in this hunt, I could care less for your opinion. You kidnapped me. You cannot then blame me for my mention of discomfort. Have you no decency? Leave me here, right now, I dare you, you coward."

That closed his discourse. "Where are you taking me and why? They will be after you soon. My husband has resources to hire the best trackers, I'm sure."

"I figure we had about a thirty-minute head start before they could have stopped the train and notified the sheriff in the next town. I would have had two hours if you hadn't interrupted my assignment."

"Assignment? Is that what they are calling robbery these days?"

"You don't understand and I cannot tell you more."

"I don't care to understand. You will be caught. And hung," I threw out for good measure. "My husband will be furious." I regretted the pain I must be causing him. I filled my misery on that godforsaken ride with thoughts of Theodore and myself, together in our new home, and our new lives. I pictured his hands, which would hold me, and imagined I could hear his voice, which would soothe me. I missed a life I hadn't even begun.

"Where are we going?"

"You'll find out soon enough. The lawmen don't have any idea of who I am or where I am headed, so we should be safe enough. It's a big country out here. In case you hadn't noticed."

126   *Dee DeTarsio*

"I noticed this country is filled with miscreants and godless savages who have no respect for their fellow man."

"I wholeheartedly agree," he told me.

My spine was jerked, my battered body a match for my shattered heart. I did not know what tomorrow held, only that it didn't have me in my new home with my new husband. I pictured a welcoming, lovely home, with Theodore and myself seated on our new divan, filled with a happiness that glowed in a golden haze. And a fern. The horse stumbled. Without my captor's plumped disguise in his shirt-front, my ride was even more uncomfortable. I bumped into his rigid form behind me. It was indecent.

The odious man finally spoke. "Look. I can't have you thinking the worst of me." I stayed silent.

"I can feel your disapproval right through your shoulder blades."

"Quit breathing on me."

"Please don't make me gag you." That shut me up.

"I need to do everything I can to prevent a railroad strike. It would cripple our nation and bring this country to its knees. Surely you can see that? Transportation, communication, commerce…the railroad is what's driving our economy and re-covery."

I feigned nonchalance. There was a kernel of sense to his defense. "Dang it, you are the most formidable woman."

I'd been called far worse.

"And the government doesn't have money to prevent any strike. Nor the power to lay low the robber barons. It's going to get mighty ugly, ma'am. And that's all I can tell you."

"Let me get this straight," I spoke my words to the ears of the brown hairy beast before me, with not a shred of consideration for the one at my back. "You robbed a train, to do good. You kidnapped a poor defenseless woman, a newly married one at that, to save the country. Heaven help us all."

"Well, ma'am, I just don't want you thinking poorly of me, or worrying I was going to kill you, or worse."

"What could be worse than being killed?" I sassed. As I pondered my ill-chosen words, just then, the horse clopped up over a rocky path, knocking the man closer into me; his left hand tightened protectively around my waist to prevent my fall. How in tarnation did that feel chivalrous? How could I feel the warmth of his hand through my garments? How did I end up in this sorry state?

We rode until nightfall again, when I slept on the ground, again, on that prickly horse blanket, next to that man. To show the state of my utter exhaustion and desperation I did indeed fall right to sleep, but only for an hour or so.

The shock of the past two days had caught up with my limbs, which trembled as if I were old Mrs. Steward, spilling her soup. A fine rain had begun to fall and though we were sheltered be- neath a tree, wet drops had conspired to make me even more miserable. I heard the exasperated exhale from my captor.

"Sorry to be an inconvenience." My teeth chattered. "Imagine, a kidnapped bride having the temerity to find these accommodations unacceptable." I heard him roll near me.

"Turn on your side."

As I was so miserable and would have done anything to feel warm and comfortable, I complied. He placed his jacket atop of me and then slid next to me, his bottom arm cushioned my neck and head, his top arm heavy over my side. He pulled my back tightly against his chest. I was mortified. It was most unseemly, though I soon stopped shivering. I cannot believe I fell back asleep. I hesitate to remember what happened next.

Can one person absorb another's nightmares? Is it possible to feel someone else's heartache? As a dark dread invaded my chaotic dreams, I was cradled in a somnambulant embrace. At some point, I must have turned toward him and nestled in closer, seeking and, God forgive me, finding comfort. We were not who we pretended to be. My cheek rubbed across the warmth of his neck. Whiskers at his jawline scratched near my eye. My lashes fluttered but were far too heavy for my eyes to open. We were never fully awake, of that make no mistake. I assure you. I have no pity for the plight of the train robber, and as much as I would dearly love to lay that particular sin at his doorstep, in fairness, I cannot. There was nothing more than an unaware embrace that gently rocked us back to the much-needed respite of unconsciousness. Some cosmic connection, as if stardust recognized stardust, was given and received. His lips may have brushed against mine. It was a dream of a kiss, a promise of an understanding. It was an entirely innocent surcease from earthly worries in a charitable exchange of comfort. Save the prurient perversions for the dime novels. Truth be told, Lucy and I loved dime novels, though we hid our passion for them and would look down our noses at those who had no such qualms. Of course, the irony is not lost upon me that my very misadventure in which I found myself would have been grist for the mill—a sure-fire bestseller, that Lucy no doubt would have gobbled up. I prayed to think it would be called *Kidnapped Bride Outsmarts Outlaw!* One can only hope.

I woke to the smell of no coffee brewing. I jerked myself up and would have leapt to my feet, had I not been mortally bruised. "I am in agony." My arms ached as I tried to rub my elbows. I inelegantly needed to push my hands off the ground to rise to standing and face my captor. "You have ruined my life. I demand you return me to my husband. Immediately." It seemed far too much trouble to stamp my foot.

"Good morning," he said. "Sleep well?"

"How dare you? You pig."

He was crouched by the small fire he had restarted. "Ma'am, please? I'm sorry. Don't make me go through all of yesterday again. I will take care of you, and I will deliver you, safe and sound, back to your family. You have my word."

Did he honestly not remember what did—and did not—happen last night? I was befuddled. None of my mother's etiquette had prepared me for this. My sister would have known how to handle it, of course. My cheeks flamed at the memory of that most intimate kiss.

"Your word." That's all I could come up with. Shaking off the last fuzziness of sleep, I was mortified. I was hungry. I was angry beyond measure. And I needed to take care of necessities. I stomped into the bushes. Trees. Grass. Bushes. Rocks. Birds daring to chirp. And I had no idea where I was or how to get out of there.

As I returned, he offered me a cup of water. "Drink this and then I will heat up some water for tea. I just finished mine, while you were still sleeping. It's not bad. There's a little bread and beans leftover from last night. I promise you a hearty meal by this evening."

I grabbed the tin cup; as badly as I wanted to fling it in his face, I knew I needed to drink it. "Where will we be this evening?"

"One more day of riding should do it, and I promise I will provide you with warm shelter and a fine featherbed."

Suellen

129

My face flamed at his words and I fumbled the cup as I returned it to him. "I cannot, I will not, get back on that horse. There is no way on God's green earth that I am getting back on that nag with you."

As his back was to me saddling up the horse, I did not hear his response clearly. "What's that?" I called out. I know he said something about his nag. Without a word, he turned, picked me up and lifted me onto the back of that horse.

"Such a gentleman you are."

"High praise, coming from such a lady," he said. "Aren't we a fine pair?"

Chapter Twenty-Four

As he joined me on the horse, I managed to elbow him in the stomach, taking great joy from his expulsion of air. I seethed at the memory of that kiss. Whereas my captor acted as if nothing untoward had happened. Nothing did, of course. I was an innocent victim. His manner toward me was as proper, if you must know, indeed mostly respectful, as it had ever been, as if he never…I could not finish my thought. I licked my lips and pressed them tightly together to prevent another useless tongue-lashing. How dare he take advantage of my person and kiss me? Indeed, I didn't even know if he remembered.

"Come on, now. We're almost there. Why, if you just look at it as an adventure, something to tell your grandchildren, we'll get along just fine. You know me now. You know I'm not going to hurt you. You know I'm a good fellow. He actually patted my shoulder, as though we were companions. Maybe he doesn't remember, I thought. My face flamed.

I tried to apply a journalistic sensibility to my captivity, at least the where and when parts.

Before long, however, the trees, hills, rocks, boulders, streams, green plants, gold plants, yellow and blue flowers under the shimmery blue haze in the distance, all began to look the same. Forgive me. Our country is beautiful beyond belief. But discomfort burdened upon misery deflates the desire to compose a fatuous appreciation of paradise.

The oaf misinterpreted my sigh. "It is surely a glorious vista. Makes you glad to be alive."

"Just how thick are you?" I snapped. "My heart would be gladdened only by my freedom to enjoy this scenery on my own terms, not held hostage to an evil man. If this is so glorious, where are all the people admiring the scenery?" We had come across no one, another pretty hope dashed.

There was no misinterpreting his answering sigh. Good. "I regret the circumstances of your presence, and I will make it up to you. I take it you are not a

Suellen   131

country girl, as this land of ours is so vast one could go seemingly forever. I've gone many weeks without encountering another soul."

"Never mind where I grew up. I prefer civilization where neighbor helps neighbor, and doesn't take what isn't theirs."

The shadows were lengthening. I was farther and farther from home, and from my husband. The doctor. The late afternoon sun reminded my rumbling stomach of what it had not eaten all that long miserable day since breakfast. We finally arrived at our destination and my heart sank. What had I been expecting? A stately manor situated next to a sheriff posse?

"What is this godforsaken place?"

"Everything is not always as it seems. I'd like to think there are still a few pleasant surprises left in the world."

"It's not enough you are the most horrific man, ripping me from the loving arms of my husband…"

"The doctor," we said at the same time, which made my hatred blaze anew.

"Oh, you are the most infuriating skunk. I demand to be released, unharmed, and not to be locked up in that," I lost my words as I pointed to the rickety, rotted board dwelling he seemed to expect would shelter us.

"I know it's not what you are used to," he said dryly, "but then again, we weren't expecting visitors."

"We?"

He gave a sharp greeting of some sort that I could not understand. A young boy, probably around Ila Rose's age—dear Lord, how I missed that recalcitrant child—came running out of the ramshackle dwelling.

"Mr. Manford! You're back. Whoa." He stopped short upon espying me, riding in front of the esteemed "Mr. Manford."

"I'm here, Bud. With a visitor. Hope you have some food for us."

The child widened his eyes and turned around and ran back inside. "Grandpa," I thought I heard him holler.

"Is that child Chinese?"

"Yes," said, "Mr. Manford." We rode up to the side of the shack and he slid off the horse, helping me down. Roughly, I might add.

"So is his grandfather, whom you're about to meet." He stopped and looked me in the eye, with concern. He brushed his hand over his own hair and tried to send me a signal of some sort.

"Are you actually trying to tell me to fix my hair? I have been kidnapped, pushed from a moving train, thrown off a horse, tied up, muffled, and set to by none other than yourself, and you are worried about my appearance?" I puffed myself up to get good and ready to give him the business when I saw a small elderly man over his shoulder. I was so hobbled from the journey it pained me to straighten my spine to stand tall. The outlaw turned and started to speak loudly in what I can only assume, journalist that I am, was Chinese to the grandfather. Based on the worried look on Mr. Manford's face, that old man might be able to help me.

"Help! Help!" I flapped my arms and tried to look more woebegone than I felt. Lucy would have been proud of my acting. "Oh, please." I wrung my hands together and beseeched him to understand my plight. "I am hurt. Badly." Plus, I was hungry. My stomach growled so loudly I hoped that didn't take away from the drama of my performance.

The man came near and peered at me. He was much older than I had thought. He moved spryly and spoke with a decibel defying insistence, on what I have no idea. I may not speak Chinese, but I know a good dressing-down when I see one. I couldn't help but shoot a victorious look at Manford. He was in trouble now.

As is often the case, it appeared I judged too soon. The old man grabbed me around my waist and threw me over his shoulder and carried me into the shed. I will not dignify it by calling it a cabin or cottage. From the outside, it had weather-beaten boards, nailed together in a haphazard fashion. One good storm would be its last, of that I was quite certain.

Imagine my surprise as we entered a fully furnished domicile. From my upside down perspective I first noticed a lovely rag rug covering wide planks of polished pine wood on the floor of the main room. From the corner of my eye, I noticed a waist-high wainscoting below a painted wall of soft, robin's egg blue. The table and chairs that rapidly passed my gaze appeared newly made, simple, but with a neat elegance, definitely hewn from the same tree.

The residence—den of iniquity?—had a large front room and two bedrooms behind, as I was about to find out. The old man carried me with seemingly no great effort into the back of the structure and into a room off to the left side. He threw me on a bed. I began thrashing, kicking and screaming. My limbs shook as if I suffered from ague. The man yelled at me and I yelled back. Loudly. I saw the boy cover his ears as he stood in the doorway.

That old man dared to put his hands upon me. He felt my forehead as if checking for fever and for a second, I thought he would cease his ministrations. I thought I read sympathy on his features, perhaps I did have a fever. But then he stood over me at the top of the bed and squeezed my head with hands so powerful I felt they could crush my skull as easily as if I were a baby bird. I grabbed at his hands but could not ease the pressure. He came to my side, finally, the pressure removed as I tilted my head back and forth to make sure my skull had not been damaged, and turned me unceremoniously onto my stomach. I pushed myself up but he ground my torso into the mattress with one hand. He began squeezing my neck in an agony of pressure.

He was torturing me. I would never survive. He was going to strangle me. "Help me," my voice came out reedy from being smothered into the bed under the push of his hands. Surely that small boy wouldn't be a witness to my demise. "Manford," I called out. None of this made sense. He wasn't a killer. That much I knew. Or thought I knew.

I began to lose consciousness. My thoughts swam and spun in a whirlpool. I ached from my bruises garnered throughout these disastrous days and quivered with exhaustion. I was losing my will as the old man continued with the torment. His hands left my neck as the weight of his entire body crept upon my torso. "What manner of madness is this?" I was able to turn my neck. He was kneeling on my body. He kept up a stream of nonsense syllables, not quite so loudly, but what did I care? Surely, he was too old to ravish me? I was mortified at his touch upon my body. He rocked indecently back and forth, and my body held onto its tenseness for dear life. I moaned and no one cared.

The man shouted something to the boy who scurried away before he finally clambered off of me. I whimpered, afraid to move lest something worse befall me. And then he took my foot, undid the buttons of my boot and pulled it off and started squeezing my poor foot, paralyzing me to incapacitation. I howled, it hurt so badly. "What do you want?" I screamed, pushing myself up.

He merely shoved me back on the bed and continued his assault. "I know nothing. I'm not even supposed to be here. I beg of you, dear Lord, let me go. Stop."

He must have finally understood because I had never been happier than when he released my foot. Imagine my disappointment upon remembering I had another. Which took the same abuse. I was nearly delirious. Squeeze. He was breaking the bones in my foot. I would be a cripple. I would hobble, if I lived, the rest of my days on earth. Whatever the cretin had been doing to my left foot resulted in a cramp, the likes of which I had never felt before. I shot off the bed and limped, trying to bear weight on the foot to soothe the cramped, debilitating pain. My teeth were bared against any more intrusion upon my person, but the Chinese man kept coming. He yelled something and then, as if I were a horse, he put his fingers in my mouth. My mouth. He pinched, but hard, my upper lip and squeezed as I grabbed at his arm, but for some strange reason it only served to make his pinch tighter. But then my cramp disappeared. Praise the Lord, it was gone. I wiggled my toes and stepped lightly, testing to be sure. I sagged with relief as my tormenter loosened his grip. I sank to the floor and curled into a tight ball, preparing for more abuse.

I heard footsteps. My body had lost its fight. I no longer cared what became of me. "KK. Help her up," Manford said. "How is she doing, my friend?"

KK, my tormenter, yelled. Manford laughed at whatever it was he said. What a sadist. How had I come to this state? What great sin on my part propelled me into this Hades? I wanted to cry. Though the tears wouldn't fall, a strangled sound escaped my throat.

"I had to see to the horse, ma'am. Sorry about KK, he was trying to make you feel better. You looked ridden hard and put away wet when we arrived, and KK was concerned. He is some kind of doctor and wanted to help you. Do you feel better, now, ma'am?" Manford inquired. What new hell was this? He reached for my arm and pulled me to standing. I peered up at those deranged men. KK was bobbing his head and bowing at his waist and actually smiling at me as if I should thank the lunatic for his manhandling of my body. Manford at least had the good sense to look a little chagrined. "KK can be a little much at first."

All I needed to get my strength back was the stupidity of another. I shot up to my full height and screeched like a banshee. "First you kidnap me, harm me, buffet me on a horse with total disregard for my safety and well-being, toss me into a hovel in the middle of nowhere, and allow this heathen," I pointed my finger, with every bit of rage and disappointment for the general state of affairs my dismal life

Suellen 135

had plummeted to, at that so-called KK, "to torture me? What harm could I, a pitiful lone woman, cause you? Why do you wish to injure me so?"

Manford pumped his palms up and down in front of him to protest. "Oh. No. He was trying to help you. He is mad at me, and accused me of hurting you. He was doing a Chinese massage to help ease your aches and pains."

"I am so weak," I said. I flopped back on the bed, barely hearing his excuse. "Help me?" I said incredulously. "If you think beating up a poor, unarmed woman is of help, then yes, I suppose so. What backward raising did you come from? Who were your parents that guided you so?"

I ran my tongue over my teeth, still tasting the flesh of that Chinese man. He deliberately harmed me and made my foot cramp, painfully so. I wouldn't have run away, honest. I knew I wouldn't have gotten very far anyway.

"KK knows about healing, though it may not be what we're used to here in this country. Your cramp is better now, right?" Manford actually looked at me as if concerned. His neatly combed hair with not a strand out of place seemed incongruous with the violence of this entire encounter.

I nodded, not trusting myself to speak any more, afraid of the punishment.

"See, the crazy thing is, he believes if you press on one part of the body it actually helps heal another part."

"And if wishes were horses beggars would ride."

Chapter Twenty-Five

Manford shook his head, and then had the nerve to brush at dirt on my dress. "We need to start over." He escorted me to the front room.

I sealed my lips.

He gave a short bow. "I apologize from the bottom of my heart for the pain and distress I have caused you. It wasn't intentional. You're safe now. But believe me, I had no choice."

"We all have choices." I turned to the Chinese fellow and the boy, hoping against hope they would understand me and heed my plight. "My name is Suellen Kincaid. I am the new bride of Dr. Theodore Kincaid who will surely be along shortly to rescue me from you and that madman." I pointed at Manford. The Chinese man, quiet now, had his hands folded at his heart and gave an even larger bow toward me. I was gearing up to go on when I was interrupted by the little boy.

"And I'm Bud," he said. "That's my grandpa; he doesn't speak English, though I think he understands more than he lets on. Just so you know. He came to America a long time ago and worked on building the transcontinental railroad."

"That's nice," I interrupted, not caring one way or the other.

"But, Manford, Mr. Fitzpatrick, is trying to help all the men who work on the railroad. Even the Chinese. My grandfather and I are Chinese."

"So I surmised."

Manford abruptly left the room and I couldn't help myself, I followed, as to not remain in the presence of the heathen Chinaman. Bud and his grandfather followed me. Manford had taken out a white crisp folded handkerchief from the inside of his suit jacket pocket and dipped it in a bucket of water that was next to the fireplace. He came at my face with it.

I made to protest when Bud bade me to stop. "Manford just wants to tidy up, ma'am. You have some," Bud waggled his fingers over his cheek and temple. "I reckon he has to clean you up. He most likely got you into this fix, but it's a little more than that."

Suellen 137

"Bud. Go on now, son. Get some more water. Scoot."

Manford was attending to my face as Bud did not obey his directive. "Manford's fussy. Fussy as my Ma was. He likes things neat and tidy, Manford does."

"Bud."

"Why, if you're here long enough he'll even style your hair for you."

"Bud."

Bud took off the corduroy cap he had been wearing and ran his hands over his head, through surprisingly clean-looking hair, cut with some style that seemed to suit the child. "He did my grandpa's after some bad men cut off his braid." The old man was very… I wouldn't go so far as to say stylish, but his snowy white hair wouldn't have been out of place on a political dandy.

"And just look at Manford himself. You can bet he'll cut his hair and shave before tomorrow."

"How nice," I said. I pushed Manford away with his handkerchief, smeared now with swipes of blood and dirt on it. "Personal hygiene is always important when robbing a train."

Bud laughed. "You're funny. Isn't she funny, Manford?" The grandfather laughed too.

"I told you. I'm not a train robber. Circumstances forced me to take advantage of a most unfair situation."

"Tell it to the judge."

Bud laughed some more. "She's a smart one. Do you cook?"

"I will not be here long enough to cook or partake in a meal with any of you." I stomped my foot.

"Well, it's dark now, and I would imagine you have to be a little hungry. We have some rice and chicken. My grandpa made it," Bud said. "It'll stick to your ribs."

My stomach growled loudly.

"I knew you had to be hungry."

I lifted my skirts and went to the table and sat down. "Is there anyway I could have a bath? A prisoner gets some demands, right?"

"Bud, get her some food. Miss Suellen, you're not a prisoner. We'll talk as soon as we've eaten. KK has water boiling and you can have that bath."

I ate and did not speak. Bud filled the pauses. He was nine years old and said he couldn't wait to go back to school in the fall. He was an engaging child, I suppose, who obviously never learned any real manners. He watched me carefully, and after I saw him change hands to hold his fork as I was, he imitated me dabbing at my mouth with my ring finger.

He peppered Manford with questions. "Can I ride your horse tomorrow? Did you bring any candy? Will you play crow-ket with me again?" He turned to me. "Have you played before?"

I set down my fork. Though I was unaccustomed to the spices used, the chicken had been surprisingly tender, and the rice had, as Bud promised, stuck to my ribs. Of course, I had been so hungry I would have eaten pickled cabbage and thought it sweet as spring strawberries.

"Have you, ma'am?" Bud asked again. "The crow-ket?"

"Bud, Bud, if you're able, take your elbows off the table. This is not a horse's stable," I said in a sing-song voice.

Bud immediately sat up straight and put his hands in his lap. I saw Manford, the bandit, hide his smile as he wolfed down his dinner. Heaven only knows what the grandfather was carrying on about. Each syllable assaulted my eardrums.

"It's pronounced crow-kay," I told him. "Croquet. People would think you were wanting to set about playing with pestilent crickets."

Bud laughed. "I sometimes do that, too," he told me.

I don't remember much of that evening, I was that tired and battered. However, I will remember that bath for as long as I live. The hoodlums located what seemed to be a large, wooden feeding trough from the barn and dragged it into the kitchen. Bud brought in several buckets of water that KK mixed with the boiled water to create a steaming soak. Manford strung a clothesline with a blanket tossed over it in the corner of the kitchen by the fireplace for privacy. The grandfather poured a whole canning jar full of soaking salts into the tub, five times as much as I've ever used. Good. I was filthy. He bustled to a shelf and came back with a piece of soap he placed on the ledge. I didn't need to be told twice to shuck off my ruined traveling suit or my stained, reeking under garments, and climb in. It was too hot to bear, and I loved every scalding bit of it. I inched my way down into the water and leaned my head back against the rim. My legs were almost able to

Suellen 139

stretch out the full length. I was submerged, and was about as happy as I'd been since I said "I do." I heard a soft thud beside the tub.

"Ma'am," Bud said from the other side of the blanket. "My grandpa says to put this in the water with you." Over the edge I saw a small bundle. I couldn't bear to leave my haven. However, I also couldn't bear to not know what it was. I had to half-climb out to reach it and the goosebumps nearly finished me off. I splashed back into the water, holding a cheesecloth tied up in a ball the size of pie crust dough before it's rolled out. I sniffed; it was filled with dried herbs. The only thing I recognized was a whiff of lavender, which was good enough for me. I soaked the bundle in front of me, and used it to scrub. I could have died a happy woman right then.

I dried off in the sheet when my teeth started to chatter. The old man had also left a nightshirt for me, probably his. It smelled clean and I could have whistled. I ducked around the blanket where the three sat at the table.

"Thank you."

"You can sleep in the back bedroom," Manford said. "We'll get this all straight-ened out in the morning. Just promise me you won't do anything stupid. You could get killed out there, or lost, especially in the dark. Give me a couple of days, I'll make sure you are safe and I will get you back to your people." He looked at me. "Your husband. And children."

With relief, I sank onto the mattress with its clean-smelling sheets. My tortured yet sweet-smelling limbs relaxed into gravity's embrace. I felt strangely languorous, which I most certainly did not ascribe to the torturous manipulations of that Chinese grandfather. I did not have a care where the men and Bud slept, together in the next room, I assumed. I felt I had an ally in Bud, and I would plot to make my way home to my husband in the morning.

I could not imagine the turmoil the good doctor must be in. Or my poor Lucy. Had the circumstances been reversed, I would have been out of my mind with worry. Did they get off the train when they found I had gone missing? Did they set about looking for me? Of course not, I chided myself. They had the children to consider, and a new household to set up. The most practical solution would have been for them to continue on. Leaving me behind.

I believe I had earned the right to feel sorry for myself. I tossed in the bed, yearning for my aggrieved thoughts to release the strain of the past days' harrowing journey and ferry me into a dreamless sleep. I heard the sharp quick notes from a fiddle. Seems Manford, for I could only assume it was him, was playing. I concentrated on the notes and the melancholy air covered me more than the scratchy blanket. I much preferred piano music, though I couldn't play one note myself; it was livelier and better for the soul. It helps no one to wallow in pain and sadness. And yet... The notes found their way through my closed door and seeped in under the blanket and proceeded to rob me of whatever armor I had pretended to wear. I was exhausted, but tiredness provided no excuse for the bone-weary grief and sadness the music conjured. I turned onto my side, away from the plaintive melody and swiped the blanket across my cheek lest a teardrop meander its way into my ear. What sounded like clapping from Bud encouraged Manford into a livelier tune, but it didn't matter. There is a fine line between love and hate, and so it goes for happiness and sadness. Lightness and darkness. Seems my soul prefers to err on the side of caution.

I slept as well as could be expected. The sun was rising, and for a glorious second I had forgotten what had transpired the previous days. I awoke to the smell of eggs and bacon, and wondered, yet again, how I could have any appetite at all. I was a woman on a mission and would flee that cabin at first opportunity and return to my family. I found my skirt, blouse and jacket at the end of my bed. Oh, they were clean enough, as if rocks were used to pound out the mud. The lilac fabric of my travel suit with its black and mint stripes was so wrinkled beyond repair, I thought my vision was blurry. The collar and cuffs lay limp against my skin, the skirt, a washed out tattered accordion pleat of its former glory.

The three yahoos were already seated at the table when I entered. Manford actually stood up at my appearance, as if he were a gentleman.

"I do believe etiquette and manners may be safely considered thrown out the window upon theft and kidnapping," I said. I inclined my head at the grandfather to thank him for ruining my gown. He gave an odd little bow.

"How did you sleep?" Manford inquired.

"What do you care?" At a look from Manford, Bud hopped up and pulled out my chair for me.

"In spite of that screeching noise I heard last night, I managed well enough," I said, seating myself.

Manford laughed. "I apologize; Bud requested it, didn't you, Bud? He enjoys music and always cons me into playing the violin."

"Manford says there's someone up north in New Jersey who can put music on a contraption and we can hear it whenever we want. Almost as if there was a band playing, right in front of us. But nobody's there, and there's no fiddles or pianos or anything. Imagine. It's like a telegraph."

"No Bud, it's called a phonograph," Manford said. "I have heard it with my own ears. I met the inventor a few months back; he's still working out a few rough spots to get the patent. He used to work on the telegraph lines, and I reckon that's where he figured out how to copy music so more folks can hear it. I believe by next year it will be making a lot of news."

I was intrigued in spite of myself.

"They should call it…" Bud clapped his hands in a catchy tune.

"I think that would be rather hard to spell," I told him. "Oh, do stop, it wasn't that funny."

The grandfather set a plate before me and though I winced at his unidentifiable language, I was delighted as breakfast has always been my favorite, and as good as reason as any to get one's self out of bed in the morning. Slugabed was also a term, not of endearment, used by my charming family to taunt me in days gone by. In a perfect world, I would not have voluntarily risen before ten in the morning. One's thoughts are so much clearer by then, and I think those extra hours of slumber would make for more kindness in our world.

My plate was piled with eggs and bacon and a slice of white bread that KK (as they called him for the obvious reason that his full name appeared to be a tongue twister made up of the twenty-one consonants of the alphabet), had taken the time to roast over the fire, making it crispy and warm. I would need all my wits for the day ahead, I thought, as I tucked in. As the meal included some of my favorite foods, I was swept with a wave of longing for the days I now looked back upon as halcyon. If only I had bothered to appreciate the simple routine at the time. I was usually in charge of making breakfast, and Lucy declared my bacon the best she had ever eaten. We used to be shamefully excited when one of the hog farmers just outside town slaughtered his pigs and drove in with fresh slabs of bacon. We would feast for weeks, my mother's cast iron frying pan sizzled in grease, which we saved as savory for future meals.

The Chinese man may not speak English but his meal was welcomed. I was not even one mite embarrassed at the only noise in the room, which came from my crunching of a mouthful of bacon, prepared just the way I like it. Crispy, seconds away from burnt.

The cup of coffee the grandfather set near my elbow helped me to maintain during Bud's chatter. Dear Lord, he even had a pitcher of cream. My bumps and bruises, and even the throbbing of my head, responded immediately to the restorative powers of the coffee. I spared a thought to ask Bud later how to say "thank you" in that man's infernal language.

"Manford says the travesty of war did cause some good things. Doctors had to come up with so many new medicines, and trains are able to go even faster than ever, There are so many inventions being dreamed up. I wish I could invent something. What would you like to dream up, Miss Suellen?"

I dabbed my napkin at my mouth. "I don't know. I never really thought of it. I never really had time to think of myself as an inventor." I gave a shrug. "How about I blink my eyes and end up back with my family."

"Ma'am. I promised. I will get you there." Manford looked disappointed. He cleared his throat and coughed. It looked as if it pained him. Good.

"Well, what's your least favorite chore? What would you like to make better?" Bud kept at me.

"That's easy. How about a machine that cleaned all these dishes?" I waved my hand over the table. We had created quite a mess on the mismatched plates before us. "However, as a kidnapping victim I cannot be presumed upon to have to wash dishes." I leaned back in my chair.

Manford growled. "Argh. I think that's a fitting punishment. Bud, KK, shall we make her wash all our plates?"

"Oh, you're a pirate now?"

Bud laughed. "No. That's not very fair, Manford. You did take her away from her family. I guess she's kind of our guest now. I could help Grandfather clean up."

"Well, that wouldn't be an invention, Bud. That would be a downright miracle. You hate washing dishes."

"So does Miss Suellen." Even I had to laugh at that.

Suellen 143

"What would you invent, Bud?" I asked him. I suppose he was a very nice little boy. "Flying machine," he and Manford said simultaneously. "That's all he ever talks about," Manford added. "I do believe he must have been a baby bird in some other lifetime."

"My husband…" I began.

"The doctor," Manford said with me.

I cast a scornful eye in his direction. "…says that it takes forever for a society to develop, and people shouldn't be in such a hurry. They need to be content with the riches they do have. He's skeptical of some of the progress, and thinks folks need to slow down. Why look at the trains, they are spreading out west so fast and there's all these problems. Lawlessness; towns springing up with no justice; and people getting killed. He believes if you're going to do something, do it right the first time."

"Your husband sounds a right smart man." Manford coughed again.

That ruffled my feathers. "He is more intelligent than you could ever hope to be, sir. He has forgotten more than you will ever know. He is good and kind, and saves lives. He doesn't steal, cheat or lie. Or kidnap." I fear my voice had risen.

Manford held up his hand to stop me. "I am sure he is the perfect husband. Forgive me. He sounds too good to be true."

That stung, but I refused to give him satisfaction. I glared at my abductor. "Say what's on your mind," I told him. "You just can't help yourself. Go on, now. Show us how educated you think you are."

Manford tilted back in his chair. "I don't necessarily disagree with your good doctor, but I think it bodes no one well to be too comfortable in this world. We have to keep moving, growing, changing, helping. Can't ever let ourselves get too complacent. That's plain lazy. Besides, I don't think I'm skeptical of any-thing…comes right down to it every time I was, I was on the wrong side of things. Sometimes, it's worth taking a chance on the unknown. Even if you don't get it right the first time."

KK refilled my cup of coffee. I gave a curt nod of my head. The man did make a fine breakfast, and his coffee had certainly managed to fuel my intentions. I took time to look about the place.

"What kind of desperado hideout is this?" I asked.

144   *Dee DeTarsio*

Bud laughed. "We live like kings. Manford is the best carpenter in these parts, and anyone wandering up here where they shouldn't would just see a ramshackle hovel on the outside. But, weren't you surprised when you got inside last night?"

I sipped the nectar of the gods. "A great many things surprised me last night," I said.

Manford did not even have the decency to appear shamefaced. "Many things are not what they seem."

"A little too early, or, shall I amend that, too late, for that cryptic sentiment."

"Manford is helping a great many people, ma'am. Don't be cruel."

"Impertinent. Where I come from children are seen and not heard."

Bud grinned. "I'm not such a child anymore." He took a sip of his coffee and, noticing my napkin in my lap, folded with the angle pointing forward, readjusted his own.

I reconsidered, remembering my plan to have Bud help me. "Sure, and you're not. Where are your parents?" I felt a pang at the look on his face. I reached out to pat his arm, "I did not mean to dredge up uncomfortable memories."

"They're gone."

"Heavens." I said as Bud continued to stare at me. He leaned in closer.

"You are the first woman I can remember being around." His hand reached out to pat my hair. "You should let Manford fix you up."

I scooted away in my seat. "Honestly. You have the manners of a cracker. Sit back in your seat, speak only when spoken to, and do not deride the appearance of guests in your house." I looked around. "Such as it is."

Bud clapped. "I knew it. You can help me learn. I want to know how to act right." He straightened in his chair, picked up his coffee cup with his pinkie extended. At my frown, he withdrew the offending finger immediately but sipped with a fine manner. "You can teach me." He gently replaced the cup on the table. "But you have to admit, the house is very fine."

"Hush, Bud," Manford scolded, as if afraid of my reaction to Bud's pride.

"He used tongue-in-groove boards to keep us as snug as a bug in a rug. You'd never know it outside though, would you? And isn't your bottom just perfectly content in that chair?"

Suellen 145

At the look on my face, he corrected. "Beg pardon, ma'am. Manford figured out how to make wooden chairs fit like a glove, almost as if they were a fancy arm chair like rich folks have in their houses. In fact, I'd take this place over a mansion," he declared dramatically.

I surreptitiously investigated. That Chinese boy was right. There was something about this space that was comforting, for lack of better word. Had I been able to, I would have wanted to purchase this very table and chairs. The smoothness and light blonde color of the wood went together. I tried in vain to remember an old art history lesson about size and scale, but all I knew was that the vision in front of me was just right. The space was clean and organized, with very little fuss. No knickknacks or artwork of course, or the feminine touches that make a house a home, but what would one expect from three men?

For goodness sakes, there was a handful of wildflowers tucked in an old tin can at the end of the table. And it looked lovelier than many a tiresome flower arrangement I have seen. Weeds of Queen Anne's lace filled the spaces between lovely purple flowers I wasn't familiar with.

My belly was full, the coffee had been divine, and when KK began to gather up the dishes, for an instant I nearly offered to help him.

"Manford likes things just so," Bud said, watching me look around. "In fact, you should let him fix your hair. You would look nice with it up higher." His hands waved over his own head.

"Bud. Enough." Manford pointed the child out the door.

Bud wiped his mouth with his napkin, set it upon the table and meekly asked permission to be excused. God help me, I almost smiled.

Manford's voice was hoarse and he winced upon swallowing. I narrowed my eyes at him. "Don't get any big ideas, ma'am. I am heading into to town to deposit this money securely. See, what kind of thief would put their ill-gotten gains into a U.S. bank?"

"A con man, I reckon."

"I'm asking for your word not to leave this place. It will all be over soon. You are safe here." I snorted.

"Your word?"

"I don't care much to die from exposure," I said. He nodded. It was enough.

He took his satchel, a packed lunch that heathen grandfather shoved at him accompanied by a string of clucking chicken noises, and hopped on that godforsaken horse.

"Manford works for the federal government." Bud was at my side and timidly took my hand. I decided to allow it. "He's even met the president."

I sniffed. "If you believe that, why, then I met the Queen of England." Bud laughed, and I must admit it was contagious.

"You sure are pretty, ma'am."

I covered my mouth and sobered up. "Tell me more. How did you and your grandfather come to know Mr. Fitzpatrick?" Bud walked us over to a willow tree, which in different circumstances would have been charming. We sat together underneath; a frilly green cocoon half covered us.

"My grandfather worked on the railroad. He's the strongest man in the world. He helped build the Transcontinental Railroad. Manford, there, kept an eye on things and reported back to the government. See, lots of bad guys try to cheat workers out of their pay." Bud paused, looking older than his years. "And the Chinese got the worst of it. Your language is so hard to learn," he told me. "Your ways foreign, and your laws don't shine an ounce of kindness on my people."

That I could believe.

"Anyway, Manford gets around." He looked around. He leaned in and whispered to me. "Words have wings. Manford is a spy."

I hooted. "Come now, child. He's pulling your leg." Bud, offended, stood up and brushed at his pants.

"Don't be angry. Sometimes grown-ups keep children unaware of their true natures," I explained.

"Beg your pardon, ma'am, Manford has helped more people than you will ever know."

Chapter Twenty-Six

When Manford, that terrible man, returned from his outing to bank his ill-gotten gains, it was near on suppertime, and he continued to cough. The rain, cold nights, and several days of traveling with my ungracious self had not done him well. Good, I thought. He said very little at supper, and his eyes had a glazed look. I nearly reached with the back of my hand to feel his forehead. Gracious.

"Ma'am?" His voice was raspy. "I took the liberty of having one of my contacts telegraph your people, to let them know you are well, and will be returned home to them within a week, ten days at most, God willing."

I was surprised, and appreciative of course, but would not give him gratitude. It did help knowing that Theodore and Lucy were apprised of my well-being. Disconcerted as I was, being held in that cabin against my will with a train robber, I couldn't wait to lay my head on my pillow and dream about how they received the news, and how they must be praying for my safe return.

That odious man stood up and gave a short bow, then sneezed. Lord knows I was surprised as anyone I hadn't caught my death on that foolhardy ride after he snatched me from that train. KK screamed at him, something that sounded like angry crows discovering a harvested field. As screaming was the only tone of voice KK had, I wasn't too concerned. But Bud frowned.

Manford sneezed a few more times, and allowed KK to put him to bed. KK bustled back to the kitchen and brewed a hot tea that smelled vile. I took myself outside and Bud joined me. I looked longingly at the path that wound around a forest of pine trees down the way, wishing I had the gumption to take the horse and follow the path to my freedom.

Angry at my lack of courage and my circumstance, I stomped to my room and waited for darkness to fall. I could not sleep due to the incessant coughing coming from the other room. Inconsiderate. I tossed and turned, and was in no fine mood when morning came. I dispatched Bud to round me up some camphor and eucalyptus oil, if there was a druggist that they were not telling me about somewhere near that godforsaken spit of property.

"Yes, ma'am," Bud told me, doffing his cap while speaking to me. "I'm sure they have it. Can you make him better?"

I sniffed. "We'll see." At the look in his eye, I would have had to have been made of stone. I ruffled his hair and told him, "It's just a bad cold. I'll have him right as rain in no time." I added, "It's not my fault he's such a big baby."

"I heard that," came a croaking voice out of the back room. Bud laughed, appearing much relieved, and ran down the hill to fill my order. I watched as long as I could, but lost sight of him in the tall grass 'round a short hill. Meanwhile, I watched KK brew a nasty concoction, guaranteed to take your breath away. I did not envy Manford as KK forced him to drink the hot tea.

No more than two hours had passed when Bud returned. He had a small jar of the pungent camphor wax I had requested and a brown vial of eucalyptus oil. "Perfect. Now where did you go, Bud? And how close is town?"

He sucked in his lips.

"Bud? I asked you a question," I said, gently. "I think I deserve to know. I'm not going to run away, and I'm not going to kill Manford," I paused, "just yet," I said, to make Bud laugh. He smiled.

"Why, we're right outside of Columbus. It's the capital, you know. Of Ohio?" I nodded. So we had arrived in Ohio. My bruised body surely felt like it.

"We're a ways south of High Street, where the druggist and pretty much everything else is. Keep going a few miles and you'll hit the Ohio Agricultural and Mechanical College. Manford says if I study real hard, I could be the first Chinese boy to go there."

"Well, you're certainly smart enough," I told him. "What are you going to do with this stuff, ma'am?"

"I'm going to make Manford suffer a little; do you want to help?"

Bud shrugged his shoulders to his ears and his smile nearly reached them, too. Lord love a child with a sense of humor.

With two fingers, I swiped a goodly amount of the camphor onto the paper the druggist had wrapped the jar in. I added ten drops of the eucalyptus oil, then a few more for good measure. "Bud, do you think you could bring just a splash of kerosene?"

His eyes were big and he was delighted to help. I added a few drops of the pungent oil and worked it into the mixture. "Go on, smell." We both leaned in and inhaled. Bud started coughing. I rubbed him on the back with the heel of my hand, keeping my sticky fingers in the air. "I think it's ready."

We went into Manford's room and I directed Bud to open his nightshirt, making room for me to apply the mixture to his chest. I tamped down any thoughts of impropriety, grateful for Bud's presence. As I rubbed the unguent over his skin, I could feel the heat of the man's fever. "You're burning up. This will help." I closed Manford's nightshirt and pulled the blanket up high to his chin.

"Now your feet."

"No, thanks, ma'am," he croaked. "I appreciate it. It surely smells terrible and if this doesn't kill me, I do believe you may just cure me."

"Bud, I need your help." I was not about to touch that man's feet. "Take your two fingers, just like you saw me, and rub the rest on the bottom of his feet." KK, who had been stirring what smelled like a savory soup by the fire came to watch. His old nose quivered, but he nodded at me.

"Good," I told Bud. "Go on."

Manford's foot kicked out as the greasy cold salve made contact. "Did you just giggle, sir?" I asked for Bud's amusement, "or is there a little girl in here somewhere, that you also kidnapped?" Bud valiantly captured the wriggling foot and applied the ointment. "Now put his socks on. Ask your grandfather if he has anything to help him sleep." KK was one step ahead of me and returned with a steaming cup of what Lucy would have called road apple tea.

"Dear Lord, that smells atrocious," I said approvingly. KK nodded and then proceeded to holler at Manford, forcing the brew down his surely swollen throat. We trooped out. I thought about making a run for it, then realized I was not in danger. I had given my word, to a train robber; I agree that makes no kind of sense, but I stayed put. I believed he would, with his own convoluted code of ethics, honor his promise and put me on a train to my beloved soon, perhaps within a week if he was to be believed. However, the good Lord does help those who help themselves.

I was restless inside the cabin, and I suffered for the anguish I was sure poor Lucy and Theodore were undergoing. I went outside to see what Bud was doing. I snatched part of the morning's loaf of bread and a piece of ham, and wrapped them in a napkin, and shoved them in my skirt pocket. I had been tempted by the sight of the lane worn in the grass at the bottom of a short incline at the property's

150   *Dee DeTarsio*

edge. I had a half-baked plan of aimlessly wandering there, escaping Bud's notice, and then making a break for freedom. Bud had been to town and back in a very short time; it had to be close. Surely, I was in as fine a shape as a nine-year-old boy and could find my way. Optimistically, I imagined I would encounter neighbors or farmers along the way who could help me.

I found Bud in the shed, cleaning out the horse's stable. I helped him throw some fresh straw down, and as I poked around, I found the croquet mallets. "We used to play this when I was younger, before the war."

Bud smiled. "I bet I can beat you."

I clapped my hands. "We'll see about that." In the dark corner I retrieved the wooden mallets and two wooden balls, one red, one blue. The set was missing the wickets. At the other end of the shed I found a coil of rusty wire, which bent fairly easily as I worked two pieces back and forth. I did this several times to create a length of nearly fifteen inches or so, that I could bend into arches for our play. "There. Let's go build the croquet course. Do you know the rules?"

"Of course. Manford taught me. But we never played with those things," he said, pointing at the wickets. "I don't get to play that much, though. Manford travels and grandfather, well, he's usually too busy. I don't think he understands the rules, or the purpose."

I gave Bud the balls to carry and we went out into the sunshine. "I must warn you, I'm fairly accomplished."

"Yes ma'am," he said. He set about helping me shape the wires into small arcs, which I placed opposite each other across a large patch in the grassy yard. We scattered the others in between to create our playing field. I bit my tongue from taking control over the child's placement of the wickets. His happiness was infectious. We laughed as we shuffled our feet, flattening the grass so our wooden balls would not get caught up in the growth. "Here's the start. I will hit my ball first toward that goal, and then you go." I had found two sticks to mark each endpoint.

While Manford slept, Bud and I played croquet. I talked freely to the child; he was not a whiner. He even made me miss Theodore's children some. I had not yet crossed that precarious bridge from courtesy to affection, but believe me when I say I had one foot poised. You can't force feeling, yet there I was with that Chinese boy, telling him things I hadn't thought of in years.

As the rules in my memory of the game were a bit lacking, as was the equipment, we improvised. We hit those balls, ruthlessly aimed for each other's, and had a high fine time. My foot atop my ball steadied it, as I whomped my mallet but good, sending Bud's ball out of bounds.

"Victory," I shouted as my sure swing careened my ball into the winning stake at the end of the course.

"Manford doesn't believe it's sportsmanlike to preen," Bud told me.

"Manford is absolutely correct," I agreed. The little stinker had been teasing me.

Our game ended, he peppered me with questions: "How old are you? How much do you weigh? Why are you here again?"

"Hush," I finally had had enough. "You are a hooligan."

He let out an Indian whoop in response. He chased me, then I chased him, then he bade me teach him how to dance. I glanced longingly at the little path I could barely make out. I had almost forgotten my mission. I sighed. In an odd way, I was almost relieved I'd kept my word to that scoundrel Manford and not run away. What were several more days, anyway?

I took his grubby little paws in mine, not minding so much since mine fared not much better, and showed him an easy step. I hummed a tune, well aware I was no Lucy in the singing department. Bud was beginning to get the hang of it when his foot became entangled with mine, and we both tripped into the soft grass.

"We all fall down," I said. "What's that?"

"Didn't you ever play nursery rhyme games growing up?" And then my face fell at the look in his eyes. Of course he hadn't. His childhood, from the little Manford told me, must have been atrocious. I sing-songed the "Ring Around the Rosie" rhyme for him, and he immediately repeated it back.

"You're a lovely boy, Bud. Actually, I don't much cotton to children, as their manners are mostly spoiled."

"Do you have children?"

"I did."

He nodded without asking more. I plucked a yellow dandelion from the ground and tickled him under his chin. "As I thought, you like butter." He found his own flower and cast a yellow shadow under my chin.

"You like butter, too."

"I know. And I'm getting mighty hungry about now."

"Is that why you have bread and ham in your pocket? Were you planning on us having a dinner out here?" His eyes shone.

"You don't miss a trick, do you?"

"Let's go wash up." We jumped up and I took his hand as we raced for the house. We reached the door and each paused for a drink of water out of the tin cup in the bucket.

"I'm glad you didn't run away Miss Suellen."

"I am too, I guess." As soon as I was convinced I wasn't going to be murdered, and the fact that Manford Fitzpatrick was just a bumbling thief, I realized I had had worse days. "I expect to be back to my family soon enough. Mr. Fitzpatrick has some big meeting he needs to attend to first. And then he's promised to deliver me home, safe and sound."

"If Manford says something, it's gospel truth," Bud said.

Bud poured some water over his hands, and then offered to do the same for mine. We each wiped them dry on our clothes, then went and sat under the shady tree to eat my getaway meal. KK was nowhere to be found, Bud said he often went out looking for berries and plants. After we ate, I went in so that I could prepare a plate for Manford. I tapped on the closed door, and he bade me enter. He was dressed and sitting on the bed, looking out the window. I followed his gaze and saw Bud chasing one of the wooden balls, singing the song I had taught him. We could hear him clearly, and I realized Manford must have heard most of our exchanges from the afternoon right outside his window. I pursed my lips.

"I'm hungry; thank you," he told me. "I can eat at the table; I feel that much better. Thanks to you."

"Well, I believe lack of sleep, riding those miserable days, and kidnapping can harm one's health, such as it is."

"*Touché,*" he said, then laughed. Then coughed.

"You might want to take it easy, and keep drinking water and that atrocious tea KK makes you."

Suellen 153

Manford made a face. "It is that bad. Between that and your explosive liniment that you coated me in, it's a wonder I am upright. Remind me to take a vial of that next time I need to open a safe." He looked at me for my reaction.

"Mr. Fitzpatrick, I do not think enough time has passed to be making a mockery of your illicit pastime. Nor do I ever think there will be enough time."

"Sorry. However, you and KK should go into business healing folks of their misery. His tea and your poultice could make a leper whole and cause a heathen to embrace the Lord." He stood up and allowed me to precede him down the short hall to the table in the front room.

I scooped up a bowl of a hodgepodge stew KK had left in a pot, and I placed the dish on the table.

"Ma'am?"

I raised my eyebrows.

"You are wonderful with Bud; thank you for that too."

"He's a good little boy." I cleared my throat and went back outside.

KK returned with some eggs and blackberries, and spent the rest of the day tending to Manford, whose cough seemed to have lessened. After the sun set, I pointed KK and Bud toward the feather bed Manford had Bud move into the kitchen near the hearth, and told them I would check on Manford before I retired.

A kerosene lamp provided a comforting glow in the camphor and eucalyptus scented warm room. KK had helped Manford wash up, and he was propped high on pillows as I entered the room. I felt his forehead. "Your fever is down."

"I slept most of the day and feel much better. Thanks to you and that god-awful potent voodoo medicine you greased me up with. I swear I smelled like a stick of dynamite, and I was worried you were going to strike a match and blow me up."

"Why? Is there money inside of you?" I said.

"There's solid gold inside me," he said, touching his heart. "Would you sit with me awhile, I'm not sleepy and my throat is much better."

"You stink," I said.

"You do know how sincerely I regret forcing you off that train, ma'am."

I slightly raised one shoulder. Though he was sick and vulnerable, and truth be told had acted like a gentleman, more or less, an ignorant gentleman, I could not

154 *Dee DeTarsio*

find it within myself to assuage his conscience. "Tell me about yourself, that I may feel even more guilty."

"Nothing to tell," I told him. "Birth, war, death." I walked back over beside the bed and sat down on a stool.

"Three words? That's all you've got? I can do better than that. I was born in Ohio, could run faster than all my friends, and once jumped off the roof of our barn on a dare and lived to tell about it." He twisted his right hand as if offering proof. "I have three younger sisters who I helped raise, and a parcel of kin who think I'm a black sheep."

"You insult an entire breed of livestock," I told him.

"My sisters are good girls. I tried to make things pretty for them. That's where I learned to cut hair."

"And learned to don disguises, no doubt," I said.

He smiled. "I briefly fought in the war, for the North, naturally."

"Naturally."

"I was an officer, and I was able to gather some intelligence. Dark days for both sides, as I am sure you know, ma'am. Families took it worst."

He paused so long I couldn't resist a prod. "Were you married then?"

"I was."

Past tense noted. He finally continued. "My wife died. They said it was cancer."

"I'm sorry." I whispered the words.

"She was such a little thing, my wife. With never a bad word toward anyone or anything. I could lapse into melancholy, and she would always see the bright side." He looked up at me. "That wasn't always a welcome personality trait."

I reluctantly laughed. "Have no fear; I shan't jolly you with hearts and roses. That's more my friend Lucy's style anyway." Neither of us spoke for a few minutes.

"We hadn't had a chance to have children yet," he said in response to my unasked question. I had been wondering. "Her name was Lillian. Lovely Lillian, I used to call her. There's not a day goes by when I don't think of her, and try to make her proud."

I could hear the clock tick from the kitchen. Manford coughed and rustled in the bedclothes, turning on his side. I prayed he would fall asleep.

Suellen 155

"My joy in her is exceeded only by my sadness at her absence." I looked away from his pain.

"And you? A newlywed?" He cleared his throat and nestled into his pillow. "I wish you well. I will return you back to your groom, the doctor, as soon as I can. How did you meet?"

There was a devil at work inside me, demanding attention. "He wasn't my first husband." Manford nodded as if he understood. "The war."

"You don't understand."

He eased himself back up higher on the pillow and focused his attention on me. His rather nice brown eyes had a kindness that made that devil inside me quite angry. I stood to pull up the blanket for him.

"It was after the war."

"What happened?"

"My girls got sick. And passed. I lost the baby." I twisted my new wedding band. "And when my husband got sick, I don't believe he cared to live anymore."

I could feel the heat flare up my neck into my face. "Did you love him?"

"I loved him enough to kill him."

Chapter Twenty-Seven

Manford reached from his bed for my hand. That little squeeze of pressure released a dam of confession as I withdrew my hand. I sat back down.

"The doctor said there was nothing we could do. We both knew it. How I hated those words, 'it's only a matter of time, it's only a matter of time.' Life and all the bad things in it are always 'only a matter of time.' He was so weak." The excuses tumbled from my lips. "I nursed him as best I could. He was in a bad way."

My breath accelerated. "He begged me." I looked up at Manford. "But he didn't have to. We both knew it was inevitable. We both watched it come."

"You are very brave."

Though they were the very words I wanted to hear, they did little to absolve my sin. "He was the bravest man I've ever known." I squeezed my hands together, remembering.

"We were neither's first choice, you know. But, heaven help me, I did not know what I would ever do without him. One day, toward the end, when he could find the breath, we talked. We had never really talked before. He was a good man."

Manford respected my quiet as I paused.

"A heap of folks thought he wasn't good enough for me. Myself included. Turns out, I wasn't worthy of him." I looked down. "All those wasted years. My husband used to say that it's what's on the inside that will kill a person. I never really understood what he meant."

Dear Lord, I had no idea why I was confessing to that man, but I couldn't seem to stop myself. "We had come to an understanding." I spoke more slowly. "I couldn't bear to see him suffer anymore. I found I did have feelings for him and I would do right by him, no matter what. I owed him, you see? I nursed him, and made him comfortable. And I did not let him die alone. Or in pain. He was brave. I can only hope my ending is half as peaceful."

"No one should be forced to make that choice.

"It had to be done." I couldn't help but continue to defend myself. "And choice is a powerful medicine. For him, it was the only one left. When I start to repent

Suellen 157

and feel the burden of redemption is unobtainable, I realize I would do it again, for his sake. He suffered so, with no hope of survival. He was so strong, who knows how long he could have lingered, tortured like that. He was scared, Mr. Fitzpatrick. So scared of dying and what comes next. But he faced it. That's bravery." I squeezed my hands together as if in prayer.

"After the war, I know many marriages came together out of nothing but convenience. But we sufficed. It wasn't a bad arrangement. Especially with the girls." I sighed.

With great effort I stilled the quiver in my voice and swallowed a few times.

"His every breath hurt, and took far too long. It sounded like a creaky old rusted gate that you never could open, scraping against its hinges." I folded the cuff back on my sleeve. "I would sometimes lose my own breath, waiting for him to exhale, praying for that one more time." My glance flickered toward him. "If you have time to ruminate, waiting upon the sound of another's breath… It's purgatory." I shall never forget that sound. I brushed my fingers against my lips. I didn't need to tell Mr. Fitzpatrick how my poor husband had struggled so hard and fought for each gasp of air that the effort would sometimes foam at his mouth.

"I didn't know how much morphine was required. It was bitter, and nearly impossible for him to swallow. I mixed that last dose in his tea. And he knew it. And he drank it. Greedily."

"God bless you, ma'am." Manford made me hold his gaze. "You are forgiven, you know. You are a righteous woman, and you need to believe in your right to peace."

"I deserve many things, sir, and peace is not one of them."

"Your actions were a loving kindness mercy. Would you have condemned him for helping you?"

"Lord, he was so scared. He wanted more than anything to trust in my empty promises. I sang to him as I did to my baby girls. 'Hush now, all is well, all is right, mama's got her baby tight.' His pain robbed him of any dignity he once had, and magnified his fear. It was heartbreaking. I had to help him. I had to. He begged me. And he thanked me. And I held his hand until it went cold."

Neither of us spoke for a long pause.

"It was all I could do to not drink the rest of that morphine. I wanted to more than anything. I didn't have the courage after all." I have never told a living soul any of that, though I'm sure Lucy suspects. My relief at unburdening myself was bewildering. I stood up and smoothed my dress. "Would you like some tea?"

"No," he said softly. He repeated himself. "No, thank you. Nothing to drink for me. Nope, not thirsty at all." His eyes twinkled as I realized he was mocking me.

"You fear I will kill you, too?" I was mortified. Until I started laughing. The kind of laugh that hiccups out of the sobs at gravesides. I held my stomach and water streamed from my eyes. A snuffling chortle was uncomfortable in its fierceness. I walked out of the room to compose myself and to get that man a damn cup of tea. "How dare you?"

It was some time before I returned. He was sitting on the bed. He gratefully accepted the tea.

"It seems as if I need to apologize to you once again. I was in the war, and I do not mean to diminish the brave women left home to raise the families and bear the burdens, on either side of the country. I vowed there had to be a better way, and it has been my life's work to help make it better." He sipped his tea. "Thank you for your care," he told me. "I am sworn to secrecy and cannot tell you the real reason for my mission, but I work for the government. I'm one of the good guys. That's all I can tell you for now. Just know that I'm no Robin Hood, but neither am I a simple train robber. I ask you to trust me, and I ask once again for your word to not run away."

He coughed, but his chest seemed clearer. "Since you are—" I lowered my head, waiting to see what he would say. "Our guest," he managed.

"Understatement, thy name is insanity."

A slight color rose in his face. His lips curved. "Since you are here, and I cannot take the chance of any exposure to this mission, I would be greatly indebted if you would accompany me." He spoke the last few words of ridiculousness in haste.

"Insult, meet injury." I dropped a curtsy.

"It's not like that. For all that I've put you through, your presence would only lend credibility to the task at hand." He held up his own hand to prevent my answer. "If you help me three days hence, I will see you to your door, to your people, to your husband. You have my word."

"Help you what?"

"You would be my assistant, my secretary if you will. You will not be in any danger. It makes sense to have a government agent travel with someone, and helps people believe what they want to believe anyway. All you need to do is present some contracts for the men I am to meet for their signatures, and then when the time is right, reveal the cash."

"That you stole," I interrupted him.

"That I have secured in a safety deposit box at the bank," he finished. "Just a simple business transaction."

"Nothing is that simple."

"Can you do it? Your assistance will get you home that much sooner. Will you help? Do you I have your word you won't run?"

"I don't know how I can help, but I promise I will try." I don't know if he noticed that vow allowed for leeway.

Chapter Twenty-Eight

Over the next two days and nights, I had gradually relaxed, realizing I was not going to be harmed. In spite of my circumstances, and my fear for my beloved's worry and that of Lucy's, I shamefully enjoyed myself, knowing I would be home soon.

KK was an exotic cook and showed me a rice dish that I believed I could recreate once I was safely installed in my new kitchen up in Oberlin. He also showed me massage points as a protocol for healing certain ailments, which I could not wait to visit upon patients in my new role as the doctor's wife.

Manford had decided we needed to "lay low" in the parlance of a gangster, for the past several days; good thing too, since he had been indisposed. He again gave his word that if I but accompany him on his journey and assist him in his mission, he would personally escort me to the front door of my new home in Oberlin.

I made my deal with the devil.

"If you travel as my secretary," he was up and dressed and sitting at the table, "it would serve me that much better in my disguise," he told me.

He began cleaning his gun.

"Dear Lord, I am not carrying any gun."

"Do you want me to teach you how to shoot?"

"I believe I already know how," I said, remembering the giant hole I had somehow managed to blow in my mother's cameo in my bedroom back home.

"Would you care to try?"

"How do you know I won't just go ahead and shoot you?" I asked him.

"Because you're a lady," Bud said answering before Manford. "And a lady always honors her word. As does a gentleman."

"Another useless talent, much like whistling and croquet playing, which has yet to improve my life."

KK returned at some point, and as they had sugar and flour and butter, I made an only half-bad attempt at a blackberry cobbler that crumbled every which way

Suellen

161

and had sunk in the middle. The gentlemen at my soiree were delighted with my effort.

Manford explained my role in the next day's transaction. "I'm only telling you the basics, I don't want you compromised any more than necessary. You won't be implicated, that I promise you. I can offer you that much protection."

I folded my arms. "Go on."

"I have a meeting scheduled with two of the principles of the Baltimore and Ohio Railroad. I am not prejudicing you to warn you, they are among the biggest robber barons there are. They, and their other 'Associates' as they prefer to be called, hold a controlling interest in the railroads; no one is quite sure how much exactly, and that's the way they like it. If you pretend to be my secretary, it helps add one more layer of protection, not tying me to the robbery. I'll be using my own name and back to my own self, well, as close as possible," he said. "As I used a disguise and an alias on the last trip, we will not be recognized."

"I don't understand why you just don't give the money back. Give it to the sheriff, or the governor, and tell him why those men are so evil."

"Doesn't work like that. Corruption abounds, ma'am. It's my job to offer to deal with them, offer them a subsidy and negotiate with them. With the backing of the U.S. Government, I can engage them in dialogue with the workers, to help them see how if they provide better wages, better and safer working conditions, and compensation for the families of workers who are killed or injured on the job, everyone wins. Profits actually go up; workers are happy, safe; and everything runs as it's supposed to. It's 1877 for heaven's sake. We are in modern times and it is the most dangerous job of our time, and yet imagine, these workers are lucky to get one dollar a day to support their families."

"Where do I come in?"

"As I said. Anything that can help allay suspicions. Just adding respectability, as well as another witness to help keep these gentlemen honest." He paused. "I fear if my identity has been compromised, your presence will add a layer of protection. And it is perfectly safe, I assure you."

"They won't know I was kidnapped? Is anyone even looking for me?" I fear I sounded more poor mouthed than I intended.

Manford sheepishly pulled out a folded paper from his pocket. The smeared black ink headline—WANTED—was crooked. It featured a rough drawing of a grotesque old man, a horrible monster with an eyeball dangling from its socket, and he held a bag of money. Under the Wanted headline it read: Train Robber Monster Kidnaps Bride. In the lower corner of the wrinkled paper was what I assumed to purport a cringing bride.

"This is supposed to be me?"

Bud and Manford exchanged a look.

"Was the purveyor of this handbill a blind gentleman? My nose is not that pointy. No one's nose is." I stared with distaste at the drawing of the "bride" featured next to the monster. I was shown as a haggard-looking woman, albeit with a fringe of hair scribbled in, in an attempt to highlight my stylish up-do. A dark dress choked up to my neck in a most unflattering caricature.

"Be glad, ma'am, no one will recognize you. We'll just get through this and I will have you on a train to Oberlin to your family in two more days. I checked the schedule; a train leaves at noon Friday to head up north. You could be home in time for supper in three days."

I read the handbill. "I should turn you in for the $100 reward. It would come in handy, but I fear no one would believe me." I rubbed my nose.

"You have very proportional features, Madam, with one of the loveliest *retroussé* noses it's been my pleasure to observe."

I looked at Bud. "That, my young friend, is a cavalier gentleman trying to undo the damage he has done by buttering up a simple female. However, this woman chooses not to purchase what that man is selling."

Bud laughed. "You are pretty ma'am, especially when you smile. And I like your nose, too."

I sniffed loudly. "As do I." We all laughed. Manford folded up the dreadful handbill and put it back in his pocket. Good. I cared not to see that ever again.

I tossed and turned that night as my conscience wrestled with the strange camaraderie I had begun to feel in regard to this fool, and his errand, versus the law. Right versus wrong. I had overheard Mr. Fitzpatrick telling KK that I would do "quite nicely." Whatever did he mean by that? Was I a patsy for going along with this? A pawn in his wicked scheme? Why, I could be put in jail. Stealing breaks the eighth commandment. Every bone in my body rebelled against the wrongdoing and my being any part of it. And yet. And yet, I just wanted to go home. Safe and sound. The sweetest words ever.

When the inhabitants of the cabin were all fast asleep—and by fast asleep I mean engaged in some manly snoring contest, Bud included—I crept to the kitchen in the dark and on my tiptoes, found a pencil stored in a tin can on a shelf next to the stove. People who fail to plan should plan to fail.

Chapter Twenty-Nine

The next morning, fortified with the coffee that KK brewed to my liking, strong and dark, he had even obtained more fresh cream from the unseen neighbor down the way. I was ready. Manford had obtained an outfit, a skirt and blouse, suitable for a government secretary, I expect; truth be told I liked it very much. The fabric was lovely and rich under my fingertips.

Whatever dignity I thought I had once possessed had been tossed out the railroad car upon my kidnapping. I put on the clothes that man had somehow procured for me, not even ashamed for smoothing down the creamy silk blouse, impossibly embroidered with as fine a detail as Lucy ever could. The dark serge skirt fit me reasonably well, but the patent leather belt made the ensemble complete. As I looked down, I could only get a partial visual, but believed I looked much unlike myself.

I went into the front room, where Manford offered me a seat. Bud whistled as Manford smiled. Manford loomed over me as I tilted my head away from him. "What on earth, sir?"

"I'm going to fix your hair. It hasn't been brushed in several days."

I grabbed his wrist. "You kidnap me, then chastise me for not grabbing my valise containing my brush and personal items as I was being thrown from a train?" I made to stand up.

"Sorry. That's not what I meant. You are a right handsome woman, and I will do your hair. Tell her Bud."

"He's good. He'll fix you right pretty. Not that you need it, ma'am."

"Bud," I said. "You are well on your way to becoming a right little charmer." And to Manford I said, "I made a deal. I will see it through. Put your spy disguise on me as you will." And I submitted to him to brush my hair.

His clumsy big hands had a surprisingly light touch, and did not once pull a snarl to torment my sensitive head. I bit my lips when he pulled out a pair of scissors.

"Relax. This won't hurt a bit." Bud laughed at Manford. "I just need to even out your fringe. It suits you." He made a few snips. He put down the scissors, then gathered up my hair. He fussed and fluffed it, winding it around itself in a loose and wavy topknot before securing it.

"Ouch. Did you just stab a spike into my skull?"

Bud liked that. "He used two of my grandfather's chopsticks, broke them clean in half, and whittled them down. He crisscrossed them to hold your hair in place."

My head had stopped stinging and I gingerly rolled it from side to side. The arrangement appeared intact. Manford escorted me to the small mirror. Yes, the man owned a mirror, in a shanty in the middle of nowhere. My eyes widened. He nodded encouragingly. "Beautiful."

I turned this way and that. The fringe, with the extra height of hair on top of my head, transformed me. My skin, which had received more sun on the trail the first two days of this madcap adventure than in my whole life, had healed. I looked a woman of substance. "Thank you," I said without thinking.

Manford laughed. "No take backs."

"Oh, pray forgive me, dear kidnapper. I do take back my thanks. I should be at home with my husband and family."

"And miss all this glamour?" he teased.

"Scoundrel."

"Now, now. I need you in your role. Remember. You are a successful, accomplished woman, and nothing will stand in your way. That's how I see you; you just need to let others see that too."

I inhaled the snobbery and conviction of feminine wiles from my sister. My shoulders leveled, my spine lengthened, my bosom thrust itself out into the world. I exhaled superiority.

"That's it," Bud said, clapping. "You are pretty, but I wouldn't want to tangle with you." "That's exactly what we are going for, Bud," Manford said.

"Where in the world did you learn to do all this?" I asked, as I swiped my hand in front of myself. I liked the feel of my hair gathered high, and I could see from the mirror the fringe in front of my face had been softened into fragile wisps. "What kind of man knows these things?"

He bowed in front of me. "Jack of all trades." "Master of none."

"Ma'am, would you like to take your wedding band off, to help further the disguise?"

I reared back. "I will not. I will never, ever remove this ring." I clenched my fist tightly, the feel of the metal still a new habit. Suddenly, nothing about this whole operation felt right. My gloves were either lost on the train, or secured with my belongings, waiting for me, along with my family.

"Ah, no offense meant, I assure you," Manford said. "Please. You look wonderful. And I can't thank you enough for helping with this."

"Do I have a choice?" I wish I could say those were the last words I spoke until we arrived in the town of Columbus, but that man has a way of getting my goat. He handed me a pair of gloves.

They were a lovely ivory-colored soft cotton material. I slid them on, over my oh-so-offensive wedding band. "I expect once a woman marries she's supposed to forget every little ounce of knowledge she has gathered over the years and succumb to her husband's superior intellect. I guarantee, no matter how spectacular one's wedding night," I paused, with a flicker at my own somnolent bridal evening, "a lady does not forget her accomplishments." Indeed, women, especially married women who worked in trade, were as rare as hens' teeth. As I buttoned the small button on my glove, for a split second, I wished I were a secretary, involved in the mysterious machinations of business.

Manford crossed over to the small mirror and performed before it. I pity his future wife. She would play second fiddle in any relationship to that reflection.

He smoothed down his dark brown strands of hair. He hunched inside the worn suit jacket and, if I didn't know better, I wouldn't look twice at him in a crowd.

"How do I look?"

"You look like a circus performer."

"I shall miss you."

Manford grew serious. "Now, ma'am. You will hold up your end of the bargain? I need your assistance, and for that I gravely apologize. I cannot tell you more, but know that a nation will be grateful for your service."

I pinched my lips together. "And you will see me home?"

He held up his right hand. "I swear. If all goes well, we can be on the next train headed north."

It stuck in my craw to be of service to Manford. He was a thief and a sinner and did not deserve my cooperation. I see things black and white, good and bad, whereas I determined Mr. Fitzpatrick played fast and loose with the truth. I believed him in possession of such a flighty character, skeptical of nothing and able to reorder his conscience with whichever way the wind was blowing.

"I will not swear," I said, "however, I will accompany you on this fools' errand and perform to the best of my ability." My declaration held enough loopholes to see me out of this mess should I encounter a law enforcement official and be able to blow the whistle on this sham. If circumstances did not comply, well, then, I would go through with this playacting and rely on him to see me home. A few more days and then my new life could begin. I chomped down upon my worry for in a strange way I trusted this heathen. Yet, I was uneasy. Defying the law, it didn't sit right with me.

Manford hitched the horse to the wagon and then escorted me to my seat. "Hyah," he said, and, with a jolt, we headed toward town.

"Good luck, now, ma'am," called Bud. KK as usual raised his voice in a gargle of sounds that wouldn't be inappropriate for a very angry dying man. What a bizarre language, I found myself thinking and not for the first time. Sometimes I thought it was mere trickery to mock me, yet Bud always responded to his grandfather's commands. Even Manford could understand him and answer back, though his tongue wasn't quite as forceful as the old man's. I waved at Bud. I sent up a silent prayer for that child.

"Heavens," I said after only a fifteen-minute ride. "You mean I could have run here and escaped all this time? This town is so close. How dare you let me think we were in the middle of nowhere?"

Manford touched his fingers to his hat. "For that, I apologize again, Miss Suellen. I would never have let you come to harm. Sorry it has come to this, and again, accept my gratitude for the role that you will play."

He tied the horse to a hitching post and helped me alight from the wagon. My heart sank as there were so many folks about that no one paid a bit of attention to us. Horses and buggies kicked up dust in the street, as riders and drivers created a clamorous racket, bellering for right of way. I felt a headache throb behind my eyes and nervously smoothed my skirts. I noticed two women approaching, their heels made a satisfying click in cadence on the wooden sidewalk. I perched a thin smile upon my face and felt my chin lift. As they neared, my eyes widened. Dear Lord,

168   *Dee DeTarsio*

they were pretty women. How were their cheeks so rosy? And their mouths? Painted? Oh my. They must be women of ill repute. I'm sure I goggled to warrant the sneer dispensed my way by the one with blonde hair curled high atop her head. Her dress was red as sin with a creamy silk underskirt, but her hat was a lovely creation that featured strawberries and flowers. Lucy would love the thing. Her companion was dressed in a high-necked, deceptively simple-looking gown of the palest blue lace, which, upon closer inspection was scandalous in its daring fit upon her form. It is little exaggeration to say I saw that woman's heartbeat.

I fumbled at my belt and pressed my right hand into a loose fist. Manford took my left arm and helped me onto the sidewalk as the ladies passed. I made an effort to lightly brush against the woman in the red dress, lowering my arm just so and slipping her the small folded piece of paper I held between my first two fingers. It all happened very quickly. She looked down, scanned her eyes over the paper I had pressed upon her, then cut her eyes back at me. She muttered, "How lovely for you." Manford pulled me along quickly, oblivious to my silent plea for help, as I heard the crisp taffeta of those women's skirts swish away.

She had read the wrong side of the note. My love note from Theodore. The one he had placed in my valise on the train, vowing to never dishonor me. It was my most prized possession. And it had just been sacrificed in my one escape attempt. For last night I had found KK's pencil and written on the back: Help! I am being held captive by a train robber. Mrs. (Doctor) Theodore Kincaid, passenger, B&O, July 6, 1877.

Perhaps I expelled a sigh because Manford chastised me. "Chin up. It will all be over soon."

"One way or another," I muttered, hoping I wouldn't be killed.

Chapter Thirty

"I owe you more than you can know, Miss Suellen," Manford said, as I cranked my neck back one final time at the women with the swaying hips. They disappeared in the bustle of people, hurrying to do their business.

"I should have told you before, but I didn't want to embroil you any deeper than necessary." "Embroil me? I am here, held captive, against my will. I am embroiled in nothing, sir." "Well, the fact is, you've been such a good egg about all this, I feel I owe you a neater explanation. Heck, I don't know many women who could go through all you have, with such a brave disposition. You're a drink of water—calm, cool, and just what's needed after a hot pursuit."

"Well, quit robbing trains and you wouldn't need to be holed up, as I guess they call it, thirsting for cold water."

"Holed up? They call it that out West, ma'am. Save that talk for Jesse James."

"Do you know him?" My eyes widened.

"I know of him, certainly." Manford fumbled his words. "Look. I'm not who you think I am."

"As I don't think much of you at all, that certainly matters to me none."

We were almost near the bank, as Manford had described. He slowed his steps. "No matter what happens..." he began.

"Why do men keep saying that to me?" I asked, thinking back to my very first bona fide love note from my husband, which I had just discarded.

"Well, see, it's like this... I am an agent for the government."

"A spy? You expect me to believe this? Is what Bud said true?"

"Yes, it's true. I am part of the Secret Service, a federal intelligence agency set up at the end of the war. We had to crack down on all the counterfeiting going on, which led to—" He waved his hand, "Well, you wouldn't believe me if I told you about all the financial improprieties schemers dream up. We go where we're needed, when we're needed, and do whatever it takes to keep our nation united. And safe."

170   *Dee DeTarsio*

"Do you know the president?" I mocked him. "And he put you up to these shenanigans?"

"Yes, I know him. And, in answer to your second question, he didn't exactly put me up to what you call shenanigans. It doesn't work like that."

"Like what?"

"As an agent," he paused, "I am actively gathering information for the president."

"Why can't you say the word spy?"

He paused. "Theoretically, you could call it that. I work for the president, it's very top secret, and before you ask, no, he did not authorize a train robbery or kidnapping. It's just that I have the authority to do what needs to be done."

"And what needs to be done?" I prompted him.

"We are going to outsmart the railroads. We're going into that bank, as I said, and meet with gentlemen," his mouth turned down at the word, "who are the real criminals. They are wealthy men with an agenda to become wealthier upon the backs of railroad workers. Men are dying, their families are starving, and right now, it's the railroad that is pushing our country forward and out of the depression. The panic of a few years back has slowed things down, and unemployment is crippling our nation. We need to protect the railroads, and their workers. Manufacturing, commerce, trade, it all depends upon transportation. Where do you think wheat, cattle, and lumber come from? And more importantly, how do you think it gets to folks? Cargo is being shipped to places that were out of reach, and the U.S. mail is making our world smaller and more united, as we can now communicate much easier with states all the way out west."

We paused on the walkway which fronted a market, a barbershop, a tannery, a saloon (of course), and a diner that advertised rooms. I heard the whistle of a train and dearly wished to be on it. We were nearly at the bank. "Heavens, what a busy town." A street car sped by us, a unique contraption that looked like a rail car being pulled by a horse. It was filled with people. "Doesn't anyone walk anymore?" I asked.

"We're on High Street," Manford told me. "The railroads giveth and taketh. Columbus is a booming town thanks, in part, to the railroads."

"Yet you propose to bribe wealthy powerful gentleman, who own the railroad, with their own money that you stole?"

Suellen

"They stole that money first, off hard-working Americans, with their unjust acquisitions. I need them to agree to a stipend from the government—a subsidy, if you will—as being part of their own best interest in preventing the strike, giving into workers demands for better wages and safer working conditions. They can use this money as a down payment on improving the men's pay. They already know why I'm coming, so this will be a short meeting. All we need to do is get them to sign the contracts in exchange for the money."

"And you think they will do this?"

He sighed. "Of course, it was the government land grants and subsidies to the railroads that started this mess. Land values are falling, new construction has all but halted, and corporate profits are vanishing. The greedy bastards, beg pardon," he touched the brim of his hat, "want their loot." I felt his fingers tighten upon my elbow. "That's where you come in. They just need to sign a contract, honor the wage increases starting immediately, and we can prevent a crisis of national proportions. I don't do any of this for them, even though they will benefit."

He looked me over and nodded, as if liking what he saw; a woman of some sense, I presumed, very handsomely turned out in a blue serge skirt, black patent leather belt, and lovely cream blouse fastened with pearl buttons. A small blue felt hat perched atop my hair completed the outfit, which served to make me feel quite accomplished. Confident maybe; an emotion I was unused to experiencing. Confidence surely is an emotion—without it, a good woman could weep, and with it, as I was newly discovering, a flawed woman could do the unthinkable. I stretched my posture so severely, my deceased grandmother could have felt my spine reach for the heavens.

"You are doing a very good thing, Madam, and I, and your country, thank you."

"I am a journalist and a citizen, Manford, and understand the importance of our railroads. What I don't understand is what I am doing here. Making a spectacle of myself in the middle of a street in Columbus, Ohio, arguing with you. You stand there with who knows how much money hidden inside that bank, stolen, for some infamous purpose, and I'm supposed to believe you are doing it for good?"

Manford shifted the leather pouch over his left shoulder. "That money, in a safety deposit box inside that bank, is basically a bribe from the U.S. Government to try to force their hand in providing better wages to the workers and preventing more bloodshed."

"A bribe?"

"Basically. They don't know it's their money. Which, as I repeat, they stole in the first place. Even if they did know it was their own money robbed from their very own safe, they do not much care, as they keep coming to the well of the U.S. Government for more. And it's not officially a bribe. Consider it a supplement from the government to keep the wheels turning."

"Grease the wheels you mean?"

"Suellen, there's more politicking that goes on in this world than you can ever understand. There's always a deal. Someone always wins, someone always loses, but someone always pulls the strings. It's the business of compromise. Lest you think I'm some kind of crazy conspirator, armed with radical ideas and disturbed notions of power, I hope these past couple of days have changed your impression of me."

I would not give him the satisfaction, but in a surprisingly short amount of time, the man had grown on me. Not unlike a blister upon my heel. I listened intently, trying to untangle those convoluted threads.

"An audacious plan to rob a train, kidnap a woman, then boldly face your victims?"

"They are not the victims here. And furthermore, it takes a bold plan to face their audacity. The Railroad acts were legislated to construct railroad lines and telegraph lines across the country, and in doing so, allowed for the government to use them for the post, the military and transport," he went on with his explanation. "These railroads, Suellen, are the making of this country. There are thousands of new avenues with folks migrating all over the interior. And these railroad barons are not stupid. They are smart businessmen, working within, and sometimes without, the law, and selling their land to settlers at a handsome profit. Land closest to the tracks draws the highest prices, of course, because farmers and ranchers want to be near railway stations to ship their produce and cattle. Homesteaders want to be nearer towns, and to the goods they can buy and barter. This growth will save and heal our country, but it's an undertaking that needs to be regulated. You can't trust the big money men to be charitable. History does repeat itself, and it's never a fairy tale ending. Power corrupts and absolute power corrupts absolutely."

Suellen 173

"And I'm supposed to be glad there are train robbers to keep them honest?"

"Things aren't always as they seem. As I've mentioned before, I am trying to make the best of a bad situation. I apologize to the end of days for embroiling you in this mission. Now, if you bear with me, I appreciate your help in providing a little added padding to my story of being a representative of the Transportation Department in town with my assistant. With you by my side, I'll look the part of a government patsy, sent to muster a paltry deal." He straightened his hat and slouched a bit, completing the picture of a timid clerk sort of fellow. "They'll see what they want to see anyway. If they accept this money..."

"Bribe."

"Subsidy."

"Supplement. Taxpayer's money. Pirate's treasure." I waved my hand in dismissal. "What then? What happens next?"

"The government provides the railroad an incentive to increase wages, provide medical care and compensation, and help for families whose providers have passed. And a full-blown strike is averted. Rail work is incredibly dangerous. Those workers are the backbone of the system and need to be properly compensated."

"The crazy thing is, I reckon I believe you."

"You do?" He raised his eyebrows. "I mean, you should. It sounds farfetched but I swear on my mother's grave, it is the gospel truth." He shifted the leather satchel. "I did not, I would not, ever entangle you in opprobrious dealings, ma'am. It's a little shaded, and my supervisors in the government can't necessarily claim me, or allow me to besmirch them or their reputations, as I'm sure you understand?"

I nodded. Of course there had to be spies, good ones, working for justice, I supposed. And for the first time in a long time, my heart beat with a patriotic fervor. Lucy and I had actually helped a few of the railway families back home, and if I could help more, so be it. "I am ready." I was. I felt the slow burn of indignation against bullies who should know better. Oh, dear Lord, how happy was I that my note seeking help was misunderstood by that woman. I was mortified for ever having written it in the first place. Why, what would I have done if the authorities raced in to rescue me, and lit into Manford, knowing what I knew now?

I should have trusted my instincts that Manford wasn't truly a bandit. I knew it. But my stiff-necked pride got in the way, and I felt I had to be a law-abiding

174   *Dee DeTarsio*

citizen. "There's a whole rainbow of colors in this world," I could just hear Lucy telling me, trying to point out that nothing, but nothing, was ever black or white. Yes, for goodness sakes, I was going to help this spy, and my country. I stood tall, proud to be of service.

"God works in mysterious ways, Mr. Fitzpatrick," I said, nodding my head wisely and feeling most virtuous. When will I ever learn not to tempt the fates like that?

He handed me the satchel, which was filled with contracts of some sort, wordy government documents that Manford said the men would not read and most likely not sign, unless we were incredibly lucky, and good at our task at hand. It was uncomfortably heavy, or perhaps my guilty conscious was leaning upon the scales making it seem of greater weight. He handed me the small key for the safety deposit box, which I held tightly in my fingers, prepared to complete my task.

"Put your hand down," Manford told me. "Act natural."

"Telling me to act natural has the effect of making me wonder how to put one foot in front of the other." Lord, I was nervous.

"Well, don't walk in the front door of this bank with that key pointing up and out like a gun. You look petrified. Remember, this is a dull government job."

"I was just trying to be prepared."

"Take it down a notch. A little incompetence would be appropriate here."

We had arrived at the Wells Fargo building. "Wells Fargo used to offer overland stagecoach delivery of gold, money, mail, what have you," Manford said. I think he was trying to calm me down. "And its agents developed a pretty nasty reputation for protecting their valuable cargo. Thanks to the transcontinental railroad, more stationary offices like this one are cropping up for businesses and regular people alike."

"I've been inside a bank before."

We walked inside into a darkly paneled, silent-as-a-church vestibule. "I feel as if we should pray," I whispered.

"This is the worship house of choice for many," Manford whispered back to me. We walked by the two clerks standing duty behind their railed windows, waiting for customers to put their money into savings, or write a check, or, imagine, transfer funds by telegraph. What a world we lived in.

Suellen   175

"Mr. Fitzpatrick?" A tall gentleman in a dark brown suit that matched his mustache approached us.

Manford nodded. "And my secretary, Miss Robinson."

I shivered a touch, waiting for lightning to strike at these blatant falsehoods. "Madam." He inclined his head but did not introduce himself.

"The gentleman are waiting for you in my office. This way." He held out his arm toward the back of the bank and the three of us proceeded to his office.

We entered a large room anchored by the largest desk I have ever laid eyes upon. What, I wondered, did that poor man do with such a large desk? It was dark as ebony, carved with curlicues at the corners atop beast claw feet, and neat as a pin. I suspected not much work actually occurred atop its pristine surface.

Through a haze of smoke, I saw two gentlemen off to the right. They stood to greet us. They were smoking cigars, this early in the day. Cretins. The caricatures of robber barons did them justice. Oiled hair, rich fabric suits, one wore a signet ring on his pinkie! It sparked with an actual diamond. I didn't know how rich they were, or how they amassed their fortunes, but I intuitively sensed their smug bonhomie.

"Mr. Fitzpatrick," said the banker, Mr. Wilder, according to the large brass nameplate on his cotton-field sized desk. "And his secretary."

The banker didn't say the names of the railroad men, I noticed. They shook Manford's hand in that excessively male way, as if to determine who is top dog. Manford, in his new costume matching his servile government employee demeanor, spoke to me, not taking his eyes off the two men. "Miss Robinson, if you will?" He glanced at the banker. "Safe depository?" I saw the gentleman share a quick look.

"Let's get down to it," the one wearing the ring said. As I do not speak robber baron, I could not be sure of its import, but it did not sit well with me. Why, even their fingernails looked shiny and buffed as if they had never done an honest day's work.

"This way," Mr. Wilder ushered me back out the door as Manford took a seat next to the two gentlemen. My observations were interrupted as Mr. Wilder closed the thick office door with a muted click. As prearranged, I was to go to the safety deposit box and retrieve the stash of money that Manford had secured there several days ago.

176 *Dee DeTarsio*

My heart beat so hard. Dear Lord, if my sister taught me anything, I prayed, let me put it to good use now. I stood up ramrod straight and pursed my mouth. I felt the contents of the leather purse, the accursed contracts, and worried they would explode in fire at the untruths being bandied about.

Mr. Wilder allowed me entrance into a giant vault, guarded by a many-layered steel door, with a spinning handle for its lock combination. He had seen me grip the key between my thumb and first knuckle, and opened a door off to the left. "I will be waiting outside."

I barely nodded, a gesture I am sure my sister would have approved.

He shut the door of the small room lined with rows of locked brass numbered boxes. I found the correct box, number 356, that Manford had described to me, slid it out and set it on the table, making a loud clunk, to show I wasn't a fraud. I had no time to even remove my gloves from my trembling hands. I slid in the key, held my breath and opened the metal box. There were five thick packets of green-backs, all $100 banknotes, with President Lincoln's ugly face peering right back at me from the upper left corner.

To this day, I do not know what guided my intentions, but as I looked at that money, I felt a pang. Perhaps I was more like my sister than either of us had realized. I picked up that money and fanned its crisp bills. I took a deep breath, knowing I had not much time left. Minutes later I slammed the lid down on the box, locked it and slid it back into place. I clasped the satchel to my chest. I smoothed down my skirts, patted my hair, and hoped my face was not as red as it felt.

I flung open the door and Mr. Wilder ushered me back to his office. Manford was in the middle of some joke, as the three men laughed. It appeared their meeting was going well. I stood just inside the door, unsure what to say or do. Mr. Wilder closed the door and took his seat behind his desk.

"Do we have an agreement?" Manford said. He flicked his fingers at me for the contracts. I removed the papers from the pouch and handed them to Manford.

"Rutherfraud is going to pay us extra to do our job?" The two men looked toward each other and smiled, as pure evil a smile as I had ever seen. I felt ill. How much money do they and their kind need? What did they know of the hunger, and illness, and the struggles of mothers trying to keep their families together, always fearing there would never be enough. One person's definition of enough was another person's embarrassment of riches.

Suellen 177

"Let's see the money first, and we've got a deal."

Dear Lord, what was I going to do? My loathing was tempered with the fear of handing over the leather pouch. I was trying to catch Manford's eye as well as my very own breath, but he would not look my way. Perhaps I had not thought this through. Surely someone was going to notice I was near ready to faint. Before they could shake on their agreement, there was an interruption.

"Open up. Wilder, you in there? Open this door." Thumps pounded the door.

"I apologize, gentleman," then belatedly, "Ma'am." The banker hurried around his desk to the door. It opened before he could reach it, revealing the barrel of a gleaming silver pistol, attached to a man of law.

I screamed and slumped to the floor. I could not breathe. Manford was by my side in an instant.

"Hold it right there," hollered the sheriff. "Raise your arms and turn around. You too, ma'am."

I panted from my crouch on the floor and struggled to catch my breath. The sheriff pulled me up, scrutinizing my face closely.

"Sheriff Daniels. What is this?" Mr. Wilder himself looked guilty as sin. Manford had told me he was most likely getting some sort of kickback from the whole unsavory deal.

I turned slowly. Behind the sheriff stood a deputy, and the very same fancy blonde-haired woman in the red dress, whom I decided was not very pretty after all. She must have read the back of my note seeking help. I am cursed.

"You are under arrest for the train robbery, July 6th, B&O, and crimes committed against the United States government," the sheriff said to Manford. Manford lifted his head, wary, calculating.

"I assume you are the wife of Doctor Theodore Kincaid? Suellen?" At my nod, he continued. "Are you hurt or in any other way compromised? What this man did to you is beyond the pale."

"I'm fine," I said weakly. "He didn't hurt me." I struggled for breath.

"Pass over that satchel nice and slow now, and we'll take a little walk over to the jail and get to the bottom of this." I gave them the satchel and tried to speak. "It's, not, there's… " Was I dying? My hands were clutched at my heart.

The sheriff took the leather bag and sat it on the desk. He looked through it, thoroughly, turned it upside down. A few typewritten papers fluttered out, extra copies of the signature pages of the contracts to be signed. "Where's the money? There's nothing in here but papers."

Manford's eyes flew to my face. I imperceptibly shook my head.

"She has the key to the safety deposit box," Mr. Wilder said. He took the key which I still held in my hand. With a gun at Manford's back, the sheriff, his deputy, the woman and railroad men, trooped next door to the safe.

The deputy grabbed Manford by one arm. Before they started moving, the sheriff turned to me. "Ma'am?"

Oh no. Oh no. Don't say anything, I bargained. Please God, I'll make it right. Don't let Manford know it was me.

"Are you sure you are in good health, ma'am? You are looking peaked. Did this outlaw harm you in any way?"

"No. No. No. He was a gentleman, through and through. I'm fine," I gabbled away. "Right as rain. Just a misunderstanding."

He looked at me queerly. "You're coming along with us anyway, until we get this straightened out. Thanks to you, we got our man. That was right quick thinking, you writing that note and tipping us off."

I couldn't bear to look at Manford. If truth be told I guess I knew him well enough to decipher the hot rage that was burning through his very skin toward me.

"Wilder? Sheriff? What's this all about now? Where's our money?" One of the railroad men was very agitated. Welcome to my misery.

"We got word," Oh, dear God, the sheriff looked right at me, "that this here gentleman is the very one and same who robbed your train. I'm guessing he forced this woman, this newly married woman, to go along with his schemes."

"Outrageous," said the taller, thin railroad tycoon.

"Reprehensible," agreed his crony. "Hang him. But first, where's the money?" I hazarded a glance at Manford. He was poker-faced.

"Ma'am, I'm sure you understand many laws were broken, not the least of which, your very kidnapping. Perhaps, you, Mrs. Kincaid, can help supply details. Can I impose upon you to answer questions?"

I nodded.

"I'm sure this mongrel put you up to this, but if you can please assist us in any way, that help will be greatly appreciated. Let's take a look at the safety deposit box."

Though the sheriff's gun was aimed at Manford, I was herded along with him as our group trooped back to the entryway of the claustrophobic depository room. The sheriff had myself and Manford waiting outside the vault door, but we could clearly hear the oath sworn by one of the men as they discovered the box was empty.

"Where's the money?" The sheriff nudged Manford in his shoulder with his gun. Manford shook his head. "I don't have it."

"Ma'am?"

I did not have to exaggerate the fear on my face. I trembled.

"Do you know where he hid the money?"

At least I could answer that honestly. "I do not know where he hid the money."

"We'll figure it out, gentleman."

"See that you do."

"We're headed to the prison to get to the bottom of this." The sheriff indicated to his deputy to grab Manford. "We'll get the money back, rest assured," the sheriff said to the two gentlemen, who had donned their hats. They didn't appear as upset as one might expect concerned businessmen who'd lost fifty-thousand dollars would be. "We'll need your statement, and we'll get to the bottom of this."

"Of course, of course," one of the men said. "We have an appointment we must attend and we will stop by the jail forthwith." The sheriff gave them a squinted eye but said nothing more.

And while I officially wasn't arrested, the deputy placed me in the cell next to Manford's. "Just so you can sit a spell until we figure things out. You're safest in there and we can keep watch over you."

"This is horrifying. I demand that you release me. At once." It was not hard to feign indignation. My voice was breathless and I felt faint. I detected a pungent odor that reminded me of a tomato withering on its dried green vine. As Manford kept his distance on the other side of the bars, I could only deduce my own fear was the culprit. "You cannot lock me in here." Could they really suspect me of being in cahoots with Manford? With a train robber? Who stole fifty-thousand U.S. dollars? Then tried to ransom it back in some despicable spy deal? Which oddly enough, did not seem to discomfit the very men who had a stake in that money to begin with. I would assume their hands are none too clean either, and could not bear much scrutiny. As I struggled to inhale, I wondered anew at my own self-righteousness.

The sheriff who had stayed behind at the bank burst through the door. "Lawson? Get her out of there. That man kidnapped her. Do you know who she is?" The unfortunate Deputy Lawson fumbled with the key to remove me from my incarceration.

"Thank you, Sheriff." I was not acting, though perhaps my sister's helpless female act did shine through. "It's been an ordeal." I placed my hand to my forehead and thought about swooning. At the last moment I decided I could not pull that maneuver off.

"Tell me what happened." He seated me in his wooden desk chair while he perched on the corner of the desk. It was difficult to sit, and the constriction of my garments conspired with my helpless hysteria. "Lawson, get her some water." Lawson poured me water out of a jug on his desk in a none-too-clean tin cup. It didn't matter as I was only able to take small sips. Conscious of Manford listening to every word and inflection, I kept it short and to the point. "I was not harmed, simply in the wrong place at the wrong time. He is not a bad man and dealt with me as fairly as the situation warranted."

"Pardon me, ma'am, I have to ask. You were not engaged in any funny business with this outlaw, were you?"

"How dare you?" My breath came in short gasps. "I thank you to keep your scurrilous accusations to yourself."

"Sorry. Please forgive me. Do go on. Is there anything you can tell us?"

I folded my hands in my lap as if recounting great suffering. "I was just married," I pleaded. "Please, I don't know anything. Let me go home."

"Any accomplices? Where is his hideout?"

Oh, dear God. The thought of them going after KK and Bud nearly paralyzed me. "No. No one else. I am in misery and just want to go home." Like Manford said, a con game relies on playing the part your target wants to see. A simpering,

Suellen

181

simple-minded female came on me a sight too easily. "We were many miles from here, perhaps two days. In a cave."

Sheriff Daniels nodded grimly. "Probably in Kentucky somewhere." His beefy, liver-spotted hand with filthy nails patted my arm. "There, there. We were just lucky Miss Celeste had the good sense to come to your rescue."

"You rescued me, sir, and I will be forever grateful." As long as I got out of that jail as quickly as possible, with no more incriminating questions asked, that is.

"Yes sir, that Miss Celeste," the sheriff continued. "Why, I was that surprised and only too happy to help. She is one of a kind, and to stand up and do her civic duty to help us solve this case is commendable. There, there." He patted my arm yet again, not very gently, obviously quite pleased with himself. "To provide succor to a damsel in distress is what I'm here for." He puffed out his already dangerously puffy chest.

"How can I ever thank you?" I said.

He cut his gaze to mine. Oh, dear Lord, he had been talking about the blonde wretch, Miss Celeste. The woman in the red dress, to whom I had passed my note. He was sweet on her.

I gave a tersely worded statement to the sheriff that he laboriously printed, brief with a very kindly report of Manford, though I knew it would do no good. I ended the interview after only some five minutes or so by bursting into a fine display of tears, more wind than water, claiming exhaustion. My sister would have been proud of me.

Chapter Thirty-One

"Why don't you head on over to the telegraph office, up ahead at the train station, and send off a message to your folks. They must be worried sick. Deputy Lawson will escort you." He paused to gather breath enough to scream out, "Lawson!" He jerked his head toward Manford in his cell. "We heard about this outrageous train robbery and kidnapping, of a new bride, just the other day."

"Yes. A tragedy. Thank you for your service. I do need to go send that telegram now, if you don't mind. My family must be arrived in Oberlin." I paused and deliberately did not look in Manford's direction. I didn't know what to do and clasped my hands as if at prayer to hide the shakes. I was responsible for his arrest. I was responsible for his mission failing, and as it turned out, he was the good guy all along; which deep down I supposed I had figured out shortly after he kidnapped me.

"We will make arrangements for you to stay in a room above the diner with Mrs. Waggoner, and then you can take the train to your home. Oberlin, is it? Tomorrow a train is going back up that way. Go on now, tell them Sheriff Daniels sent you. I expect they know everything anyway, can't keep any secrets in this town. I will let you know if I need more details." The sheriff ran his hands through his over-long gray greasy hair. I didn't give a Confederate half dollar for his chances with Miss Celeste.

"Miss Suellen," Manford said. He was furious.

"Nothing from you," the sheriff hollered into the cell. "It was thanks to this fine upstanding woman that we caught you. You've done enough damage and you do not have the luxury of wasting her time with any more of your depravity."

I looked back at Manford in his cell. "He's not going to hang, is he?" The sheriff, honest to goodness, told me not to worry my "pretty head." He managed to stoke my already carefully banked embers into a much-needed blaze. I knew I didn't have much time to figure out what in the world I was supposed to do next.

"Don't waste your pity on a roughneck bandit like him. Your Christian charity need not bother with him any further. You're lucky to be alive."

Suellen 183

"It wasn't like that at all," I said, my words intended for Manford. The tense line of his mouth was his only tell at my betrayal. "I'm sorry," I said as Deputy Lawson marched me out the door, leaving Manford there no doubt thinking the money gone, as well as his freedom. Heaven knows what was going to become of the railroads. He had convinced me a powder keg was about to explode. I was mightily ashamed.

The deputy escorted me to the train depot to send a telegraph to the doctor. The deputy sent one to authorities in Fremont back in Tennessee. My adventure, it seemed, had come to an end. I would be departing to Oberlin and into my beloved's arms in a very short amount of time.

"I am safe. Stop. All is well. Stop. I will be home tomorrow. Stop. Love to you and Lucy." I signed off as my husband had in his love note to me, a fine circle of events that I hoped would not go unnoticed by him. "Yours affectionately and forever, Suellen."

The telegrapher was kind enough to point out that the editor of the town's newspaper, the *Columbus Dispatch,* was one Mr. Thomas Sinclair, and he was indeed in his office next door. I had noticed the establishment as we walked past from the jail, whence a half-baked idea began to form. Taking one more deep breath, I asked Deputy Lawson to wait out front. This is for Manford, I thought. Posture perfect, I walked in and introduced myself to Mr. Sinclair.

"My name is Suellen Kincaid," I said. "Surely you've heard of me?"

"You were kidnapped from the B&O about a week ago? I'll be darned—pardon my language." He stood and came to greet me. "What happened? How is it you come to be here? Have a seat. Margaret, bring some tea," he told a well-dressed woman in a light blue plaid dress seated at the desk next to him. She was about my age and looked at me appraisingly.

"That would be lovely," I told him. Though the charade wasn't the one I had intended to play, I used it anyway. With my bosom thrust forward—please don't judge, needs must—I strived to feel as feminine as possible to play upon Mr. Sinclair's sensibilities. Sensibility is probably not the right word, for if the man had any sense, he would realize his not-particularly-clean beard provided nil in terms of alluring enticement. I suspected he was unaware of this and used it to my benefit.

"It's true," I shuddered, and delicately dabbed at my eyes. He handed me his handkerchief, yellowed and smelling of cigar smoke. "Thank you," I said, sounding exactly like my sister trying to charm birds out of the tree. "It was a terrible ordeal," I told him. "I just sent my dear husband, the doctor, a telegram. He and the children must be out of their minds worried sick about me."

"Oh, you poor dear. What happened?"

"Well, I will tell you once I can compose myself. The sheriff just arrested the outlaw responsible." I sighed heavily as if I could no longer go on. That part was quite true. I could barely get the words out. "I am a journalist, and I will write you the biggest story of the year," I told him. His eyes bugged out. "You have heard of Auntie Ques.?"

"Yes, of course. You are she? Fine job, Madam. Our paper recently started carrying your advice column. Folks enjoy it. Now what about this story?" He raised his hand and waved it in the air. "'Kidnapped Bride Outsmarts Outlaw!'" He beamed at me. "It'll do. It'll do. I can't wait to read your story. But you have to hurry, now. I'll have my typesetter," that must be Margaret, the tea-bringer, "have it ready to lay out for the whole first page, and it will be printed before dinner tomorrow."

Margaret appeared by my side with a cup of tea, sheaf of paper, pen and ink. I rather liked the look in her eyes and thanked her. She nodded as if sizing me up, verdict to be deferred.

Oh my. "Of course," I said. I stood up and grasped the paper and pen. "It is a most adventurous story. You will be intrigued," I said, as if I were used to conjuring up one thousand words of a true-life crime story, which I planned to embellish with the whole truth and nothing but the truth.

First, I needed to get to my hotel, to which the deputy kindly escorted me. He explained my situation in very great detail to the proprietress, one Mrs. Waggoner. It was all I could do to respond to her wide-eyed yakety-yak questions. "Please, ma'am," I said. My voice quivered, as I had reached the end of my lung capacity. "It has been an ordeal. I need to rest." I could not wait to shuck my costume and breathe again.

"Of course, I understand." She waved her hands above her head, as if I were some kind of royalty come to call. "I will send up your dinner, and you just holler if you need any ol' thing."

Suellen 185

As the door closed behind me, I unbuttoned my blouse, unhooked my belt, pulled my skirt off and fairly wrenched loose the laces of my corset. I leaned over the bed, gulping in great breaths of air as fifty-thousand dollars bound in their packets landed on the coverlet.

"Now what do I do?"

I had very little time to write my story, do my part to save the railroads, and make sure fifty-thousand dollars went where it could do the most good. And while I set about saving the world, I might as well also see if I could free Mr. Fitzpatrick from jail.

Chapter Thirty-Two

I considered best how to organize my thoughts, knowing no one needed to know of every single, little exchange between myself and Manford.

I knew Bud and KK would be worried, but I waited until after Mrs. Waggoner came up to my room with a pitcher of warm water and a bowl of green bean soup seasoned with ham. I washed up and ate the delicious soup, which heartened me. I slipped out the back as if I were dejected, which I was, and needed a breath of air, which I did. The sheriff had absconded with the horse and buggy, so I hitched up my skirts and found the trail, then disappeared into the golden light toward the woods and ran as if I was beating the setting sun, which I was, and Manford's life depended on it. Which it did.

Bud must have been keeping watch all day and stood up under the willow tree when he saw me. He knew all was lost. He helped me inside where I told him my story and he translated to KK. "I can't stay," I said, catching my breath. "I came back for a few things." I was not being dramatic as I bent clean in half, wondering when exactly it was that I had lost the ability to run fast and jump high. "I have a plan."

Bud escorted me back a short while later, and I drew solace from the company of that nine-year-old child in the twilight. I shooed him off as we approached the hotel and he slipped away into the darkness. But I heard his beating feet come back upon me as he threw himself into my skirts, hands around my waist. He ran off just as quickly, the pattern of his retreating steps a comfort. Our plan just might work.

I returned to my room above the diner and commenced writing my story until the cramp in my neck bade me to rest. The bed was clean and soft enough, but truth to tell, I missed Bud and the delicious rice and eggs that KK would serve for breakfast. In a short amount of time, it seemed Bud was the son I never had, and KK the grandfather I never wanted.

I was mortified about my role in Manford's capture; but, the fool, it was his actions that accounted for his capture in the first place. I hoped he was able to slumber, because Lord knows I could not get comfortable. Had Lucy been near, she would have hollered at me to stop my puffing and tossing and let those with a pure heart get some sleep. My heart was not pure, but I would try to make amends come morning.

I dropped off my page-one story to Mr. Sinclair, first thing. I never dreamed when I was doing my Auntie Ques. advice column that I'd be writing my own risqué, dramatic escapade at the hands of a wanted gunman. It would have made a most scandalous dime novel. Mr. Sinclair scanned my cursive on the five pages of paper I delivered. He quirked his eyebrows at some points, exhaled a breath at a part that let me know exactly where he was in my saga, and then whistled at the very end. "You sure about this?"

Upon writing my escapade, I realized that truth is not absolute. Not where emotions are concerned. Truth is how you feel one day, not the next. Truth can't take into account the many facets of an obstacle and it's just human nature that the perception of truth changes like the sparkle of a diamond. I confess, something that makes me laugh one day can serve me spitting mad another.

So while I reported the facts, I admit to taking liberties, and enjoyed such purchase. Every journalist, despite whatever protestations of reporting objectively, takes liberties colored by their prejudice. No such beast that answers to the name Truth exists. Bias is as truly inherent in our genes as is breathing. I imbued the words with my donation to fairness. I hoped to spare Manford, it's true. I hoped to subdue my minimal role, also true, but mostly, I hoped to make these stubborn Southerners and negative Northerners recognize a cause behind which they could unite. At the ripe old age of thirty years, it has come upon me that education and intelligence and all the money in the world isn't worth a hill of beans. Treating folks fairly—and as the Good Book says, as we would want to be treated ourselves—makes a heap more sense. I know I only had a short-lived trip on that train more than a week ago, but taking care of people who work hard is the type of country I want to live in. I am far from an expert, but Manford had me convinced that the railroads must be cared for, as well as the men who worked on them.

Mr. Sinclair rattled the papers. "You don't have their names?" I shook my head.

"No matter. Well done. I give you thanks."

"Of course. You're welcome." I accepted my five-dollar payment and it felt like riches beyond compare.

He stroked his beard then escorted me to the door. I saw Margaret slip into his vacated seat to read my story. She never looked up. "If you ever want to write for the *Columbus Dispatch* again, ma'am," he told me, "we'd be right honored to have you." He cleared his throat as if unsure how to proceed. "You tell a good story. We'd welcome you on our paper."

I laughed, at him and myself. For a second, it seemed such a novel, enticing proposition. "I must get home to my family." The seven sweetest words in the English language.

"Have a safe trip ma'am. You're a brave one. Now get on home safely to that bridegroom of yours, hear?"

I nodded and proceeded toward the train depot. I had plenty of time. Fortunately, the jail was along the way. Good luck had never been a friend of mine, so it was with trepidation I entered the dusty front office. The sheriff was finishing up his breakfast at the desk. The deputy was nowhere to be seen. I do believe I owed the Lord a rosary, or several. "Good morning, sir."

"Ma'am." He rose and nodded at me before seating himself again. "What can I do for you? Don't you have a train you want to be on?"

"I'm headed there now," I replied, gaily. Remnants of my sister clung yet, and once again I was grateful. I swirled my skirts, noticing Manford sitting inside his cell at the back of the room. He refused to look at me. "I wanted to thank you, ever so much for rescuing me. I don't know what I would have done. I didn't have opportunity to bake you one of my pies."

He held his hands up, "No thanks needed, ma'am. Just doing my job. It's good citizens like you, and Miss Celeste of course who got your note, who we vow to protect and keep safe."

"Miss Celeste, that's right, you mentioned her name. She is lovely, and I am so grateful to her, as well." I patted my hair. I was wearing my outfit from yesterday, looking respectful and feeling feminine. "Pardon my presumptuousness, I couldn't help but notice, she seems sweet on you."

The sheriff's face reddened. "Go on. Did she say something to you?" I felt Manford's attention.

"Well, time is short, and I was thinking that even though I couldn't bake you a pie, maybe I can show you my appreciation in another way. Since I am a bride, it would be my pleasure to continue in the cause of love and unite two people, star-crossed as it were, who belong together."

He narrowed his eyes at me. Too much? I held my breath. "What's that? What exactly did she say?"

"She didn't have to say a word," I told him, crossing my fingers. He wiped his mouth with the back of his hand. Dear Lord, he must have been born in a barn.

"Well, before I am late for my train, would you like me to give you a haircut? I'm known as something of an artist." I paused, then made myself giggle. Manford, I noted, had come to the bars of his cell. His attention was focused. For Pete's sake, I could not read that man's mind. I plowed on.

"I could do a very nice job, and maybe tell you a few things that I think Miss Celeste would find hard to resist." Manford became quite still while the sheriff sat up straighter. I hurried to set any illicit ideas straight out of their heathen heads. "Like roses and a picnic. By the river."

The sheriff rubbed the front of his shirt. That a boy, I thought, rub those crumbs in deeper. Ladies love that.

"I never thought much about it," he said. "Do you think it will help?"

How did I not know how simple men are? Could it really be this easy? And how did my sister arrive at this knowledge?

I briskly walked behind him, as if we had an appointment. I set my bag on the desk and pulled out Manford's scissors I had taken the previous night from the cabin. "This won't hurt a bit." I did wonder if soap would ever cut the oily residue that slicked my fingers as I made myself lift strands of his greasy gray hair that nearly touched his shoulders. I tugged and tousled one side first and then the other, and threw in a French phrase to heighten my air of credibility, "*Sacre blue, vous êtes un cochon.*" No offense meant to pigs. "Please, slide your chair back, just a bit more, almost there, I need the light. Yes. Perfect." I had him situated near the bars of Manford's cell.

"Suellen," Manford started. I held up the scissors to silence him. And I began to cut. It was most enjoyable. For me. I saw the sheriff's gun hanging in its holster on the opposite wall, right near the keys, which I presumed would unlock the cell. Snip, snip, snip. "Very nice. Very nice. You should wash your hair, at least once a week, to keep it looking more young and vital."

The sheriff kept quite still as I walked in front of him, still seated in his chair. I shamelessly brought my bosom quite close to his face and concentrated on pulling up a hank of hair high off his head and cutting it short. I kept my arms up as I peered down to admire my handiwork.

The sheriff's piggy brown eyes looked up at me and I was taken aback. I abhorred this man. I had labeled him a bully, which he was. An ignoramus, and not someone I would ever enjoy spending time with. But, to my surprise, I found myself hoping Miss Celeste would feel differently.

Without looking at Manford, I nodded. He reached through the bars and grabbed the scissors, holding the sharp blade at the sheriff's throat.

"Oh, dear," I said, especially loud. At those words, our prearranged signal, Bud bolted through the door, locked the latch and pulled shut the curtain to the front window. I played helpless female while Bud grabbed the keys to unlock the cell.

"Oh my," I cried. "What is going on? Help, Help."

"Grab the gun, too, Bud," Manford said. Bud tossed Manford the keys and he extricated himself from the cell. "Arms up," he told the sheriff. "And the money? Where's the money?" he said. He nodded at a safe in the corner of the office, which was open and contained the satchel, which held nothing but useless contract papers.

"Don't worry about it," I said. "I must get out of here. Oh, someone help me." I nearly forgot my role.

"I need that money," Manford said grimly.

"You will hang for this," Sheriff Daniels shouted.

"Manford, we have to get out of here," Bud said, dancing from foot to foot.

"Hold on, son," said the sheriff, arms still held high. "You don't want to do this. Don't make it worse on yourself."

"I'm not going to hurt you, sir." Manford said. "I just need the money for the railroad workers, and we can let Miss Suellen here get on with her life."

"Don't worry about the money," Bud said again. Manford, no fool he, twitched an eye at Bud and myself and came to a decision.

"Let's go."

I wrung my hands. "I was just trying to thank the sheriff, and cut his hair." I nodded vigorously at Manford, who didn't want to understand me. "Please. He's sweet on Miss Celeste."

The sheriff's face turned bright red and I highly doubt he was thinking about Miss Celeste at that moment.

"It's the least you can do, Mr. Fitzpatrick."

Manford snorted, located a set of handcuffs from the sheriff's desk drawer, and pulled the man's hands together behind his chair. He then used his fingers to arrange a side part on the sheriff, and finished cutting his hair. It took no more than a few minutes, and as I suspected, the sheriff looked a heap better.

"Go on," Manford said harshly to me. "Get out of here, ma'am." But the look he gave me clearly demanded to know where the money was.

I merely quirked an eyebrow and hurried for the door, Bud hot on my heels. I heard Manford call out to the sheriff. "There's a lime pomade for your hair at the druggist's, Dr. Wilber's. The ladies like the smell." He ducked out the door and disappeared between the buildings.

I lifted my skirts and ran toward the train depot. I could hear the whistle. The train had arrived and was disembarking passengers onto the platform. Steam was rising from its smokestack. I had time before they would begin boarding. I would not miss my train; however, the noise of its engine hurried my footsteps nonetheless. I couldn't even look back to see what happened to Manford and Bud. I was sure Bud had a horse, as he had told me not to worry about that, and that they were well on their way to safety.

Chapter Thirty-Three

Even though I could have purchased my ticket with my own money from the article I had written, the sheriff had given me a voucher to ride the train for free. I had also allowed the great city of Columbus to provide my hospitality for the evening prior, and pay for my meals. Parsimonious indeed was my middle name. I chose a seat and clutched my hands to my chest, trying to calm my breath. What a morning.

All I could think about was the fact that I would be seeing Theodore in a few short hours.

And begin the rest of my life. And Lucy. Oh, how I had missed her.

I have a small confession. That wasn't all I could think about. I worried dearly about poor Bud. And KK. Truth be told, I even spared a prayer for Manford. It was my hope that the sheriff would be discovered well after those boys had gotten far away, and that the railroad officials would resign themselves to not pursuing Manford as an outlaw.

Other passengers took their seats, and in a little more than an hour the clamor of the steam engine roared to life. A mighty three whistles were emitted as the train jerked toward my future. Before long we were picking up steam, heading north. The zig-zag of my person in that seat as the train careened over the rails was soothing in an almost prayer-like manner. I barely registered when a filthy beggar sat in the seat next to me.

I pulled my skirts closer.

"Did I really need to cut that man's hair? Don't look at me."

My fingers flew to my mouth as, of course, I turned in my seat. "What madness is this? What are you doing here?"

"I said I would escort you to your home, and I aim to keep my word."

"Manford. You can't be serious. You'll be caught again."

"You didn't even recognize me."

I looked him over. His hair was gray, again. His face, hands, and clothes looked as if he had been working on the railroad all the live long day, covered with soot and coal. He slouched like an elderly person with achy bones, and no strength left.

"I don't understand. What just happened?" "I owe you my gratitude. You rescued me." I cleared my throat. "After I turned you in."

"I figured out you felt like you were doing the right thing. I should have trusted you earlier and told you the truth."

"I probably wouldn't have believed you." I could hardly believe he was sitting there beside me.

"I headed south out of town, made sure a passel of folks saw me. Bud had a horse and my attire," he swiped his grimy hand in front of himself, "waiting for me, and then I did a quick change, and circled back. Here I am."

"Will they come after you?"

Manford patted his jacket pocket. "Thanks to your article, I doubt the robber barons will make a stink out of pursuing this. They would dearly love to catch me, of course, and would love their money returned, but honestly, those varmints mostly want to go unnoticed. So they can continue in their schemes. Besides, the president and Secret Service have it all under control. I won't be pursued." He hacked a loud phlegmy cough as the conductor passed us by. My head was turned toward the window, in distaste.

Manford reached inside his jacket, his elbow boring into my side. He pulled out a folded paper, the ink smudged. "'Kidnapped Bride Outsmarts Outlaw!'" he read. There was a sketch within the article of that distasteful flyer seeking his capture and my return, featuring the caption, "Triumph of The Kidnapped Bride!" He cleared his throat. "Barely out of my wedding dress, I was ripped from the embracing arms of my husband as we embarked upon our honeymoon and life of love together." He raised his eyebrow at me. "I feared for my virtue as a newly married bride, a woman who had just pledged her body, mind and soul to one good man. I was wrenched from the safety and security of my family and violated by a dastardly coward filled with the lust of criminal intent."

Manford frowned. "I did not violate your person, Madam."

"Keep reading," I said in a bored voice. I stared out the window. I may have mouthed along to a few of my favorite phrases.

"Three terror filled nights, spent with the madman, torn from my loved ones, not knowing if I would live or die, left me inconsolable. I prayed to the good Lord above, I bargained with Lucifer. Spare me from the gates of Hell, I beseeched the stars at night as I lay below them, an insignificant supplicant, tied up on the cold, hard ground, with nothing more than thorny twigs for my pillow, unforgiving rocks and clods of dirt for my bed. Fear makes the night air frigid."

Manford snorted. "You had a blanket, and my padding for your pillow."

I waggled my finger at him. "You're not Robin Hood just yet, sir."

He continued. "Prisoner to my tormentor, captive to his every whim, I could not keep my terror at bay. My body shook, my limbs shivered. Would I be slaughtered? Would I be Ravished?" His voice had gone melodramatically high.

"You found it necessary to capitalize the word 'ravished'?" He rattled the paper. "Would I ever see my family again? Would I ever feel the touch of my dear, dear husband and cherish our pure love once more?" I hid my smile from Manford.

His finger skimmed the paper down a ways, past further licentious accounts of my abduction through to our arrival at the hideout, before he read on. "My tale takes a turn, as I who had been a victim, torn asunder from vows of love spoken with lips fresh from my beloved's kiss, became a victor. I champion the very crime committed against me. I was kidnapped from a train, taken against my will, and forced to accompany the thief who robbed my innocence, along with a great cache of money. In spite of my heartache and certainty of doom, I discovered a greater evil that lurks deep in the heart of certain masterminds of destruction. It should come as no surprise that unseen railroad magnates, robber barons, many of whom find themselves indeed barren—of moral compass—are to blame. Shadowy figures, slippery men behind the scenes who create chaos in the name of capitalism. They are cloaked in a conspiracy that shivers in a desolate landscape hewn from the backs of good, hard-working men. I say no names as I have none to use. It would matter little if I did as they would be as false as the very men themselves. Profit is their prophet; power is their opium."

Manford shot me a look.

"I didn't have much time," I told him. I reached over and folded the paper in half. He didn't need to read any more.

"It's very good," he said. "And will sell many papers." "And will do no good."

"The truth is always good."

"Not always."

"And that money, ma'am, thanks to your quick thinking is safely with KK and headed to the labor leaders for the men and their families."

He looked me full in the face. "Why'd you do it? What possessed you to take the money? And help me?"

"I don't quite know myself. I just knew I did not trust those men. They are evil. And I'd do it all over again."

He nodded his head, a gesture so small it should not have caused my heart to swell like that. He sighed a great, sad exhalation. "Mark my words, there will be a strike. There will be violence and deaths, and husbands and fathers not going home to their wives or children. The ones who aren't harmed will suffer an even greater indignity by not being able to put food on the table." He frowned. "I failed. I failed the government, but worse, I failed the workers."

"You did your best. You're no gentleman," I tried to tease him, "but you take the cake."

He shifted in his seat. "The profiteers will want to keep a low profile while they continue to do their damnedest to tighten the screws on the workers. It's going to get a lot worse before things get better. There's been mobs and violence and shootings from West Virginia all the way to Chicago. Wages cannot keep going down. And the conditions are barbaric. Men losing their hands and fingers, feet getting tangled up in couplers on railroad cars. It doesn't have to be this way."

"But you tried, Manford. You put those robber barons on notice."

"That I did," he said. "And mark my words, like most things in history, it has to get worse before it can get better. And it will get better, God willing, in our lifetime. Change happens by degrees. While radicals want to see a 180-degree spin of progress by our lawmakers, the actual amount is closer to maybe five degrees, and that's only if we're lucky and have a fairly honest government in office."

"I am distraught your negotiations never had a chance."

"It is probably for the better this way. The money will be put to good use, instead of back in the pockets of the railroad. I knew chances were slim that the plan would work, but we wanted to serve notice as to what will eventually come to pass. It takes time, Suellen, and unfortunately it will take much sacrifice by many good, hard-working men."

Manford disappeared before we pulled into Oberlin that afternoon and returned to his seat a new man. Clean, groomed, wearing a very nice suit of clothes. I sniffed. "Is that Dr. Wilber's lime pomade?" He smiled. He asked if he could fuss with my hair a trifle and I allowed him. The man was annoying, infuriating, obnoxious, but also someone who somehow managed to bring out the best in me.

"There. Your husband will be enamored anew."

I don't know about that, I thought. I just hoped he would be as glad to see me as I would be him.

Chapter Thirty-Four

I do not think my heart returned to its sedate, reliable rhythm for many days. Perhaps not since my first meeting with my husband. That personal pronoun even still caused a flutter as I couldn't help but imagine our reunion. I blushed at my thoughts. I did not know what to expect. I couldn't picture what "home" would look like, and I was impatient to find out. Theodore must be mad with worry. And Lucy. We had never been apart before, and I could only hope the good Lord above had seen fit to allow her and my beloved to seek and find solace with each other. If they could but put aside their differences and realize that I, who love them both so well, prayed they find their way to discover in each other the goodness, and yes, even brightness of their souls. I would make it my mission. How was I to know how well and thoroughly my prayers were to be answered?

Our train steamed into Oberlin, in the upper northwestern part of the state of Ohio. We pulled alongside the newly built depot just off of South Main Street. The dark gray board-and-batten walls were a tidy welcome to what I had heard was a most progressive town. A sizable crowd of folks gathered to greet their loved ones, or to wait for the next departure from this bustling station. Depending upon which timetable you used, our train was nearly two hours behind schedule. I had sent a second telegraph to Theodore and told him not to wait for me at the depot, especially with the children. In spite of my direction, I found myself harboring a hope that perhaps he would have been so urgent to greet me he would have defied my wishes.

I saw a young man, whom I recognized from our coach. He was hard to miss as he appeared to be nearly six feet tall, and made entirely of elbows and knees. In fact, it was as though an elbow jutted from his very throat. His lack of beard and exuberance in greeting his mother gave away his age. He lifted that poor woman clean off the ground and swung her around, hooting and hollering. "Ma, I'm home!" Fortunately, the woman's face was hidden in her offspring's chest, lest I observe her tears.

"Oh, for heaven's sake," I said as Manford thrust his handkerchief at me. I used it to wipe the soot and travel dust off of my face, and pressed it over my eyes, ignoring a suspicious dampness under my lashes that I was sure no one noticed. Why, I had no acquaintance with those strangers.

"It's so good to be here, at long last," I reprimanded Manford for what he counted as the one hundredth time. "Traveling, and all the accompanying bothers—strange food, dirty pillows, the inconvenience of not having one's routine, is such a nuisance." What was that twinge then, realizing I had come to the end of this journey? I folded his handkerchief and tucked it into my drawstring purse. Just nerves, I decided.

It was late afternoon when Manford escorted me inside the gas-lit waiting room while he obtained a buggy to transport me home. How different this train ride had been. Before, I had been naive and filled with hope. I cast a smile in Manford's direction. I must admit a certain fondness for the rascal. An emotion I could well-afford, headed as I was into the welcoming arms of my family.

I looked about, trying not to fidget when in truth I wanted to burst into song. Play the piano.

Lift my skirts and run and play a game of tag amid the shady trees in the grove just outside.

Manford escorted me out front and handed me into the small carriage, pulled by one brown horse. He joined me on the other side and took up the reins. "Ready?"

"More than ready, sir."

"Come now, Miss Suellen. They tell me we are but fifteen minutes or so away from your family and new home." I could not interpret the look in his eye.

"You will miss me," I told him.

"As a toothache that plagues me no more."

"The old me would have bristled."

"The new you sure looks like you are bristling."

Manford slowed the horse as we neared the turn onto Sycamore Street where the doctor's house was located. I looked at the houses on either side, noticing the well-tended yards, cheerful red geraniums, and gardens with beans and snap peas. Most were two-story, wood-sided affairs with some brick. All had front porches, peaked roofs, and were filled with what I hoped were kind folks.

Suellen 199

I smoothed the expression on my face. My mouth watered for Lucy's bean soup with dumplings. I would be the doctor's wife. I would have friends, social standing, and host teas and soirees, do good works and help the poor. I would be a community leader that other women would envy, but I would be gracious and dole out guidance and advice. I would raise the moral flag high. My glance flickered toward Manford. I wasn't entirely sure I had that right to be waving around any moral banner. Well. Nevertheless. I would be like my mother, in finer, more gracious times. Lucy, of course, would assist me. She could help with the children, too. She was better with them than I, though I supposed I, too, could learn to like them. And maybe the good Lord would see fit to bless my union with the doctor with a child of our own.

My heart felt as if it were trying to escape right through my stays. My eyes drank in the neighborhood. My new home. It was lovely. I hoped to find welcome.

"Don't ever sell yourself short, ma'am." Manford interrupted my thoughts. "You are one tough woman, brave, with brains and beauty."

I am sure I blushed. After Manford's ministrations, when he had helped smooth my hair and adjust my outfit before we disembarked from the train, I felt fit. I was wearing the same cream blouse and navy skirt he had presented to me. I lifted my rib cage. I couldn't wait to see Lucy's reaction to my new hairstyle and outfit. I did hope Theodore would notice.

We turned onto Sycamore Street and I tried to assess the houses, to determine which was the doctor's, but I couldn't seem to focus.

"We'll be there in a minute, Miss Suellen. Are you feeling right?"

"My nerves cannot take much more of this."

"And as profusely as I have apologized for the inconvenience I have caused you, I am glad that I met you, and I'd like to think that maybe, now that you are nearly home, it wasn't such a terrible detour."

"Are you mad?" I asked him. "It was horrible," I said. "Honestly. You must be joking. What I've been put through would see a saint kicking and screaming."

"So, you are a saint now?"

We both contained our smiles, rather enjoying each other's bluster.

"If the halo fits."

Manford continued. "And before I say goodbye—" he started.

"So help me, do not make me use your handkerchief." I waved my hand next to my face, hoping to forestall any sappy cliché he might be wont to use.

"Before I say goodbye," he repeated, looking ahead at the horse, "I just want you to know, you make an excellent spy. I couldn't have done any of this without you. It's been a pleasure. And," I saw him swallow, "your country thanks you. The president would want me to be sure to tell you."

"President Rutherford?"

"That would be the one."

"And you just now thought to tell me this?"

"I was preparing a speech and thought it deserved a prominent place."

"Has anyone ever told you timing is everything?"

"Why, yes, I believe I have heard that mentioned."

He pulled up on the reins and the buggy rocked to a halt. My memory seemed to want to catalogue the moment and I felt I would always remember the deliberate care and slow-motion stop of the horse. Manford's forearms and strong hands flexed as he pulled on the leather leads. My eyes were blinking something fierce. That train had been filthy, and I was sure I still had soot particles in my eyes. "This must be the place," I said, needlessly. I double-checked the address. I turned to him and held out my hand, a forthright effort to thank him, in spite of the condemnation he deserved for setting me about this predicament in the first place. Funny. That anger had long been spent. My wonder about that lost the battle in my eagerness to greet my husband. I had ruminated for many long hours about my husband, Theodore. He was such a good man. A quiet man. A man who had chosen me, for we shared a bond, our unspoken silences filled with meaning. How I had treasured his love note that had played such a central part to this drama.

"Regards," I said, helping myself to the ground. I hopped into the street and as I stepped up on to the sidewalk I couldn't resist a parting shot. "Thank you for kidnapping me."

Manford laughed, a sound I would miss. He tipped his hat, clicked at the horse and rode off.

I turned my back on him and my wayward adventure. I was ready to reclaim my life. My dreams. I would go inside. Let them greet me and welcome me and cluck over my travails. Mother, or maybe it had been Manford, had once warned me that things are never as we anticipate.

I must have exhaled five breaths standing there on that sidewalk, or at least as many as needed to make me feel dizzy. I couldn't explain my nerves; I should have been racing up the walk. I took a step. No one could ever say I was one who put things off until tomorrow.

Chapter Thirty-Five

The gate creaked as I pushed through and my footsteps clomped with purpose on the walkway. It was a solid, two-story white house, with steps leading up to the front porch. I lifted my skirts to climb the steps, but paused. Through the front window I saw the doctor standing next to Lucy. She was holding Baby Gus, who was as cantankerous as ever, I noted. A warm gush of gratitude flooded my heart. Theodore and Lucy had found their way together at last, turning to each other in light of my misfortune. I clasped my hands together at my heart. The two people I loved most in the world had bonded. Oh, how they must have worried about me.

The brightly painted red door flew open. Two children came clattering down the porch stairs. Their hair was combed. Ila Rose's soft, pink cotton dress was tidy and clean, and her stockings were pulled up. Her dark hair was neatly braided on either side of her head, and I was pleased to note I could see no outlines under her nails. Vaughn was in short pants and a sailor shirt, tucked in, though goodness knows how long that would last. He ran furiously ahead of Ila Rose, arms flying. Baby Gus toddled on the porch, clapping his pudgy hands with each step. Lucy streamed right behind them, beaming with pride as if they were her own. I saw Theodore on her heels, holding her elbow to help her down the first step. What a gentleman.

I do not know whose tears began first, mine or Lucy's, though I do know mine saturated the ground before me. We united standing out front with a hug that exceeded my homecoming expectations.

"Suellen. Suellen. It's really you. We have been so worried. We got your telegraph, and I thank God you are safe. You are here," she paused. Only I, the closest thing to a sister she ever had, noticed a flit of a shadow.

"How you must have suffered," I comforted her.

She shook her head and tried to dry her eyes. "You are home."

"Suellen. Welcome. Pleased to find you looking so well. We have been quite worried." The doctor and Lucy exchanged a look. He stiffly leaned to embrace me in a too-brief formal hug, negating the need to offer a public kiss to my lifted cheek. "I trust you are well?"

Though his words and greeting were all I had anticipated, his tone and delivery were not. I nodded, biting my tongue against replying, "I trust you do know how to embrace your wife better than my great Aunt Serafina?" I didn't want to upset Lucy. So soon.

The children gathered around Lucy, as her arms dropped from mine to shelter them on either side with a hug. "It's Suellen. She's back."

"I don't like Suellen," Vaughn said.

"Hush." Lucy tapped the back of the child's head. "Gus Gus, come back here." Her attention followed the toddler's path.

Under the setting sun on that warm afternoon, standing in the grass-filled yard, with three children who were to have been mine, it was so quiet we could practically hear the butterfly flit in front of the house. Full blown white and periwinkle hydrangeas, heads nearly as large as cabbages with their dark green leaves, nestled against the porch. "Gus Gus," as Lucy had seen fit to call him, waddled back toward us, and dived head first into Lucy's skirts. Did that child call her Mama?

I laughed a little through my tears. All would be well. Lucy, the dearest friend of my heart. And Theodore. And the financial security of never having to worry about food or shoes, and a well-built roof over our heads, complete with comfort, and coffee. I had made it home.

I looked at Theodore. "You look well, too, sir." His shirt was clean and freshly pressed. His hair newly trimmed. His nails were clean and even, the hands of a doctor that I loved so much.

"Come inside, honey, you must be starved. Let me take care of you, get you some coffee, and you can tell us all about what happened." Lucy squeezed me tightly.

The house smelled of lemon and that special wax Lucy loved to use. In a glance, I could see Lucy's talents, from the children who were no longer ragamuffins to the arrangement of the parlor, complete with treasures from back home.

"The house looks beautiful," I told her. "I see your touches everywhere." I bent to smell the pink wild roses gathered in a pitcher, placed on a bureau in the front hall.

"I know how you love flowers, Suellen. We wanted to make you welcome. The children helped me pick these. They grow wild, out back." She took my arm. "Oh, Suellen. It must have been awful. Are you really doing fine? You weren't," she paused, before whispering, "harmed?"

"No." I laughed. "It was actually an adventure."

"An adventure? A madman kidnaps you from a train? Do sit down, here," she pulled out a dining chair and eased me into the seat. "I must say, you do look well. Very pretty." Lucy studied me and I drank my fill of her beloved face, pleased at her concern. Over her shoulder, my husband seemed ill at ease with our sentiments.

"Theodore, dear. Please sit with us," I said. "Tell me how you have all been. I regret any worry you must have been put through. Have you started seeing patients?"

He took a seat at the head of the table. "Of course."

"Theodore, the doctor, was out of his mind with worry." She telegraphed a look at him. "We all were, honey. And now, you're home. Where you belong." She ran to the mantle. "Look, we have your wedding photo. Mr. Roth sent it special, when he heard you'd been taken."

I reached for the photo, remembering back to that day, and how excited I had been. "Dear Lord, it feels like a lifetime ago." I studied the image of Theodore, who had been seated while I stood behind him, my hand on his shoulder. He was such a handsome man. I waited for that fluttery feeling. I guessed I would have to go on waiting, I decided as I greedily looked upon my own image. Who on earth was that woman? What did happen to me these past ten days? I had the wind knocked out of my sails, as my father would have said. I barely recognized the solemn-faced woman staring back at me. My cheeks and mouth, with its hint of a smile, had been tinted pink, and my newly cut fringe of hair had framed my face. I do not know what I was expecting from my marriage photograph, but whatever it was, it wasn't that. I smoothed my cheek with the back of my hand and patted my hair. Surely, I was a little more comely than this photographic evidence bears witness. Before I could judge myself too harshly, or be caught staring in an unseemly manner for far too long at myself, I placed the photograph, face down, on the dining room table.

"It's a beautiful picture," Lucy said. Then she burst into tears. She searched both sleeves of her dress, looking in vain for her handkerchief.

The scrape of Theodore's chair startled us all, as he went to Lucy and crouched beside her, offering her his neatly folded white handkerchief. He awkwardly patted her back. "We're right glad you are here, Suellen, and sorry for your troubles."

I had had a kinder reception at the Columbus County jail. The dear man was tongue-tied. Lucy leaned forward in her chair to shake off his hand. Theodore stood up. "Well. Welcome home again, ma'am. Let me know if you need anything. Maybe you want to eat, or lie down. I need to go finish a report. The children are out back playing. Lucy's prepared her famous roast chicken, with that cornbread she tells me you are so fond of."

"I'm not overly fond of cornbread," I protested. "I mean, I will gladly take a slice, but it's not my favorite." Theodore nodded his head and walked out of the dining room, I presume to the front room where I had seen a desk with his writing papers.

"You seem to have a good rhythm here, Lucy." I'd only been gone less than two weeks and it looked as if my prayers had been answered. "Who knew the power of my prayers had such strength and fortitude?" I teased her. "I told you, you would like it."

"You'll like it here, too, Suellen," Lucy said. "The people are very nice. Good neighbors. The children are doing well, too. It's a peaceable town."

"Who are you trying to convince, Lucy?" My eyes narrowed. "What about you? Do you like it here?"

"Yes." She paused. "But, maybe I should go on back home, and give you and Theodore a chance to get to know each other better, and be a real family."

"This is your home, silly goose." I started to feel better. Of course, the situation was an odd one. I had been gone for days, kidnapped, murdered for all they knew. "I know it seems strange, but I am fine. We'll all be fine. Why, you had to be so brave helping the doctor settle in and deal with the children, and figuring out a whole new life in a whole new town."

"He's a wonderful father," Lucy said. Through the window I could see Ila Rose being chased by Vaughn, Baby Gus watching them, jabbering and spinning in circles.

"Gus is walking better, I see. And the children all seem clean, and no one is crying." "They are dears" she said. "You'll see."

"You old softy," I said. "You're in love."

A look of panic crossed her face. Her hand went to her heart. "What is it? You've always loved children."

She nodded.

"I'm the one who should be tearing up like a summer storm, Lucy." Then it was my turn to lean and rub her back, imitating the motions Theodore had made a few minutes ago. Comforting her. Loving her. Her hands hid her face and she sobbed so loudly, Theodore returned to the dining room.

"Is everything fine in here?"

I laughed at his flustered look. "Do come in and sit with us a while longer," I said, before adding, "Dear. I've missed you so."

He nodded and sat down. I was going to save my thank you for our private time, but, shoot, Lucy was part of this family and knew everything anyway.

"I received your note," I told Theodore. I pursed my lips and ran my fingertips over the tablecloth.

"What note?" Theodore said. He looked perplexed. "A telegram?"

"No. The note you wrote to me, right after we were married. It means the world to me. I don't have it anymore, that's another story, but I will never forget those most beautiful sentiments. We're going to have a good life, Theodore."

Neither he nor Lucy said anything.

"You tucked it into Lucy's case by mistake. On the train." I prodded him. "I know it's not easy for a gentleman to share his innermost feelings, but really, it was lovely, and I thank you."

I could hardly feel my cheeks, my smile was so wide, I was that glad to be home. Lucy, who had finally stopped her boo-hooing, looked at Theodore, as did I. "What is it, dear? Your cheeks are so red," I told him. He refused to look at me or Lucy.

I stood up then. I finally figured it out. My chair scooted off the rug and made a louder scrape against the wood than Theodore's had done earlier. Funny the odd nuances we notice when our world collapses. "That note wasn't for me, was it?" I took a deep breath. "The love note you wrote and put in Lucy's portmanteau wasn't by mistake, and it wasn't for my eyes. I found it on the train and I thought you had put it in the wrong case by accident. It was meant for her." I gritted my teeth. "I held on to that false hope thinking this whole time we had an understanding and a deeper connection. It was all a lie. It was always Lucy. You and Lucy." I coughed, as it was the only way I could get a breath. I had a vague notion to ask the doctor about the fatally injured nerve that had exploded in my chest. Was it connected to the handle of a bucket of tears, precariously perched behind my eyeballs?

"Lucy? Do you think history repeats itself?" I looked down at her quivering, folded hands and spoke very, very softly. "Do you?"

She stilled. She knew what I meant.

"Suellen." She parroted back what I had often told her. "History will repeat itself until we learn the lessons that we need."

"You are going to sit there before me and pretend everything is well and proper? Are you?" My voice shrilled. "Answer me."

She stood up and backed away from me, nearer to Theodore, of course. "It's not what you think."

"It's not what I think? How on earth would you know what I think?" "We did nothing wrong. Please. You have to believe me."

"We? Is there a mouse in your pocket? Imagine my surprise to find that you are part of a select intimate twosome of we." I swallowed. "And I am most definitely not welcomed." My hands balled into fists. Dear Lord, I yearned to pummel her. Theodore had stood up also, the charming apex of our little tableaux in that dining room.

"How could I have been so stupid? Why does this keep happening? I feel as if I have been kidnapped all over again. Only this time, it is my life that has been stolen away, while I am left with nothing. This can't be true. It's not right. Not you, Lucy? Theodore? Do I mean nothing to you?"

I saw the big ears on little pitchers as Ila Rose and Vaughn appeared in the doorway, transfixed. I pointed one finger out the way they had come and they ran to the back of the house.

"Again?" I raged. "How could you betray me thus? You no good... This is wrong. Wrong." I lost my words so great was my wrath. "Tell me this is not so.

What is my lot in life that this shameful history repeats itself, over and over? How dare one woman destroy another's happiness like this?"

"Suellen. I never would have told you. Believe me. Theodore and I both have done nothing to dishonor you."

I scoffed. "Except fall in love behind my back, and in front of my face."

"No," Lucy said. "It wasn't like that."

"It was exactly like that."

Theodore, who had been standing quietly, nearer to Lucy, if you must know, than to myself, his lawful wedded wife, suddenly spoke. "Suellen. I apologize. Lucy had nothing to do with this. I did not marry you under false pretenses. I wanted to marry you. I admire you very much. I cannot help it that Lucy and I..." He stopped. "It just happened. How can I explain it?" He lifted one shoulder.

I waited, in vain. "Now you lose your confidence. Pray finish, sir. Lucy and you cannot keep your hands off each other?"

Lucy gasped. I would have only felt better if I could have smacked her, but I was too overwrought. Images of all I stood to lose flashed before me: my role as the doctor's wife, Lady Bountiful; our educated conversations over coffee; sleeping next to my husband, secure in the knowledge we would be together forever; my unborn baby... "My future, all up in smoke because of some childish, outlandish emotions of the most ill-suited romance," I spat the word, "this side of the Ohio River."

"It's not like that." He had the nerve to censure me. "I respect you more than any woman I know, excepting for Lucy." The weasel hung his head. "You two are all that's good and right coming out of the war. Your strength and courage and resilience are leading us into the next generation that hopefully has learned from the past. You are one of the bravest women I know, Suellen."

I clapped my hands as meanly as I knew how, while Lucy sobbed into hers. "It's been my experience that people who are brave have no other recourse."

"I cannot help the feelings that have grown between Lucy and myself. But that does not detract from the admiration I feel for you, Suellen. However," the doctor said, "I have no regrets except the pain I have caused. I thought it was a passing fancy. I thought it would go away. I thought I could do right by you and live as a family. Indeed, I look upon you as a sister."

My mouth was agape. "Then you are the most hideous brother ever sent from above. Liar. Cheat."

"Please. Suellen. Of course I cared for you, and still do. We never meant for this to happen.

In fact, we are not sure how exactly it did happen." He had the nerve to choke a little laugh.

"You look as if your heart is broken," I said through gritted teeth to Lucy. Tears cascaded down her face as she stood there, prepared to take what I had to dish out. Looking beautiful. And fragile. Theodore stepped to her side to comfort her and that was my undoing.

"I'm the one supposed to be comforted. I'm the one who was abducted. I was missing for almost two weeks. I am your wife. Did you not want to find me? Did you even look for me? And Lucy. You. I would have moved heaven and earth to find you. Do I mean so little to you, you just stepped right up and took my place?" I sneered. "Standing in my stead like some pinchbeck wife."

The doctor stood in front of Lucy, as if to protect her. "I again take full responsibility for this scene and course of events, which I do regret. However, I need you to know that I love Lucy like no other. And while of course I realize the impediment, I want to above all else do the right thing."

"The right thing being?" I raised my eyebrow. Heaven help me, in the face of my utter humiliation, for one second I wished us back to a newly married couple, the rosy glow of nothing but good fortune ahead of us. No one answered. "What am I supposed to do now?"

"I will take care of you Suellen. I do hold you in very high esteem. I will apologize until the end of my days for this misunderstanding. It was not intentional, and, as with most things in this life, but for the Creator's whim, it was not planned. In fact, it is my hope you can find it in your heart to not only forgive us, but take up residence with us."

"You better thank your lucky stars I do not have a pistol with me." He had the decency to look alarmed.

"Suellen, please," Lucy pleaded but knew better than to reach for me. "You know me. You know I would never, never hurt you."

"And yet, you have, and with the most fatal wound of all."

"Suellen, my heart is torn in half. I can't bear your hatred. I resisted. I did everything in my power not to hurt you. I have no excuse. It wasn't intentional, Suellen. You know me."

I cut her off. "I knew you. I never knew you could be this cruel. To steal my husband? You think happiness purchased with another's heartbreak is not a sin? You will never be happy." I searched for the cruelest words I could find. "It's not as if you could ever marry."

She flinched.

My hand went to my mouth. "You've talked about it? You wished I was dead so you could move in on my husband. And you," I said to the doctor, "you chased after her, while your wife was missing? Have either of you any shame? How do you stand before me, locked in your lies? And worse. Your lust." The filthy word was flung from my lips.

My hand was at my throat, my pulse unbearable. "To think," I could hardly get the words out. "To think that when I was abducted and didn't know what was going to happen to me, I considered you, Lucy, my greatest good fortune."

"Suellen, we never... I mean nothing inappropriate ever happened. We just talked." Lucy stammered.

"Shut up."

That stopped the lovely tears coursing down her cheeks. As for myself, I was far too angry to cry. I wanted to kill, maim, destroy. I saw the reflection of us, scattered off the mirror hanging on the far side of the dining room table. The reversed image showed a shattered life. Theodore leaned in protectively beside Lucy, who stood tall, accepting my abuse as her penance, which infuriated me even more. I was unrecognizable. My face bleached of color, my eyes lashed with hatred. It was ugly, even for me, and I was glad. "I hate you. I hate everyone. I hate everything."

I headed for the door. "A curse on you both." I ran down the steps toward a meaningless void of nothing. I turned the corner back toward the train depot. Somewhere along the way I espied a boarding house. I was exhausted with the burden of dashed dreams and unshed tears. I don't fully remember obtaining a room for the night or paying my two dollars, but I fell upon the bed gratefully. I am not ashamed to say how I screamed into the pillow and kicked and clawed until the tears finally came.

It was well into darkness when a whisper of sound roused me, and announced I had somehow managed to sleep. The spirit is willing, the flesh is weak. I rose, prepared to turn away the interloper who dared intrude on my grief. I saw a folded piece of paper on the floor at my door. I lit the lamp by my bed table.

"My Dearest Sister," I read. It would have made an entrancing tale to say that I shred that paper to ribbons without reading another single damning word, but alas, curiosity kills the cat, and I deserved no less.

"Pray hear my plea, my apology, my devastation at ever causing you pain. You know we are as twin shadows in the events of our lives, and I have never thus far betrayed, by word or deed, my feelings for you. I have no excuse except that of fear, shrouded in longing, covered with a blanket of that most shameful human emotion, desire. I am ashamed and will be forevermore.

"By the time you read this, dearest of my heart, I will be headed back to Tennessee and our home. I will never be the source of your unhappiness, we have shared too much—secrets and sorrows.

"I remain your grateful sister,"

At that, I sobbed.

"Lucy."

Her signature wobbled, and I wouldn't have put it past her to deliberately wipe her salty tear on the page for effect. So, she thought she was leaving, did she? Good. Good riddance. I folded her note and crawled back into bed, the words of her shoddy excuses bled onto my fingers and chased around my head. My heart? Defeated like the capture of Atlanta.

The sun would treacherously find its way into my poor room. I felt a creak from the floorboard outside my door and through narrowed eyes discerned two small shadows, the rounded toes of leather of someone hesitating before my doorway. I still had my boots on, preferring to die that way like a good solider, I guessed. I smoothed back my hair, rubbed my eyes and went to the door. I opened it a crack, convinced my visage would frighten away whoever was on the other side.

"Lucy." Never had her name been so hateful, so hurtful.

She shoved her foot into the opening even as I made to slam the door. "You need to listen to me, Suellen."

"I need to never see you again." I would never do her the favor of saying her name again as long as I lived.

"I know I've betrayed you, and you have every right to never forgive me. I know your history. And irony of ironies, it seems it does repeat. It is the ugliest, most unforgivable sin, that I, who know you best of all, caused your heartache. I cannot live like this. I know you read my note, but I could not leave without seeing you one more time. I will move back to Tennessee, and you can have your life back." She swallowed. "You can have your life back with Dr. Kincaid. Your husband. You will live a beautiful life together, that was meant to be. We can move on from this, Suellen. You have to forgive me."

Her hair was tumbled to her shoulders, for once her cried-out eyes looked haggard, and her green cotton dress, that was one of her favorites, hung wrinkled on her shoulders.

"I have to do no such thing. You dare ask me for forgiveness?" My hands clenched into fists.

"Go ahead. Hit me. Just please talk this out, Suellen."

"Talk about what a cheat and liar you are, you mean?"

"Yes. You hate me only a little less than I hate myself."

"You have no idea."

"Please. Believe me. It just happened. Not to hurt you. I would never hurt you for the world."

"My dream came true," I looked her straight in the eye. "For someone else. And I had a front row seat. You tried to tell me this whole marriage was a bad idea. How long? How long has this been going on? You didn't even like him at first."

"I know. I didn't. Honest, Suellen. It just slowly happened. I can hardly explain it myself. And then, that day of the storm, right before your wedding? We just got to talking and it felt right. Like we were so comfortable together and were meant for each other. I knew he wasn't right for you, but I knew you were so happy to have a husband, who was a doctor, and offered security. I didn't want to deprive you."

I pinched her then. Hard. She rubbed her arm.

"We did nothing untoward, Suellen. Just talked. And by then, you were engaged and it was too late. And, well," she shrugged, "as you know, he and I couldn't be together anyway. Especially in the South."

She waited but I had no words left. "I love you. More than anyone. That's all I wanted to say. I hope one day you can forgive me."

She started to turn away, but I grabbed her roughly by the arm. I then squeezed her hands in mine, wanting her to feel the obliteration of my life. I put my face close into hers. "How could you?"

She shook her head, her bloodshot green eyes made all the more precious for the tears swimming in them. I gave a great sigh and shoved her from me.

In the blink of an eye, which is all it really takes to discern a life's truth, I considered the ramifications. No amount of preparing will do you a lick of good when a universal reckoning shows up. You can't ignore what has been made known.

"You really love him."

Lucy hung her head. In spite of my harping on about how the worst thing a woman could do was to steal another woman's beau, how could I have ever dreamed Lucy would have betrayed me thus? The dagger in my breast twisted deeper. "And he loves you."

Lucy didn't answer.

"You even love those brats." My mouth twisted as I waited for the pain to savage my heart. It burned, but not as badly as I feared. I examined the crimes again, throwing a tin of kerosene on that hateful ember, the wrongs done me, by the people I loved and trusted most. To my surprise, the flame failed to take hold. I clenched my stomach and furrowed my brow, intent upon meeting this calamity head on, and woe be unto those traitors.

Then a funny thing happened. My rage flickered. I wasn't feeling anger so much as a weighty depression. "I don't know what to say. Or do. I don't feel much of anything, one way or another."

She sniffled.

"Oh my stars, you need to stop crying or by heaven above I will strike you." I twisted off my wedding band, the one I had mistaken for my talisman, and held it out to her. "Make him buy you a new one."

She just shook her head.

"It's such a rare gift that two people ever have the honor of sharing the word love." I tossed the ring on the bureau. "Folks will talk, but I suppose you will have a better chance in this town than most others."

I stared at her. "We've been together so long, you and I." I took her hands again and held them between us, her soft light brown skin a shadow of my paler, freckled hand, and tried to instill a photographic image of her face to my memory. We weren't much for touching, but I was reluctant to let go, knowing it was probably our last time together. I rolled my fingers straight against her hand, so we stood there, face to face, palm to palm. She went along with my touch, probably hoping against hope for forgiveness. Knowing what an improbability that would be; she was forever calling me a stubborn old mule.

I pressed my hands into hers. Her left, my right. We could have traced around the fingers such a match were we. I would miss those hands. "Even your pinkie finger has that crooked little notch in it. Just like mine. I got that from my daddy," I said, before the lightning bolt hit. We were truly sisters.

Her eyes widened. I dropped her hands and took a step back. "You knew?" I asked her. She nodded.

"All this time?"

She bit her lip. My tears had long since dried. I will not tempt fate by declaring I would never cry again, but it does seem as if that reservoir had to be drained after all this time.

"Imagine. Betrayed by my sister. My very own sister. Who stole my husband. Fancy that." The irony robbed my sarcasm of import. I crossed over to the window, my back to her. I slid open the sash, as if I could release the heavy scent of grief from the room. Something Manford said came back to haunt me, an arrow fired into the universe that found its mark. He said I was an unhappy woman pretending to be happy. I didn't want to be that woman anymore. I didn't want that to be the epitaph of my life. I took a good hard look at what was inside of me all along. We all know the right answers, but I guess some of us just don't ask the right questions.

I replayed the shocking news in my heart. "I am flabbergasted," I told her. I looked over at Lucy, who stood before me, wringing her hands, but trying to seize hope that I was at least talking to her. Lucy was my sister. My real sister. The hard knot of anger and betrayal was mine for the taking. I knew I could grow it into magnificent proportions. I could rule as the Queen of Bitterness; no one could deny me my right. Lord knows the South is filled with such harridans, matriarchs of many a family, the one whose kinfolk deftly maneuver not to be seated next to at the dinner table. The one children justly fear greeting, since it occasionally includes a knuckle on the noggin. And as for holding a grudge, the South is made of world-class grudge holders. That perverse joy of family feuds, the savoring of delicious drama, and the salacious delight in insults, imagined or misunderstood, it made no matter.

I was quite sure I had the orneriness to never speak to Lucy again.

Or, as the Good Book says, I could forgive. Probably wouldn't ever forget. I could understand her transgression and still be part of her life. I was not blameless. I was presented with a handsome package: a man, a doctor, a family and security, and though it was my foot set upon that easy path of least resistance, I had to admit, that was not love. I could forgive myself for thinking it was, and who could blame me for wanting that dream? If Theodore had truly loved me, he never would have looked Lucy's way.

"Theodore's a good man," I finally told her. "Just not my good man." Curiously, I was not knocked flat by that declaration. He wouldn't have made me happy once I got over my infatuation. And there it was. He was simply an ideal of what the perfect man should be, instilled with qualities I only thought I wanted. A whisper of a breeze ruffled my hair. I like to think it was Mr. Infatuation, heading out of town, looking for some other poor girl's head to turn.

"I know there's no bigger sin in your eyes, Suellen," she said softly.

"But there are far bigger sins, dear Lucy, as you well know. The years after the war taught us that. And then, there's the sin of going against fate, going against what feels sure and right, deep in your gut."

Lucy managed a shaky laugh. "And what about your heart?"

"I think folks would be a lot better off if they checked with their gut before gallivanting off with their heart, don't you? Oh, for heaven's sake, stop looking at me as if you're saying the rosary." I never could abide false piety. "It won't be easy," I told her.

"I know," she said. Her eyes searched my face, and never faltered. "But it would be impossible back there in the South."

"You don't even call it home anymore?"

"I think this could be my home."

"You could say you are my sister."

She looked away then. "We have." She jerked her head up. "We had to. It just wouldn't have been right. Me being there in the house with Theodore. And the children. And Theodore needed help with them, and they needed me. Oh, Suellen, these past days have been just terrible."

"And folks believe it? That we're sisters?" She nodded.

"Why not?" I said. "Since it's true."

"What about you, Suellen? Please stay. There is plenty of room. I need you. We'll get through this. We're family. And Theodore wants you to stay."

"Even I am not that much of a martyr. I suppose I'll go back home." But as I said it, I felt dismayed. I didn't want to go back there. "Or maybe, I'll go back to Columbus. The editor of the *Columbus Dispatch* offered me a job. He liked the article I wrote about my kidnapping."

"We could see each other. It's not that far apart." For the first time since I'd been back, Lucy was my Lucy again. She rushed to hug me and I let her. Our cheeks pressed together. Sometimes it took that chemical compression of skin against skin to make right what words never could.

Chapter Thirty-Six

We said goodbye then. I sent her back to Theodore's house, while I, who have never been described as jaunty, walked briskly with a happy enough heart and retraced my steps back down the sidewalk, headed toward the train depot. After twenty paces or so, my steps slowed and I faltered. "Oh, dear Lord, what have I done? Maybe I should stay. Lucy is all I have."

I meandered across the street to turn right at the intersection. Several horses and carriages clopped along the busier roadway, and I could just make out the train station ahead. No. I could not go back. One step in front of the other. As frightened as I was about what tomorrow would bring, I had my dignity, which I was happy to see contained a kernel of curiosity about the future. Either I was in shock, or I had one more trick left in my reticule. I imagined it, tucked in there, wrapped in a freshly laundered handkerchief, and was filled with relief. How was it I could be relieved? More importantly, why would I cry for a dream, spun from a figment of my imagination? While I would waste no more time on wishing, I was that pleased to find I still had wishes left.

A carriage slowed near me and I cast my head lower. "Can I offer you a ride, ma'am?"

I faced forward and kept walking, not turning my head. "I do not accept charity from a stranger. A virtuous woman could be kidnapped in these trying times, after all."

"Your smile seems familiar to me," he said. "Could it be we have met before?"

"As I am not smiling, perhaps your vision is impaired."

"I am certain we are kindred spirits. Surely, we have a common cause. We've spent enjoyable time together?"

I patted my hair. "I find that hard to believe, sir, as I am not in the habit of fraternizing with common criminals."

"Or of smiling," he agreed.

I lifted my chin and walked on. For the first time in my life, I felt free. I felt as if perhaps, for once, gravity had forgotten about me. "You may take your audacious solicitations and ill-bred manners and be on your way." My hand shooed him.

"Ah, Madam, you wound me." He clicked his tongue at the horse, slowing its pace to match my progress. "The only so-called bad habit I have had of late is wondering what it would be like to be blessed with the companionship of another man's wife."

I stopped in my tracks, in the middle of that sidewalk, my hand to my mouth as Manford continued spouting nonsense.

"Nestled together that cold night, she was a perfect fit in my arms," he said. "She has the softest hair I have ever felt, and it tickled my chin, but I would never make the mistake of thinking her a helpless female." I could feel my cheeks blister. Though clouds had overtaken the day, I was warmed by a most invisible sun.

"She is as smart as a whip," he continued, "with the snap and crackle of humor that hits its target, and protects me from myself."

I stood there at the side of that street, in that godforsaken berg of Oberlin, Ohio. My thirty years of hopes and dreams degraded by loss and disappointment. I squared my shoulders and lifted my gaze to his.

"Are you throwing down a gauntlet?" I asked.

"Are you picking it up?"

"I never walk away from a challenge."

"I believe you've been known to run down, hogtie, and disperse of any hardships that come your way."

"That hardly sounds like a compliment."

"Compliments are cheap, ask any huckster. Would you prefer I mention that I particularly admire the shine in your eyes? And, if I may be so bold, I know your hair is as soft as it looks this fine morning."

I am sure my open mouth looked like a gawping fish.

"And when you smile, you capture the charm of a ray of sun in an Irish fog."

I was flummoxed as he continued. "In spite of it all, the robbery, the kidnapping, my time languishing in jail after you turned me in..." He melodramatically folded his hands at his heart.

"Manford. I apologized. And rescued you, too, since you happen to be in such a reminiscing state of mind."

He laughed; a delightful sound, truth be told. His lips seemed to part against their will, as if too big an imposition, but the crinkles at his eyes held the upper hand. "I can't get you out of my thoughts. I can't help it, I've tried. I feel as if it was destiny, our meeting, as if it was all meant to be."

"I suppose next you'll be saying a preacher told you the Lord above said we were fated to be together? Sure, it's not writ large in the Good Book?"

"That's not what I am saying, Miss Suellen, and you better than anyone know that. I don't know what I believe, except that in this horribly unjust world in which we find ourselves, spinning in a whirlpool of disappointment, there is good to be found in the most unexpected of places, from which shines a most holy light."

He looked down and pushed at the brim of his hat before he wiped that smile off his face. "And as for kissing you when we were on the trail that night, well, that's an experience I would greatly enjoy repeating, over and over."

"Such a gentleman you are." The look in his eyes recollected me saying that to him upon more than one occasion. I should have expected his deliberate misunderstanding.

"High praise, coming from such a lady," he said. "Aren't we a fine pair?" He held out his hand and I climbed up and joined him.

HISTRIA BOOKS

HISTRIA FICTION

Other fine books available from Histria Fiction:

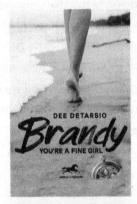
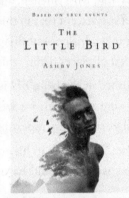
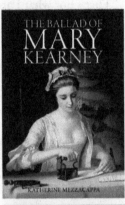
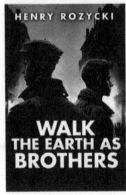

For these and many other great books visit
HistriaBooks.com